He
then Me
Comes You

Rutledge, Alabama

He then *Me* Comes You

Jennifer Brown

Copyright © 2018 Jennifer Brown

All rights reserved. No part of this book may be reproduced in any form or by any electronic or mechanical means, including information storage and retrieval systems, without written permission from the publisher or author, except in the case of a reviewer, who may quote brief passages embodied in critical articles or in a review.

He, Then Me, Comes You
Jennifer Brown
AtL Publishing Co.
Copyright September 2018
ISBN-9781723992551

Acknowledgements

First and foremost, I want to acknowledge Yahweh, my first love, glory to Your name.

Second to my son, Tre'Vion, may grace be given to you abundantly.

Lastly to all the chosen who struggle to take heed of their purpose, it belongs to you. Strive to endure.

About the Author

Jennifer Brown was born and raised on the Eastside of Detroit, and grew up with the hopes and aspirations of becoming a successful writer and motivator.

She has a calling on her life that started from when she was a young girl. She wrote short stories about her childhood and what she saw and endured growing up. She entered into many writing contests and won, not knowing that God has placed this gift on her heart.

As she grew older and life intervened she was once again drawn back to her purpose and began writing with the intent to glorify God. With that, she has accomplished raising a young black man with very little resources; she pushed through to write her truth and perspective to help those who need to hear this story.

Jennifer has many more books in development and on the way; she hopes that each one reaches those who need to discover their own truth.

A Note from the Publisher

This is one of the most "real" stories I have ever read.

Yes, there are some strong words in it- but sometimes real situations call for strong words.

I would encourage anyone who has lived through tough times to read this book; soak up every bit of it- because this story can impact *your* story.

One of my dear friends is an evangelist- he reminded me that Isaiah 40:31 has a message for everyone, and most people skip over it.

"*but they that wait upon the LORD* **shall renew their strength**; *they shall mount up with wings as eagles; they shall run, and not be weary; they shall walk, and not faint.*" (emphasis added)

While we are waiting on the Lord to do what He will do, we should always take time to renew our strength. It is our prayer that this story will help renew your strength.

Beth M. Rogers

Table of Contents

Chapter 1 15

Chapter 2 31

Chapter 3 43

Chapter 4 53

Chapter 5 73

Chapter 6 89

Chapter 7 97

Chapter 8 109

Chapter 9 123

Chapter 10 147

Chapter 11 161

Chapter 12 171

Chapter 13 183

Chapter 14 201

Chapter 15 217

Chapter 16 235

Chapter 17 239

Chapter 18 245

Chapter 19 251

~ *Chapter One* ~

Mistakes can be lessons to those who adhere...

"No, stop... please don't go! We can work this out. I can change... I can show you that I'm a different person, that I'm what you want," Jada says as she clings on to Caleb's leg.

The disturbed home is in disarray from Jada's deranged behavior.

Caleb struggles as he tries to kick her away but is unsuccessful. His hands are full of his things and are unable to remove Jada's strong grip from his leg. He breaks away for a moment, but Jada grabs hold of his ankle again trying to keep him from leaving the home.

"Get off me Jada! You are insane, you know that?"

"I'm not insane! I don't want to lose you! I need you right now!"

Caleb drops his things all over the floor as he tries to get Jada off his leg. He sighs hard with frustration. He continues to push her away as she adamantly tries to hold on to him to keep him there. He tries to collect his things once again to leave. Jada becomes very persistent and quickly grabs his bags and begins to unpack them. She begins pulling his clothes out piece-by-piece, throwing them across the room.

"Jada, stop acting like this!" Caleb shouts as he grabs his clothes from her.

"No. No, you can't give up on us because of a mistake."

"Seriously? You really think what you did was a mistake? It was a

Chapter One

choice, Jada."

"Caleb, please,... I don't want to lose you."

"This isn't healthy. You need help, and I can't help you."

"I don't need anything but you. I'm okay when I'm with you," Jada pleads.

"That's just it Jada; you need to be okay with or without me."

"But we love each other; we can work this out."

"Love isn't enough Jay," Caleb says as he grabs the rest of his clothes and heads toward the door. Jada immediately panics and surprises him by jumping on his back clenching tightly to his neck. Caleb stumbles as they begin to wrestle. He continues to struggle as he tries to get free from Jada's strong grip. They tussle for a while, and Jada grips him tighter with each movement. Moments later he manages to push her off onto the floor.

Jada stares up at him disappointed he will not yield. She begins to tear up as she watches Caleb gasp for air. He looks back at her shaking his head with disappointment of her behavior. He grabs his belongings, watching her closely as he continues to walk towards the door.

"Caleb please... stop! Please! Don't leave me - I can't take someone else leaving me."

Caleb doesn't acknowledge her plea as he continues to leave the disturbed home. He had hopes that Jada would get the help that is clearly needed because he does, in fact, love her. He, however, could not be there to see if she takes the steps to receive it. He had had enough of Jada and her issues. He takes one good look at the woman he loved as she stares back at him with hope in her eyes. He walks towards the door holding the last of his things.

"*Grab the gun,*" the injurious voice commanded.

Without pause, Jada grabs her handgun from the drawer next to the sofa and points it to her head.

"Caleb!"

Caleb turns back and looks to her. He shakes his head with fear for

He, Then Me, Comes You

Jada.

"Jada what are you doing? That won't keep me here. It only confirms what I've been saying all this time. You need help. Put the gun down. Stop playing around with that thing."

"No, if you leave, I will kill myself. I swear I will do it!"

"That's nothing to play with. Put the gun down, Jada."

"If you leave me, then I have nothing to live for," Jada says as she looks into Caleb's eyes. He seems concerned but not convinced that Jada will take her own life. There is an awkward silence as Caleb deliberates wondering if he should leave. He wonders if he should call for help. He felt stuck in this relationship far too long and couldn't take it anymore.

"I have to go Jada and you should live for yourself." Caleb says as he abandons the home leaving Jada to her fears and lack of quality of life. She continues to scream begging Caleb not to leave her. He drags his things down the steps, and as he approaches his car, he passes a man observing the loud plea. Jada continues to scream for Caleb. The man looks to Caleb as he passes by. Caleb loads his vehicle with his items and then gets in and drives off.

The man looks up at the door as it remains open. He continues to listen to Jada's bellows of cries for Caleb. Suddenly, there is silence, and then a loud bang echoes down the dark streets.

****

The shrill ringing sound echoes in Jada's eardrums. As she lies on the floor, blood drizzles out of her head. She rolls around on the floor while holding her head. When she tries to move, her limbs are weakened and she begins to shake, stumbling back to the ground. As she continues to lie on the floor the sound of her heartbeat weakens as she awaits death. With immediate regret, she tries to yell out for help, but no one can hear the faint sound of her voice. The darkness begins to fill her eyes and all that's heard is

Chapter One

the sound of her heartbeat slowly fading. Jada closes her eyes and prays silently to herself. Lord, what have I done? If You save me, I promise You I will give my life to You.

There is a cold, eerie feeling in the air. Her home remains silent as her body continues to lie on the cold, hard floor awaiting the sweet release of death. It feels like several minutes have passed as Jada thinks of ways to seek help. Silence still haunts the room. Moments later, she suddenly opens her eyes looking to the ceiling. Her body struggles to revive itself. At that same moment, the man that passed Caleb on the street enters the home in a panic. He quickly takes out his phone and calls for help. He then kneels next to Jada, looking to her with an emotional pain on his face as he sees her bloody face. He grips her hand, checks her pulse, then leans down and whispers in her ear.

"Don't be afraid. He's with you."

****

The sound of beeping from the heart monitor rings in Jada's ear interrupting her slumber. She awakens to an empty room confused and dazed on how and when she got to the hospital. She looks around hoping to find someone, anyone to explain her presence. She suddenly feels an ache in her head, and she touches the bandages surrounding her wounds.

As she continues to examine her head, she touches several stitches. She then looks to see if she could locate a button to alert the nurse. No sooner than she finds it, the nurse walks in. She's a tall, slim woman with her blonde hair pulled back in a bun. She has no makeup on but exudes the face of a sleepless hard worker. The nurse, who is carrying a folder and wearing floral scrubs, looks to Jada and smiles.

"How are you feeling, Jada?"

"I don't... how did I get here?" Jada said as she stares at the nurse, confused and struggling to get her words out.

He, Then Me, Comes You

"I'm not sure, but you were in really bad shape when you came in."

"I'm not sure what happened," Jada said.

"It's okay. Don't try and strain yourself. Just relax and focus on getting better." Jada looks to the nurse, tears up and closes her eyes.

"Are you in pain?" the nurse asks.

Jada shakes her head still crying. She puts her hands up to her face and begins to cry harder. The nurse has compassion for her and moves closer. Jada removes her hands from her face, shaking as she opens her red teary eyes, and looks to the nurse. The nurse holds her hand without saying anything as Jada calms herself. Moments later Jada senses a calming feeling and takes a deep breath. She takes her hand and tries to wipe away her tears. The nurse grabs a tissue and hands it to her.

"Be encouraged, young lady," the nurse says as she releases Jada's hand with a smile and then winks. She walks toward the door.

"If you need anything just let me know. My name is Michelle."

Jada smiles and nods as Michelle departs. She closes the door behind her. As Jada sits in silence trying to recall what had transpired and how she ended up in the hospital.

A vague memory from that night flashes to her mind. She shivers as she recalls the blood oozing down her face. Moments later, her mother Claudia walks in frantic with worry.

"Are you okay? Why would you do this?" Claudia asks as she drops her overly-sized purse, causing things to spill out. She looks at Jada, grabs her and holds her daughter trying to show consolation.

"Claudia, please just stop," Jada says as she pushes Claudia away.

"I don't understand. Why are you being like this, especially now at a time like this? Don't you need me?" Claudia asks as Jada's demeanor confuses her.

"No, I don't need you. I haven't spoken to you in years. Why would

Chapter One

I need you now?"

Claudia stares into her daughter's cold yet fearful eyes as they tear up with disappointment and hopelessness. She tries again to extend another gesture of affection but is again rejected. Claudia stands back and observes her daughter asking herself how Jada got to this point - to the point where she didn't want to live. How can she be so selfish to those who love and care for her? How can she take this gift of life that God has given to her so carelessly?

"I just want to be here for you," Claudia states as she stands close to Jada.

"Too little, too late, Claudia."

"What can I do?" Claudia pleads.

"You can leave."

"I'm not leaving Jada."

Jada rolls her eyes and turns her head away from Claudia, who then picks up her things and sits in the chair positioned in the corner of the room. Several minutes pass and no words are spoken. Jada becomes annoyed by Claudia's presence.

"I want to be alone," Jada says.

"I can't leave you here like this."

"It's funny how now you want to be protective of me. I know I'm not important to you."

Claudia is ashamed by the truth of not being there for her daughter. It's hurting her as she looks saddened by Jada's harsh words.

"Well, you know your sister is..."

"Here we go again. Why is it even when I'm in distress you must bring up Mia? Your favorite daughter."

"I don't play favorites."

"Oh, yes the hell, you do."

"You will not talk to me in that disrespectful tone, Jada. Now enough is enough. I am your mother."

"My mother? You gave birth to me and you're my mother? Any

He, Then Me, Comes You

animal can give birth....it doesn't make them a mother," Jada reminds Claudia with no compassion or regret. She spoke those words with the purposeful intent to harm.

They are more enemies than family. Claudia wasn't a good mother when her daughters were younger, and she's been paying for it ever since. Jada will not let her forget the things she failed at. Jada had held it over her head for years.

Claudia did what she thought was best at the time and did what she only knew how to do to provide for her daughters. She wasn't always there for Jada, but she loved her.

"Why do you hate me so much?" Claudia asks.

"I don't hate you. That would be too easy. That's the problem. If I hated you, then it wouldn't hurt so much."

"Then why can't we fix this? I miss you."

"Claudia, why are you here? Why are you pretending like you give a damn? I haven't heard or spoken to you in years."

"That's not by my choice. I wanted to be in your life. But you chose to keep me shut out. I need to be here for you."

"Stop it! Just stop, okay? Stop pretending like you care about me. Stop with this foolishness!"

"Jada, calm down."

"I don't need another person pretending to care because it will help their conscience."

"I'm not here for me," Claudia pleads.

"Yes, you are. You need to make it right with your God before I kill myself."

"You don't think it's time that we stop this madness and try to begin to heal?"

"Heal? You actually believe that you can recognize your faults just so we can attempt to heal our relationship?"

"I want to at least try, Jada. I love you," Claudia says as she tries to caress Jada's face. Jada pulls away quickly.

Chapter One

"If God loved you the way you loved me then we are all in trouble."

Surprised by her rebuttal, Claudia grabs hold of her chest as she felt instant pain from the blow of truth from her daughter. She knew that it would be a battle to get Jada back in her life. She was willing to fight for her. There was some truth in Jada's statement of

clearing her conscience. She couldn't bear the thought of losing her knowing they were still on bad terms.

"Well, I'm here at this moment, so now what? What are you going to do, Jada? Are you going to give up? Or are you going to fight?"

"She doesn't respect you. You don't need her. All you need is yourself," the injurious voice whispered.

"I'm tired of fighting, Claudia."

"You should never get tired of fighting. That's what he wants."

"Who? This adversary that we've created to justify our own messed up ways? I don't believe in some fairy tale villain. Just get out!" Jada screams.

Claudia is not giving up. She will not leave or walk away this time. Now she is more determined than ever to have a relationship with her daughter. She knows now that God has led her to this. She needed to pray for their healing. The Bible speaks about how mothers and daughters would be against each other in latter times. She was well familiar with the verse.

"I've told you before that believing in God also means believing in His purpose and His ways. The adversary is real and is strong in deceiving and destroying families. Now, I'm not leaving. I'm not going to give up this time."

Jada pushes her mother from her face. Claudia steps back, still looking to her daughter for any signs of hope.

"Look, my head is starting to hurt. I need my rest."

"You can rest, but I'm not leaving," Claudia insists, as she then begins to fluff Jada's pillows trying her best to make her daughter feel more comfortable. She looks around the room, looking for

He, Then Me, Comes You

ways to make it more comfortable with a warm feeling.

She walks around frantically trying to be strong as she begins to fidget and clean things around the room.

"If you are going to stay, can you at least get me something to eat?"

"Of course."

Claudia leaves the room leaving Jada sitting in a confused state. Jada and Claudia are one in the same. Jada shares some of her mother's stubbornness. She always knew she shared her mother's tendencies but fought them because she swore she would never be like her, closed-minded with tunnel vision. She always had to be right no matter the situation. She couldn't stand the thought of being wrong even in the smallest of terms. She would argue her way so that she would appear to be right even for a small portion of the argument. When her mother came back into her life, Claudia was a changed woman. She had given her life to God and promised Him and herself that she would never live an ungodly life. Jada had a belief in God, but it was never limited to what people always perceived Him to be. She always thought why would God want us to pursue something He knew that we could never achieve, such as perfection. Yet many people judge you if you aren't perfect, as if it were achievable. People could never be perfect or be without error. Jada felt that if that's what God was about, then she could live life without Him. However, she didn't try to have a relationship with Him to find out for herself what God wanted. She never wanted to. She wanted to live her life the way she saw fit. Jada didn't care about living a righteous life. She felt the Bible and spirituality to be archaic. She was proud and stubborn knowing that she could live a well-fulfilled life on her own. Although she failed at finding love, she was extremely successful with her talents. She was a well-known writer and made millions selling her work.

The money was great, but it could not fill the void of love, unconditional love.

Jada grabs her phone and looks to all the missed calls and text messages. She notices, however, that Caleb is not one of those

Chapter One

people who called or texted.

She decides to send a text pleading for another chance.

- Caleb, I'm in the hospital and I need you. -

She waits for a response. As she stares at her phone she notices the dots where Caleb is typing something but has not yet replied. Several minutes pass and the dots are still there. Jada thought that he might be sending a long apologetic message. Soon the dots

disappear and still no reply. Jada becomes filled with isappointment as she sighs and begins to cry, wondering if he ever loved her at all.

****

Lamar sits across the dinner table looking to Vanessa, disgusted by her lack of manners. He is staring and nodding his head as if he's listening to her speak about herself.

As Vanessa continues talking, she doesn't notice Lamar's disposition as he continues to gaze into thin air.

While Vanessa continues to talk, a small piece of food escapes her mouth and she spits on him. He bounces back in disgust and wipes his face. He decides that he has had enough and begins waving his hand to get her attention to stop talking. Vanessa smiles and puts her hand to her mouth. Lamar begins to sulk as he looks to her, thinking why he is on another date with someone he was fixed up with.

One of his friends from his business organizations suggested that they would be a great fit. He wondered how his friend could ever think that.

Sure, she was attractive, he thought, but besides the long, silky hair and pretty face, Vanessa didn't have much else to offer. She

He, Then Me, Comes You

appeared to be another woman with beauty on the outside and major issues with low self-esteem on the inside. She clearly needed therapy as she is now going on and on about how she wanted to be loved by the perfect man.

"Oh, I'm sorry, I'm just prattling on," Vanessa said.

"The talking is not the problem; well... sort of, but it's talking while having food in your mouth."

Embarrassed by Lamar's direct criticism, Vanessa grabs her napkin while consuming the last bite of her steak and potatoes. She wipes her mouth and gives a coy smile.

"I'm sorry I didn't realize. What did I do?"

"You were spitting while you were talking," Lamar explains.

Vanessa grabs her wine and sips it to cleanse her palate.

"Oh, wow! Please, excuse me. It's just that when I'm nervous I tend to go on and on until someone stops me."

"There's no need to be nervous. Relax," Lamar says.

"So, enough about me-let's talk about you. Have you ever been married?" Vanessa asks.

"Yes... but I don't really want to talk about my ex-wife at the moment."

"Oh, are you still in love with her or something?" Vanessa playfully asks.

Lamar immediately gives her a scowling look. He is completely turned off by her neediness.

"No, I just don't feel comfortable discussing my previous marital issues on a first date."

"I'm sorry. Let's just talk about something else if you'd like. You know John didn't tell me how amazingly accomplished you were or how good-looking you are."

Repelled by Vanessa's statement, Lamar refrains from telling her how he really feels. Instead he smiles and drinks his Hennessey. Without realizing, he checks his phone for the time and looks

Chapter One

around as if he's bored by her presence. Vanessa notices and gets offended by the gesture. She rolls her eyes and sighs.

"Is there some place you need to be?" she asks.

"Excuse me?" Lamar replies.

"Look, I know blind dates can be hard, but you don't have to be a jerk about it."

"Jerk?"

"Yeah, a jerk. Do you have somewhere else you need to be? Why do you keep checking the time?"

"Relax, I didn't realize that I was," Lamar explains while looking to see if anyone noticed the tension between them.

"Look I don't need this. You are obviously not interested. I was hoping you would turn out to be the one, you know?"

"The one? Are you serious with that?" Lamar asks.

"Why wouldn't I be serious?"

"You women kill me looking for 'the one'. It's not your job to look."

"If I'm not looking, how will I find him?" Vanessa asks.

"You don't find him. He finds you. You need to stop desperately looking for men. You walk around with this look on your face like a starved puppy, ready to jump at any sign of affection."

Lamar, now annoyed, looks for the waiter. He gestures at the waiter for the check.

Vanessa sits back in her seat in a shocked state. She was the kind of woman who was turned on by very aggressive and abusive men. This coincided with her having daddy issues. It seemed she was looking for men who would, in a sense, chastise her. She lustfully looks at Lamar. As he looked back, he knew what that look entailed and took advantage of the broken-spirited Vanessa. Lamar thought like most men, why not use her to satisfy his carnal needs until he found a woman of substance.

He, Then Me, Comes You
****

The sound of Vanessa's moans fill the dark room as Lamar kisses her on her neck.

Lamar grabs her hair and pulls her head away from him. Vanessa eagerly enjoys his aggressiveness while she engages with lustful intent. She removes Lamar's shirt and begins to undress herself. Lamar looks to Vanessa and notices that her face resembles a distorted demon. Startled by what he sees, he immediately pushes Vanessa off. She falls to the floor almost hitting her head on the nightstand. She gets up and looks to him.

"What the hell is wrong with you!" Vanessa screams.

Lamar closes his eyes in disbelief. When he opens his eyes, he looks to a scared and confused Vanessa. She stands trying to conceal her lustful state. Lamar, still sitting on the bed, appears to be shaking as he is trying to calm down. Lamar puts his hand to his face still confused about what he saw. As soon as he seems to be calmer, he looks to Vanessa again and sees that her face is distorted.

"What the --!" he screams.

Lamar jumps up and moves further away from Vanessa. As she attempts to come closer to console him, he extends his hands outward in order to keep her away from him.

"No! Stay back!"

"Okay, you are out of your mind. I don't need this. You are crazy! John was right about you. I'm leaving."

Vanessa grabs her things mumbling to herself about what had transpired and grabs her shoes and leaves Lamar's home. Lamar, still panicked, drops to the floor as his heart beats rapidly. If what he saw was real,then there must be something he should do.

"*She drugged you,*" the adverse voice states.

He has the thought again that Vanessa drugged him. Suddenly he's calm.

However, he is still uneasy and isn't sure if Vanessa did drug him.

Chapter One

But why would she need to? Was she setting him up? Was she trying to rob him? His mind thinks back to where and how she could have drugged him. He gets up and immediately calls his friend John, who doesn't answer. He sits still confused and uneasy. He continues to contemplate back to when and how Vanessa could have drugged him. He takes a deep breath and stretches back on the bed with his hands covering his face trying to understand, yet nothing comes to mind that would bring him a verifiable explanation. Moments pass and he is now calm. As he sits in silence, a thought enters his mind.

"*Do not give dogs what is holy...*"

Confused by the thought, he looks around the room. Lamar stands wondering where he had learned that before. Having no recollection, he brushes it off and goes into the bathroom to wash his face. As he looks into the mirror, he becomes afraid that he may see a distorted face. He continues to stare. Again, he has a similar thought.

"*Do not throw your pearls before pigs...*"

"What is that?" Lamar asks himself.

Lamar, now very nervous and not knowing why, is baffled by these strange thoughts and even stranger demonic faces.

"I'm losing my mind. This is crazy. Okay... it's okay. I'm going crazy. What I need is some liquid courage to get rid of these weird thoughts in my head," he whispers to himself.

He quickly heads downstairs to his dining area where he has a bar full of alcohol. He grabs the Hennessey bottle. The thought to throw it away surfaces. Lamar pauses as he holds the bottle. He shakes his head in disbelief because he knows that he would never tell himself to throw away a bottle of Hennessey. As he begins to pour the drink, he stops and contemplates on whether he wants to forget what he saw. He instead wants answers. He picks up his glass and before it touches his mouth, he gets a strange feeling in his gut. He has the thought again to throw away the Hennessey. He sits the glass down in front of him and stares for a moment.

He, Then Me, Comes You

Why would he have such thoughts, and especially at this particular time?

He stops and covers his mouth wondering if he is schizophrenic or even possessed because of seeing strange things. He begins to wonder if he needs to see a doctor or if he needs to take medication.

Scared by the outcome, he tries to reason with himself. But because the thoughts had so much clarity he decides to listen. Lamar takes his glass into the kitchen and pours the contents down the drain. He then gets this feeling in his spirit to throw all his liquor away. He gathers up all the bottles of alcohol, and one by one pours the contents down the drain.

Afterwards, he sits back and wonders why the sudden change in his heart. He gets a strong fire in the pit of his stomach with a yearning to understand. As he sits in silence another thought comes to mind:

"Do not lean on your own understanding..."

At this point, Lamar knew it was words from the Bible. His mom used to read it to him when he was a kid. He remembers going to church with her from time to time, but after she died, he was so full of anger that he never wanted to seek out God. He didn't believe in God, nor did he care what He was about. Sure, he had some sense of a higher power, but to have a personal relationship with God didn't seem feasible to him. He couldn't deny what he was feeling at that moment. He craved knowledge on what he saw, and why suddenly the taste of liquor no longer tempted him. He needed answers. He thought he should call one of his friends who could give some type of insight on the matter. He needed his friend who was well versed in the Bible and had a close relationship with God. Lamar begins to pace around his house looking to the ceiling wondering if he will hear more verses from the Bible.

Instead, he grabs his keys and decides to go buy one.

~ *Chapter Two* ~

Remember what you promised Me....

"***Get up.***" The sweet sound of a voice whispers to Jada.

Suddenly she awakens to a dark room. She looks to the window and then looks around the room. She looks around confused by the clarity of the voice. She sits up cautiously, wondering if someone was in the bedroom. She doesn't seem afraid but alert of a presence. She then grabs her phone and looks at the time as it reads 5:00 a.m. She lies back down and closes her eyes. As soon as she drifts off to sleep she hears the voice again.

"***Get up.***" Jada quickly sits up. The sound of the voice was so clear, she becomes afraid and leaps up from the bed and turns on the lights. She grabs her baseball bat that she keeps near her bed and looks around the room with her heart beating rapidly. She holds the bat tightly and looks in every corner of her room. She walks in the bathroom, checking the shower.

"Get it together, Jada," she says to herself as she tries to calm her breathing.

A few months had passed since the incident. Jada was still a little shaken up but seemed to be back to normal. She lies back down wide awake, not able to fall back to sleep. Instead, she grabs her phone and decides if she wants to call Caleb. She gets up and looks out of her window and then to her phone. As she hovers over Caleb's name wondering if to call or not, she senses peace and returns to her bed. She drifts off back to sleep.

Chapter Two

Jada is sitting in a chair in a dark room. She looks around and finds herself looking at two doors. The doors are closed. Not knowing where she is, she quickly gets up and looks around.

"Hello!"

Her heart begins to beat faster as she panics trying to figure out where she was and how she had gotten there. She wonders if she was kidnapped and they are holding her hostage. She then looks down and notices that she is not tied up. Moments later both doors are opened and a loud voice comes over the room.

"*Choose.*" The voice she hears is the same voice she heard earlier telling her to get up.

As she looks at both doors, she notices a bright light in one of them. Through the door to the right, she sees a light, bright like the sun, full of people having fun and laughing. As she takes a closer look around the room, she notices that the people in the room have a calamitous look to them. Frightened by what she sees she gets this eerie feeling and she immediately jumps back.

"What in the crazy hell!"

Ironically, that's what the place reminded her of. She walks over to the other

door and looks inside. Unable to see anything, she yells out.

"Hello!" Suddenly she hears the same voice.

"Faith... faith is required to enter."

Jada gets the tingling feeling through her body and she decides to walk through the door. Immediately the door closes behind her and she is in total darkness. She drops to her knees and, suddenly, this incredible urge to cry comes storming out of her.

"*You need to have faith to move forward. Trust in thy Lord with all thine heart...*"

****

He, Then Me, Comes You

The loud sound of the alarm wakes Jada from her slumber. Her heart is beating fast as she touches her face, and she appears to be crying. She sits up thinking about her dream and how real it felt. She notices her hands are shaking and she looks for her phone. She scrambles, throwing pillows everywhere trying to locate it. Confused, she gets up to get dressed. Suddenly her phone rings, and she stops to look for it again. As she finally finds it, she notices that she has several missed calls. Most are from her mother. Claudia insists on getting her relationship back and has been very persistent. She also is pushing for Jada to mend ties with her sister Mia. Jada being the oldest feels that she is in the right and does not think that what her sister did was worth salvaging. Jada ignores her mother's calls and continues to get dressed and leave for some coffee.

The chilly air graces Jada's face as she stands at the top of her stoop looking out to the world. It has been several days since Jada stepped foot outside. She closes her eyes and inhales the fresh air. When she opens her eyes, she looks to the streets and admires the people walking by going on with their lives. She steps down and walks down the street ending up at her favorite coffee shop. She enters the busy facility to satisfy her palate with some dark roasted coffee. As she stands in line, a very handsome man looks to her. Jada smiles a coy smile and then looks away. After a moment, she turns to look again, but the man is now lost in the crowd. She sighs wondering where he went as she looks around for him.

As she realizes that he may have left, she gives up and then he approaches her.

"Looking for me?" the man asks.

"Oh, hi,..., no, I wasn't looking for you; I was actually looking for, umm... looking for the bathroom," she says while shaking her head lying through her teeth.

The man smiles as he exposes his dimples and his perfect white teeth. Jada stares knowing he knows that she is lying.

"I'm Cree."

"Hello, Cree. I'm Jada."

Chapter Two

"Nice to meet you. Do you mind if I treat you to a cup of coffee?" Cree asks.

"Sure, that would be nice," Jada says with the biggest smile.

Jada, being the hopeless romantic, desperately seeks to be married. However, she was not fortunate in that department. She would always end up with a man who treated her with disrespect and who would ask her to change. She was an eccentric woman and enjoyed comic books, movies, and she also read a lot. She wasn't very prissy or girly. She was very beautiful but was always deemed as the weird one. She despised wearing heels and dresses. Growing up wasn't the best for her. Her mother would always force her to wear pretty dresses and put her hair in big curls with bows. During those times, kids would be outside all day playing, so when Jada would come in for lunch, she would be covered in dirt from head to toe. Her hair would be a mess and her dress sometimes torn from when she would climb trees. Her mother ultimately gave up and allowed her daughter to be who she was. She decided to buy her clothes that made her feel more comfortable. Jada kept that sense of tomboyish style, but most people would always think something was wrong with her. Often, she would find herself changing her style and what she liked in order to fit the needs of the man she was dating at the time. Needless to say, it never worked out.

Cree escorts Jada to a small table in the corner. He pulls her chair out trying to impress her. She smiles big as she gushes over him. She then notices other women admiring him. Jada becomes extremely giddy that he came to her.

"So... Jada, are you married or involved with someone?" Cree asked.

"No, I'm single. Just haven't found the right one yet," she says smiling, trying to be complacent and nonchalant.

"Right... 'the one'. Everyone seems to be looking for it but can never find it. I wonder if 'the one' exists."

"You don't believe in finding the one?" Jada says as she stares into Cree's almond-shaped eyes. Cree smiles and finds a way to grace Jada's hand as he reaches for the sugar.

"Well, everyone wants love eventually, but men don't necessarily look for the one."

He, Then Me, Comes You

"What do men look for?"

"The one right now."

"Oh, wow, is that right?" Jada says surprised by his candor.

"I'm just saying."

"Thanks for that."

"I know I may sound cliché but you are beautiful. It's hard to believe that you are single," Cree says with a slight smile.

"Yea, I know, right? I often wonder that myself," Jada says putting on an air of humility.

"You are funny-I like that. Why don't we have an official date? I would love to take you to dinner, get to know you better."

"I would love that," Jada says trying not to look too pleased.

Cree and Jada exchange numbers. He then gets up and kisses her on the cheek leaving Jada with a big smile across her face. As she sips on her coffee, she sits in awe and excitement about her upcoming date.

Still smiling, she notices a man staring at her. The man appears to be in his late 50's. His chocolate complexion is graced with a soft black and gray beard. Jada looks away and then back at the older gentleman. The man is now reading. Jada feels connected to the man somehow but doesn't understand why. She shrugs it off and leaves the coffee shop and begins to walk home to get ready to go to the community center where she worked with kids. She was very well off, so she really didn't need to work. She had sold some of her work when she was in college. She would ghost write for many A-listed authors. Jada never wanted the fame of being known for her work.

Knowing that her hard work did well was satisfaction enough. As she walks home she gets a text message from Cree.

- Hey, you, can't wait to see that beautiful face again -

Jada smiles and clinches her phone hoping that God sent her a man that she can live the rest of her life with. She was tired of the search. She wanted what most wanted. She desired marriage and a family.

Chapter Two

****

"Umm...so let me get this straight,...Vanessa was basically ready to do anything you wanted her to do and you pushed her away because of something you thought you saw?" John asks Lamar in a condescending manner.

"Yea..."

"Man, what trip are you on?" John inquired.

"Look, I know what I saw."

"Right, and you also threw away your Hennessey? You could have given it to me. You don't throw away Hennessey. What's wrong with you?"

"I knew I shouldn't have told you."

"Nah, bruh, you did the right thing. Now we can get you the help you very much need," John says, laughing at Lamar.

Lamar throws John a menacing look. John takes a shot of Patron while shaking his head. As Lamar sits in the bar watching everyone screaming at the game, he suddenly feels out of place. He no longer enjoys being at the bar with his friends screaming at the TV. He wonders if there is more to life than this, and if he would ever find someone again to share it with.

"All I know is now Vanessa is telling everyone how weird you are."

"Do you think I care what Vanessa thinks, including anyone she hangs around?"

"You should. If this gets around, you may never get any more women," John says bluntly.

"Man, I don't care about that."

John looks at Lamar confused and gets the feeling that he is talking to a stranger. He no longer recognizes his friend.

"Are you saying you are into men now?"

"I'm leaving." Lamar gets up from the stool and leaves two twenty-dollar bills on the bar for his meal. John has his hands up gesturing

He, Then Me, Comes You

that he was just kidding, but he continues to shake his head as Lamar leaves the bar without another word.

John then takes another shot of Patron and continues to watch the game. As Lamar heads to his vehicle, he tries to understand the change he is going through and what exactly was happening.

Maybe a midlife crisis? Surely not. He gets in his vehicle and sits for a moment, hanging his head in hopes of finding some answers. As soon as the thought of what his purpose in life was supposed to be comes to his mind, it is quickly replaced with another thought.

"Seek ye first the kingdom of God..."

Lamar knew then that he was hearing God. But he wondered why in the world would God be talking to him?

He was never much of a religious person, and he didn't think he believed in God.

"Surrender to Me and I will give you life..."

"How? How do I surrender?" Lamar said to himself.

He gets frustrated and wonders why God would speak to him in that way. Why wouldn't God give him a whole paragraph or engage in a dialogue with him. Why was Godspeaking to him at all? Lamar puts his car into gear and heads home. He enters his home feeling empty. He needed answers but didn't know where or who he could talk to. Lamar grew up in foster care. He lost his mom at the age of eleven. It was just he and his mom. He never knew his father. He was told that his dad was in the military. After joining, his dad never returned home. He often wondered what his father was like. Lamar wondered if he was anything like him.

His mother never told him much about his dad because she was bitter about his leaving her. His mother fell out of touch with his relatives and never spoke of them. When Lamar tried to search for some of his relatives, he learned that they didn't want to have anything to do with him because of his mother. Lamar is a biracial man. His mother was a white woman with red hair and a pale face that was graced with beautiful freckles. His father was a black man, born and raised in Detroit, Michigan. He had learned that some of his relatives were racists and denied he ever existed. This put a pain in Lamar's soul that he could never heal no matter how hard he tried to mask it, not even with one-night stands and alcohol.

~37

Chapter Two

No matter what he tried to do, he was never completely satisfied. He tried to find his father, but the military wouldn't provide him with any information or answers. He often wondered if he had any brothers or sisters, if his father ever remarried, or if his father had ever tried looking for him. As Lamar sat on his sofa in silence and confusion, he heard from God again.

"Come to me, you who have been weary and burdened and I will give you rest."

As Lamar listens to the words of God, he begins to cry. He covers his face in amazement of how the words of God are imprinted on his heart. He feels the love of God holding him.

"My son, pay attention to what I say; turn your ear to My words. Do not let them out of your sight, keep them within your heart; for they are life to those who find them and health to one's whole body."

Lamar then tries to hold back the pain, but he starts screaming. He shouts out in sheer pain as his tears begin to fall vigorously down his face. He screams for answers and how he should get those answers.

"Surrender to Me."

Lamar is fighting against this feeling inside him, but he can't hold back his hot tears of pain and anger. "No, this isn't how life is." Lamar tries to convince himself. He grabs his phone and begins to text a woman to come by so he could mask the pain he is feeling.

"Surrender to Me."

Lamar jumps up and begins to pace the room. He begins to smack himself back to reality.

"No. I don't want to be let down. I can't do this!"

Suddenly his breathing becomes heavy, and he feels the heaviness in his heart. "I can't breathe," he whispers to himself. Lamar drops to his knees. Unable to fight the strong feeling in his spirit, Lamar lifts his hands and falls to the floor.

"I surrender!" He yells and weeps for hours until he falls asleep on the sofa.

He, Then Me, Comes You

Lamar awakens by a pounding on his front door. He gets up and walks over to the door and looks to see who it may be. A delivery man signals that he has a package for him. Lamar opens the door to a Fed Ex man holding a box. He signs for it and closes the door. He examines it and places it on the sofa. Then, looking around, Lamar wondered why he didn't make it to his bedroom last night. He goes to the kitchen and makes himself a cup of coffee. Moments later he walks back into the den and looks at the package. He examines it to see who it came from. When he opens the package, he finds a letter, a journal, and pictures. Within the journal are old writings and scriptures. He opens the letter, and it reads:

"Dear Son, I'm writing this letter because it's time I gave you a sense of who you are and where you came from. I'm sorry it took so long for me to reach out to you, but I was afraid. I was afraid that you would hate me or reject me because I wasn't there for you. My heart ached for years because you were not with me. Before your mother died, I tried to see you, but because I had left you both, she kept me from you and told me to leave you alone if I wasn't going to stay in your life. To be honest, son, I wasn't going to stay. I was not in a good place and in no position to teach you how to be a man. I was discharged from the military and became addicted to drugs.

When I found out you were in foster care, they wouldn't let me have you because of my addiction. By the time I became clean, you were already a man, and I didn't know how to locate you. After years of prayer, I finally found you. However, I've been told that you are not ready to meet me yet, so I'm giving you my journal.

Please find it in your heart to forgive me, and we will hopefully meet soon. Be blessed, Son."

Lamar is in tears after reading the letter. He wonders how his dad found out where he lived, or why he feels he's not ready to meet. There was no return address to send a letter back. Lamar covers his mouth as he sits in utter shock at what is transpiring in his life. He gets on his knees to pray. He couldn't believe just last night how he was hoping to find answers to the real person he was and what his purpose was. No sooner than he hears from God and lets Him in, God begins to give him answers. Amazed by His grace, Lamar begins to praise and thank God. Unfamiliar with this action, he

Chapter Two

smiles with hope.

"Thank you, God! Thank you!"

He lies on the floor crying with excitement praising God for his answers. As he lies on his back looking to the ceiling, he wonders why he didn't go to God earlier. He then wonders if he had brothers or sisters, possibly nieces or nephews. He thinks maybe he wouldn't have to live his life without relatives after all. Moments into his praise he gets a text from another woman John tried to set him up with. Lamar ignores the text. He then decides to reply to the woman that he's not interested and that it was a bad time. Lamar decides at that moment to surrender fully to God. He needed to know what or how God could influence his life. Excited by all of these changes in his life, he gets up to look through the journal he received. He couldn't believe the entries that were written. They speak of his father's heart and of his intentions with Lamar. Also inside the journal were old photos of when his dad was a kid and of his grandparents. Overwhelmed by this gift, Lamar closes the book and begins to cry. He couldn't believe how much he had cried over the last couple of days. The last time Lamar cried was at his mother's funeral when he was just a little boy. He didn't think he had any true, heartfelt feelings anymore. He always felt dead inside. He felt like an empty hollow shell of a man, lost and without purpose. He then begins to get on his phone to learn about God. He decides to get in touch and set up a meeting from a close friend that was very mature in the faith. Moments into his search he gets another text from John.

-Mar, I can't believe you blew off Kayla! You didn't get a chance to see her body!

What's been going on with you? It's like I don't know you anymore -

Lamar is saddened by John's text. He knew that he was turning away from that lifestyle because his main focus now was to become a true servant of God. He wanted to walk in God's truth and purpose for his life. He could only reply that he was sorry, but to his amazement, he really wasn't sorry. Lamar knew in his heart that soon he and John would grow apart; his newfound faith may

He, Then Me, Comes You

even end their friendship. It might even bury other friendships as well.

Lamar thought long and hard about this, but he soon came to the conclusion that he could pray for his friends and hope that maybe one day they, too, would discover a new life-a life full of love, faith, and hope in God.

"***Because strait is the gate, and narrow is the way, which leadeth unto life, and few there be that find it.***"

~ *Chapter Three* ~

What's done in the dark comes to light....

Jada is lying peacefully at rest. She then gets up and heads to the bathroom. As she walks and stumbles back to her bed, she notices a change in her room. She stands there dazed not quite awake. As she looks around her room, unfamiliar with the surroundings. She noticed only her bed was there. Confused by this she looks around wondering if she was robbed? She then thought how could she have been robbed while she was asleep? How could they take all her possessions without her hearing anything? She is not a heavy sleeper. As she sits on her bed, she then looks down and notices that her sheets were a different color. It was a deep red. She then looks up and sees her very first boyfriend, Kalel. She jumps back, startled by his presence.

"Kalel? What the... how did you know where I lived? How did you get in here?" She asked as she tries to turn on a light. Kalel doesn't speak but has this look in his eyes of seduction. He walks over towards Jada. As he approaches her, she becomes paralyzed unable to move. She is now scared as her eyes begin to widen with anxiety trying to break free from her paralyzed state. He leans in and kisses Jada. She immediately becomes aroused and ashamed from feeling this for him. She closes her eyes in hopes that he will go away. She then opens them up again and looks to Kalel but he is no longer Kalel, but Tony,

Chapter Three

Jada's second lover. Shook by this conundrum, Jada eyes become widen again and she is still unable to move. She tries to scream but no sound is present from her lips. Jada becomes frightened but she's not able to do anything but allows Tony to continue with kissing and touching her. Jada is trying her best to break free and run but is unsuccessful. She then looks away and asks God to help her. When she looks back she notices Tony is now Corey, another lover of hers.

"What the hell is going on!" she screams out. Jada now erratic screams louder as she attempts to push him off of her.

"Get off me! Get off me!"

At some point, Jada did get Corey to stop and walked towards the edge of the bed and stood there almost as if he was motionless. No thoughts or emotions. When he stood by her bed, she then saw in a shadow of the room, were all of the men she had sex with. All of them were in line at the foot of her bed with Caleb in front with blood on his hands. Jada then looks down at her sheets and notice that there was blood on the bed and a dead stillborn baby. Jada begins to scream, but then is woken up to the sound of her alarm on her phone.

The sun beams in her room shining on her face. Jada is breathing hard as if she's not able to catch her breath. She is shaken by the dream and begins to cry. She doesn't understand why she would have that type of dream. She grabs her phone and notices a text message from Cree.

-Looking forward to tonight-

Jada smiles but is still uneasy about her dream. What could it all mean? She tries to shake it off. The abortion she had still haunts her. She had had four abortions since she was with Caleb. He only found out about the one and couldn't handle the secrecy. He felt that there needed to be a discussion but Jada felt it was her body, therefore her decision. She couldn't have the baby at that time in

He, Then Me, Comes You

her life. She didn't know whose it belonged to because she cheated on him. She didn't want to go through the embarrassment of testing several men. The time she slept with several men was a dark time in her life. She felt empty and didn't know what to do to fill that emptiness. Her flesh had a mind of its own. It controlled her every thought and seduced her with every opportunity that came to her. She was an empty shell of a person. At that time she didn't care who she hurt or what consequences came after.

"It was just a dream. It was just a dream." She says as she puts her hands to her face trying to compose herself.

"I am really going crazy. What is wrong with me?" Jada mumbles as she is running her hands over her face to make sense of the changes that's occurring in her life. She sighs hard with an urge to pray and ask for guidance, but soon pushes that feeling to the side. She rises and gets dressed to start her day. After she gets dressed she heads out the door and notices the older man she saw in the coffee shop sitting on the corner in front of the store. She looks around wondering if anyone is acting abnormal to the man just sitting there. However everyone seems unbothered by the man or doesn't seem to care. She wonders if the man is homeless or need help. She walks towards him and with each step there is a gnawing in her spirit.

"*Turn around, leave the man alone. He is crazy.*" The injurious voice whispers to Jada.

Jada pauses but needs to know this man. So she proceeds. She walks over to him and stands in front of him as they lock eyes. She gets a familiar feeling in her spirit and is at ease.

"Hello," she says.

"Hello. How are you this morning?" The man asked.

"I'm ok I guess. Um do you know me?"

"No ma'am I do not."

"I saw you in the coffee shop and it felt like we knew each other."

Chapter Three

"No ma'am."

Jada seems drawn to the older man. She felt like he is somewhat of a protector, maybe even a father. She looks the man up and down to observe the situation. He doesn't appear to be homeless. His salt and pepper hair is cut and trimmed with his beard lined up gracing his dark complexion. His eyes are bright with wisdom and knowledge. Maybe even with some secrets. She observes his clothing. They are very neat and ironed on point, maybe disciplined with the military.

"Did you eat?" Jada was inclined to ask but questioned herself as to why she needs to know this man.

"Not yet." the man smiled as he looks into Jada's big brown eyes. It gives Jada peace. She doesn't feel threatened but comforted.

"Would you like to join me for breakfast?"

"I would be delighted young lady, my treat?"

The older gentleman gets up and grabs his umbrella. Jada gives off a coy smile and extends her hand causing the man to pause.

"Oh no, I invited you, it's my treat I insist... please," Jada argued.

"Well ok then." The man complied.

"Were you expecting rain?" Jada asked.

"Well you never know."

"Um, what's your name by the way?"

"Oh, my friends call me LD."

"Nice to meet you LD... I'm Jada."

LD smiles and shakes her hand. She smiles back. He then escorts her up the street to this quaint restaurant a few blocks away

As they sit at the table looking at the menu, Jada keeps her eye on LD. He doesn't notice but can feel that she's starring and continues to act ignorant.

He, Then Me, Comes You

"So... I think I will have the pancakes, how about you?" LD stated.

"Uh yea, the pancakes here are really good." Jada says and is interrupted by the waitress ready to take their order. After she's done, LD sips on his coffee waiting for Jada to ask the question she has been inquiring about. Moments pass.

"So, are you going ask me?" LD says.

"Ask you what? She says trying to nonchalant.

"You seem like you have something on your mind. You are examining me like I'm your patient."

"Are you homeless?" Jada asks.

"No ma'am."

"Are you stalking me?"

"Why would I be stalking you? What reason would I have to do so? I don't know who you are."

"I know it's just... I've seen you everywhere, and now you were just sitting on the corner right where I live. I mean who does that?"

"I get it, it seems strange..."

"Strange? It's down right creepy." Jada said letting out a laugh indicating she was in agreement with the unusual way of them meeting.

"I assure you, I'm not after you. I've been led to sit and wait and I'm just being obedient."

Jada smirks, raising her eyebrow in confusion. "Ok who told you to sit there? And why would you do it?"

"Well my Father led me to sit there and wait."

"He told you to wait? Wait on what?" Jada asked.

"Well he didn't tell me that yet. He just told me to wait."

Chapter Three

Jada grabs her coffee and sips on it. LD looks to Jada smiling. She then gives a coy smile still confused by LD's disposition.

"Ok you can tell me the truth, are you crazy? Did you escape from a mental hospital or something? I won't judge."

LD lets out this haughty laugh that disrupts the entire restaurant. Startled by his response Jada moves her coffee so he wouldn't spit in it from laughing. She sits waiting for him to stop laughing. She then laughs a little herself waiting for his response.

"I'm sorry young lady, but I didn't expect you to be…curt."

"Curt?"

"Yes. You are being judgmental. Just because someone sits outside for a period of time, makes them crazy?"

"No I was more on the part of someone telling you to for no reason."

"There is a reason, He didn't disclose that information to me yet," LD said.

"Well, I'm sorry for being obtuse. Tell me... your father, is he a stubborn person?"

"No, well He can be in our eyes, but I wouldn't call it being stubborn, more like perfect timing."

"Perfect timing? Who is this dude, God?"

LD looks to Jada and nods. She sits puzzled but doesn't say anything. She only stares at him. She begins to question her motives for having breakfast with this man. She then wondered if her curiosity is finally going to kill that nosey cat in her mind. Her life hasn't been the same since the incident that she barely remembers. It's not that she's afraid but more aware of herself and feels led as if someone was pulling her towards something. Soon the waitress comes with their meals and sits it down in front of them.

"Here yah go, can I get you anything else?" the waitress asked.

"No thank you." LD answered.

He, Then Me, Comes You

LD begins to pray over his food as Jada watches for a moment. She then mimics and closes her eyes as well. When she closes her eyes, she sees a lamb wearing a crown. Startled, she quickly opens her eyes and finds LD smiling looking to her. Her eyes become widen.

"Ok LD, you keep smiling at me. Now I don't know what you think this is, but I'm not looking for a sugar daddy. Using God as a pick line is very distasteful."

"Ms. Jada, I am old enough to be your father. I'm not interested in little girls."

"Well, being old would imply you being a sugar daddy. I just want to lay down some ground rules.

"Well thanks for the heads up. But I'm good."

LD cuts up his pancakes and butters them. He takes a bite and his eyes smile as if he hadn't eaten in days. In fact he hasn't. He was praying and fasting on what God was leading him to do. He then looks to Jada.

"Are you married Ms. Jada?"

"No not yet, I would like to be, if I can find the right guy."

"Have you asked God who you should be with?"

"Ha, yea right, like God is interested in my love life. I'm sure he has wars and poverty and things like that to be more concerned about other than me."

"You think so?" LD inquired.

"Yea I know so," Jada says very sure of her statement by gesturing with her facial of expression with a condescending undertone.

"I find it funny when people speak about God and know nothing about Him."

"Excuse me?" Jada says as she is now offended by LD statement.

"I said I find it funny, people speak of…."

Chapter Three

"I heard you. I was just implying why you would say that I don't know God," Jada says interrupting LD appalled at his accusations.

"Do you have a relationship with Him?"

"No but I don't need to have a relationship with God to know him." Jada says with an attitude.

"Young lady, what person in their right mind can say they know another person and do not have a relationship with them? Now you may know of him, but to say you know him takes a lot more work."

"Look, I didn't ask you to breakfast to get preached to. I get enough of that from my mother."

"Enough? I don't think you have had any."

Jada immediately stops eating and sits back in her seat. She is shocked that he would dare imply anything. Her face is scrunched up in an offensive manner but she also intrigued by LD's bold approach. She then sips on her coffee to cleanse her palate. He didn't seem to have very much respect for her she thought. She felt ashamed, even worrisome. She was used to men eating out of the palm of her hand, no matter what age he was. She didn't like being misunderstood as a woman, it always had her at a disadvantage and she felt out of control. Suddenly she was recalled back to her dream she had encountered just this morning. She looks down to her plate and then looks to LD.

"I would say sorry and I didn't mean to offend you but I would be lying," LD states.

"Ok LD, I'll bite. How do I get this relationship with God?" Jada asks sarcastically.

"Full surrender, faith, and obedience."

"Like in a cult?"

LD sits up and looks to her, He smiles and then continues.

He, Then Me, Comes You

"Young lady with all due respect, referring to the Almighty as a cult is offensive and if you are not going to be serious then there is no point in speaking with you on this matter."

"Ok... ok. I'm sorry, I really want to know because well..." Jada pause in the middle of her statement. Concerned by her demeanor LD doesn't push her to continue but waits. She hesitates and looks away. She swallows hard trying not to tear up and cry in front of all those people in the restaurant. LD is compelled to pray while waiting for her to finish, asking God what he should do to help her. Jada then begins to cry.

"I can't do this. I don't know why, or what God wants from me, but next time you talk to Him since you have a great relationship with Him, ask Him why He would allow something so bad to happen to me? Ask Him why He continues to hurt me and let me down." Jada states angry and fearful she is being open and exposed. She grabs her things and head out of the door. LD watches as she leaves. He sits in silence wondering what he should do next. He begins to finish his pancakes and realizes Jada didn't pay for the meal. He smiles to himself.

"Well I guess it was on me."

The waitress returns with a coffee pot. "Did you want any more coffee sir?"

"Uh no just the bill please," LD requested.

"Oh, no you're all set that woman just paid for you and your daughter's meal," the waitress said while pointing at an elderly woman. She smiled and waved to LD. He waves back and nods.

"Is she a regular here?"

"Yes, she comes in here from time to time with her prayer group." LD smiles and looks up. He shakes his head and tops off his coffee and heads out.

~ *Chapter Four* ~

No one said it would be easy…

Lamar is lying on his sofa, reading his Bible he just recently purchased. He has been studying for a few months now. Not sure what he's reading, he begins to cross-reference the scriptures he reads. He huffs in frustration. "I'm trying here, Lord. What do you want me to do? Please lead me and I will obey." He says, frustrated. Lamar throws the Bible and begins to pace across the room.

"This is not who I am! I don't do this religion thing!"

Lamar waits to hear from God. Nothing comes to him except the feeling of hunger. He doesn't want to eat and instead picks up the Bible and begins reading again. Soon his stomach begins to rumble and he can no longer concentrate on what he's reading. Lamar read about fasting and praying. He thought it would be a good idea so that he could get more answers. But God hasn't spoken to him. He has fasted for three days now and still no breakthrough. He shakes his head in frustration, wondering what to do. Silence consumes the room. He then jumps up and grabs his keys and heads out of the door. He then comes back in and stands in silence.

"If I'm going to do this, I'm doing it right," he said to himself.

Lamar goes upstairs to change his attire that's more appropriate for an upscale restaurant. After he dresses, he heads back out. He goes to one of the classiest restaurants in town. Because he is well known through his organization, he didn't need to make a reservation. As he pulled up in his very expensive vehicle to the valet, he notices a

Chapter Four

woman getting out of the car. Lately, Lamar hasn't paid too much attention to women, but this woman gave off a familiar feeling. Lamar shrugs it off and enters the restaurant.

Later in the evening, he notices the woman sitting at the bar. As he stares at her face, he realizes that he knows the woman. It's Jada. She appears to look sad and lonely. He gestures for the waiter. When the waiter comes, Lamar then asks the waiter to invite the young lady to join him if she wasn't waiting on anyone. When the waiter left, Lamar watched him walk over to Jada. She begins to listens to the waiter then looks to Lamar. At first, she looks puzzled but then recognizes Lamar and heads to the table. As she approaches Lamar, he gets this feeling in his gut. He has butterflies. He felt the same way he did when he first saw her when they were ten years old.

"What the hell is going on? Why am I nervous?" he says to himself.

Jada smiles as she comes closer. He smiles back, very excited and anxious to be near her.

"Wow. Mar, is that you?"

"Hey, Jaybird."

Lamar gets up from the table and they embrace each other. He closes his eyes, as he holds on tight to her. He smells her hair as they continue to hug. The scent is of coconut oil. He leans back and looks to her enchanting face putting him at ease. It reminds him of a time when he was happy. Peaceful.

"What are the odds of us meeting?" Jada asks.

"Wow, woman you look great."

"I know, right!"

"Here you go with that big head of yours," Lamar says.

"I was just kidding, how long has it been, like twenty years?" Jada says, still smiling. Her heart is beating rapidly as her eyes dance with affection looking into his.

"That sounds about right," Lamar confirms.

He, Then Me, Comes You

He then pulls out her chair. Lamar never was a man of chivalry. He never cared about women's feelings or even thought of pulling out her chair or open doors. This one was different. Jada had captured his soul.

"Wow, well you're just a gentleman. I bet you have these women drinking your feet water," Jada says while laughing.

"Oh woman, please. What about you? You look gorgeous. Why are you here alone?"

"Well I had a date, but something came up and he had to cancel."

"I hate to say I'm sad about it, but I'm not. I'm glad I get to spend the evening with you."

Jada smiles as she grabs her glass of water sitting on the table. They both exchange looks as if they were kids again, excited. They both had that feeling of puppy love. The type of love you have when you first like someone and you are nothing but smiles and giggles.

"So... Mar, are you single? Why are you here alone?"

"I needed a night to myself and yes I am single. I've been divorced for three years now. It didn't work out the way I had hoped."

"I'm sorry, what happened?"

"Well she cheated on me and I was…" Lamar stops and pause for a moment. He becomes puzzled by his comments, Lamar sat back, wondering why he had disclosed information so quickly to Jada. Usually he would keep personal things to himself. But somehow with Jada he becomes paralyzed and smitten. He can't help but confide in her.

"You what?"

"Nothing, don't really want to talk about it."

"Are you sure? Cause it kinda feels like you do. Like you need to talk about it."

"Um, nah it's nothing we should talk about right now." Lamar stated as he clears his throat and drinks a sip of his water.

Chapter Four

"I had such a crush on you when we were kids," Jada said.

"Really?"

"Uh huh, it was massive."

"I had a crush on you too, I would find ways to touch you or be near you," Lamar stated.

"Wow I always thought you liked Sara because she was always around you, always laughing and flirting. She couldn't control herself. I wanted to punch her in the face."

"Look at you. You were jealous."

"Yeah I was."

"Sara, she wasn't the type of girl you would date. She showed all the boys her breasts if we paid her a dollar. She gave me a special for only a quarter, and she let me touch them."

"Are you serious? Ugh, I knew she was nasty."

Lamar looks to Jada and smiles. She playfully hits him and they share a look. They begin to touch one another's hand and continue to look at one another.

"Did you want some wine?"

"Yes please."

"I always liked you and how you acted like you were so tough," Lamar said.

"I did not act. I am tough," Jada smiled and said as she blushes and stare at Lamar for a moment.

The waiter comes to the table and asks if they were ready to order. Lamar politely orders for them both with Jada's approval. As the waiter walks away, Jada casually embraces Lamar's leg under table with her foot.

"Jaybird how long have you been dating? Are you two serious?"

"Jaybird? I haven't heard that in so long, it's like music to my ears. You were the only one that could get away with that."

"I thought it fit you well."

He, Then Me, Comes You

"Oh ok. But I just met the man actually. This was supposed to be our first date."

"Doesn't seem promising with him standing you up."

"Oh whatever, he said he had to take his grandmother to the store."

Lamar gives her a look wondering if she really believed the excuse that was given to her. He pauses as he stares gesturing for her to think about what was just said.

"And you believe that?"

"Well I don't know I guess." Jada says as she looks off thinking that maybe he was playing her and that he was in fact lying to her. Her thoughts become interrupted with the waiter bring them their meals. Lamar grabs Jada hand and closes his eyes and says a silent prayer giving thanks for the meal. Jada just observes wondering if Lamar could be the man that she hoped for. She shrugs off her thought and begins to eat. Moments pass as they are reminiscing about their childhood days and what they both been up to up until this point. She had learned that he was very successful with many of his business and he learned the same about her writing.

"I can't believe you remembered one of my poems."

"Oh yeah, check it. I'm a pretty girl. But I don't like to be a pretty girl. Dressed in shimmer and sass, showing off my … Put me in some Pumas or Adidas girl, showing my true colors to the world."

"Oh wow, that is amazing. You really surprise me Mar." Jada says as she graces his hand. He smiles and they lock eyes.

"Mar if you were divorced three years ago why you single?"

"I'm not really dating women right now."

"Don't tell me you are one of those clichéd dudes who gets their heart broken and is now closed off from women."

"And why is that a cliché? Men don't bounce back as easily as you all do. You all fall in love every other week."

Chapter Four

"Ok well there is a little truth there, but c'mon Mar. This is partly your fault."

Stunned by her response Lamar immediately freezes and goes into defense mode. He picks up his glass of wine and drinks, thinking of a rebuttal. Usually he would find a way to defend himself and change the subject but curious of what she might say, he instead entertains the conversation.

"Why is this my fault? My ex-wife cheated on me?"

"Well why did she cheat? Were you there for her or were you wrapped up in your own world ignoring her?"

"I didn't force her to sleep with another man. You sound ridiculous."

"Oh, I see now... is that what you do?"

"What do you mean?" Lamar asks.

"As a defense mechanism? You belittle people."

Uneasy by her discernment of him, Lamar quickly becomes angry.

"I'm not belittling you."

"Uh sure you are, I believe that's the sole definition of belittling someone, you diminish and discounted my opinion. Even if it didn't hold any truth, why did you feel the need to make me feel less to even think that way?" Jada replied.

Suddenly Lamar anger turns into conviction. He has been told that he was a jerk on several occasions, but not really understanding why. Of course, there were times when he felt the need to cut people down because of their haughty nature but he never thought it was an everyday practice.

"You have to remember I've known you since we were what... ten years old. I remember when everyone used to pick on you because you had that speech impediment. Do you remember? You felt you had to prove yourself and make people feel bad because that's how they made you feel."

He, Then Me, Comes You

Lamar couldn't believe he buried that pain from his childhood for so long. He wondered if he often belittled his ex-wife. He sat in silence thinking back at the times Kelly would give her opinion on some of his projects. He immediately remembers this very important project he was working on with teenage boys and helping them cope with living in a fatherless home. Kelly suggested he could have them role-play to get their feelings out, and somehow get them to express how they truly felt. He told Kelly that she should leave dealing with boys to him and she wouldn't understand because she was a privileged woman. He called her ridiculous just as he did with Jada. He remembers the look on Kelly's face as she walked away. He then realized her pain and somehow felt it in his spirit at that moment. Uncomfortable with his newly found realization he immediately becomes ill. Noticing the change in Lamar's complexion, Jada looks concerned.

"Mar, are you ok? You don't look to well."

"I'm not sure. I suddenly don't feel so good."

"Ok we can leave now. I'll get the check." Jada gets up from the table to get a hold of the waiter. Moments later she returns to the table and there is money left for the check but Lamar is no longer present. Jada looks around but cannot locate him. He was afraid to be seen by her. He didn't like feeling vulnerable and exposed. He did a great job at building a wall up so that he may never feel hurt or pain by anyone. She sighs with disappointment and hands the waiter the money for the check. She sits back down to reflect on the conversation. She didn't mean to upset him only wanted to understand him. Jada immediately felt the need to protect and help him but didn't quite understand the nature of the situation. Why did she need to protect him? Why did she have that strong desire to be there for him? It was as if she loved him. She thought how she could love someone she barely knew. Sure they knew each other when they were kids but as adults she didn't know what type of man he had become. She grabs her heart, as it feels incredibly heavy. She then thinks about how she may never see him again. She gets up to the leave the restaurant.

Chapter Four

****

Lamar enters his home still feeling uneasy with a sharp pain in his gut. The pain is so unbearable that he drops to his knees. He begins to crawl towards the bathroom he doesn't make it. Instead he lies on the floor in complete darkness. Silence fills the room as he closes his eyes hoping to become free from the unexplainable pain he was experiencing. Not knowing what to do, Lamar opens his mouth and speaks.

"God... I... um need you. Please help me." Lamar lies there waiting to hear from God. Hoping to get some type of comfort. He calls again. "Father, help me... please!"

Lamar is still lying on the floor keeping his eyes closed awaiting a response. Suddenly, he feels a burning sensation in the pit of his stomach. It felt like a volcano was erupting in his body. He turns over and gets up on his knees and begins to vomit all the wine he drank and food from the dinner. As his eyes begin to bulge out of his head, tears fall down his face. He lies back on the floor on his back looking up to the ceiling relieved from the pain. He thinks what could have caused him to get so ill. He looks to God for answers. Silence continues to consume the home. Lamar then gets up and heads to the bathroom cleaning his face. After he washes his face, he again feels convicted for what he may have done to his ex-wife and now Jada. He wondered if that was the only thing he did. Not sure but convinced it wasn't, he went to his bedroom and got on his knees and asked for answers.

"Lord, please help me understand my faults in my marriage. Show me what I've done that may have caused Kelly to be with someone else. I ask that you forgive me for not being the husband I should have been. Please I beg you to show me."

Lamar hangs his head down while he remains on his knees. As he sits waiting he begins to weep. The thought of Jada comes to his mind as he remembers her smile. He thinks that he may never see her again. He was rude and hoped she would forgive him and one day they will cross paths again when he was in a better frame of mind and spirit. He remembered how her smile made him feel. He felt at ease, calm and content. He wondered how could something so small change his mood or put him in a certain place of serenity. As he continues to think of her, calmness comes over Lamar. He sits in peace. He then wondered what were the odds of him seeing his childhood crush. He thought if he didn't decide to eat at that restaurant would he have seen her? He wonders how she feels about him. He wonders if she only likes him for how he looks or if she would be interested in knowing about his comic books, his love for Game of thrones or his obsession with collecting precious stones. He wonders if she wants to get to know the real him. He gets up and heads back down stairs to clean up the mess he made. After he's done he grabs his Bible and begins to read. He quickly falls asleep after only reading a few scriptures.

****

"Mar! Can you come in here please?" Kelly asked.

"What is it? I'm working on something."

"Please babe!"

Lamar gets annoyed by Kelly's bellowing. He gets up from his desk full of papers and goes upstairs to the bedroom. When he enters, he finds Kelly in lingerie lying on the bed with rose pedals everywhere. She is in a sexy position with a huge smile on her face.

"Well," Kelly inquired.

"Well what?"

"Aren't you going to say something or better yet do something?" Kelly asked still smiling.

"Kell, I have so much work to do, I have a deadline to meet. I can't right now, babe."

Chapter Four

"Mar come on, you can take a break. We haven't made love in months."

"I know Babe; please let me get through this project first."

"That's what you said the last project and the one before that."

"Kelly... what's more important? Huh babe?"

Kelly changes her smile to a disappointing frown. She gets up and sits at the edge of the bed. Tears form in her oval shaped eyes as she shakes her head in disappointment.

"Please try to understand. We wouldn't be able to afford all these nice things if I didn't work. Now let me work. And clean these flowers up," Lamar commanded.

Kelly falls back on the bed letting out a huge sigh. She hadn't had any time with her husband at all since he started his organization.

Lamar wakes up sweating. He looks around trying to calm his breathing. He reflects to the dream he encountered and suddenly more memories of how he neglected his wife comes to mind. He shakes his head disappointed in himself. He gets up and then drops to his knees thanking God for showing him. Lamar didn't realize how much God hears us and wants to help us. He is so appreciative that he gets inspired to help others.

****

Jada is sitting at her dining room table staring at her phone. She couldn't believe she had gotten excited over yet another man who's made an excuse, and a lame one at that. However, she wasn't completely sad about it given her run in with Lamar. She texts Cree and waits for a response. After several minutes, she gives up and looks outside to find LD sitting on the corner again. Jada tries

He, Then Me, Comes You

to convince herself that she wasn't rude and that she should avoid LD at all costs. Somehow her curiosity keeps getting the best of her. Jada then decides to grab a canister and pours some coffee into it. She then leaves and walks down the street where LD is sitting. He looks to Jada as she gives off a coy smile and extends her hand with the canister of coffee.

"Peace offering?" Jada asks.

"Hello Ms. Jada."

"Listen... um LD, I was going through something and I know that's not an excuse, but I just want to say I'm sorry and I hope you will forgive me for storming out on you."

"Thank you and of course I forgive you."

Jada gives LD sad eyes and looks around. As he sips the coffee, she waits for his response on how the coffee taste. She sits next to him.

"So, I guess God told you to wait again?"

"Yes."

"You think God will talk to me?"

"Well it's not a matter of if He will talk to you but a matter of will you listen. He's always speaking. We get too busy with our lives to stop, be still and listen."

Jada puts her head down. She begins to tear up.

"What's wrong Ms. Jada?"

"Well it's kind of embarrassing but I got stood up last night and I don't understand. I mean why would he ask me out and go through the trouble if he wasn't really interested."

"Did you ask him?"

"I tried but he hasn't responded yet."

"What is it that you want?" LD asked.

"What do you mean?" Jada asks, while looking into LD's eyes.

"You seem to be upset about someone you just met, why is that?"

Chapter Four

"I want to get married and have a family. I feel as if I'm getting older and soon no one will want me."

"Not to sound insensitive but, you are concerned about the wrong thing."

"Why do you say that?"

"Well how have you prepared for it?"

"Prepared?"

LD takes another sip of his coffee. He then looks up to the sky. He has a silent conversation with God, hoping to hear from Him with answers on how to help Jada.

"Ms. Jada, do you believe in God?"

"Yes LD," Jada replies.

"Well then start there. Pray and ask your Father in Heaven on what you should do and ask Him to lead you."

"Well it couldn't hurt, I tried everything else."

Jada gets up and waves to LD. As she walks to her door, she gets a text from Cree. Jada thinks how strange it was that at that very moment she decides to go to God, she gets a text from Cree, it was as if it was a distraction. She opens the text and it reads:

-Hey Jada I'm so sorry about last night, it was a crazy day. Please allow me to make it up to you. -

Jada stops and looks back to LD. He is shaking his head no, as if he knew that Cree texted her. She smiles and waves and enters her home. As Jada enters the home she contemplates on whether she should give him another chance. Just as she is about to reply a thought comes to mind.

"He's not the one."

Again, Jada thinks the voice is her thoughts in the back of her mind. And again, she ignores it and replies to his text.

He, Then Me, Comes You

****

Jada is sitting on her sofa dressed for her date with Cree. She looks to her phone for the time. Jada and Cree made plans for dinner at six-thirty. It is now over an hour past the time that they had agreed on. She is now irritated and tries to call him. He doesn't answer and Jada huffs with frustration as she tosses her phone and sits in silence disappointed. She gets up and goes to the window in hopes that LD is sitting on the corner. She is disappointed to find that he is not there. For some unknown reason to her she kept looking for him to guide her, somehow help her with her messy life. She felt that she could trust him with her thoughts and feelings. She sits back down on the sofa wondering why she keeps choosing the wrong men. She often wondered what was wrong with her. She would see women with their mates and she knew that she could make someone happy but she couldn't meet the right one to make happy. Tears start to form in her eyes as she thinks back to a woman once telling her that she would never get married and that she will always be a whore. Jada then reflected to her dream she had with her past lovers all standing next to her bed. She continues to sit in silence. She then decides to get on her knees and pray. As she gets down on her knees, tears fall vigorously down her face. She closes her eyes not sure what to say it. As soon as she begins to pray to the Most High, her phone rings, interrupting her. It was a call from Cree. Jada excitedly answered the phone.

"Hello?"

"Hey Jada, again I am so sorry, is it too late to see you?"

"Um, we could probably catch a late dinner," Jada suggested.

"Actually, will it be ok if I came over and we just hung out?"

Jada looks to her phone for the time again. She contemplates and wonders if she should reschedule. This felt all too familiar and she knew that this would lead to sex or worse. She felt so alone and needed the feeling of being wanted and desired that she ignored her gut feeling and decided to let him come over.

Chapter Four

"Um sure that's fine, I will text you my address."

"Ok I will see you soon."

After Cree hangs up the phone, Jada felt a chill through her body. Everything in her was telling her not to let this man she barely knew in her home. However, the desire to have companionship took over her common sense. Her flesh was in constant battle with her spirit. She worried that something might happen so she decides to call him back.

"Everything will be fine. He's a great guy. He could be the one. He could be your soul mate," the injurious voice insists.

Jada then stops from calling him and perks up. She thinks what if this is my soul mate. What if he's the man I've been hoping for and wanted for so long? Again, Jada not knowing what to look for from God has her judgment clouded. As she quickly straightened up the home, she realizes what LD had said and that God is answering her prayers for a husband. But again, in her gut she felt uneasy. The fact the Cree was coming over for the first time at such a late hour didn't sit well in her spirit, she wasn't at peace. At that moment, Jada wished she had LD's phone number so that she could call and get some advice. During her cleaning, she stops and has a thought.

"He's not the one. It will cause calamity..."

Jada stops and looks to her phone and the time now close to midnight. Soon after she looks to the time her doorbell rings. Again, she has another thought.

"Wait for the Lord, be strong and let your heart take courage."

The thought amazed Jada. She knew without a doubt that God was speaking to her. As she goes to answer the door, her spirit is in frenzy with her carnal ways and desires. She answers and standing there is the very handsome Cree. He has this big smile on his face and he is holding containers of food.

"I know this looks bad on my part but I brought you food."

"Oh, wow thanks, it smells amazing."

"Yea... I know I do smell good, huh." They both laugh at the crony joke.

"I didn't want you think that this was like a booty call or something."

Jada giggles. That's exactly what she thought. Not feeling comfortable yet, she keeps her phone close to her.

"So, to ensure you that this is innocent, we are going to have a meal together, talk a little and then I'm going to leave. Hopefully get a goodnight kiss if our conversation goes well but that is it." Cree says in a joking manner.

Jada smiles and suddenly she's at ease with her body. She grabs some plates and silverware from the kitchen. When she returns, Cree is setting up the food. After seeing that he may mean well, she then wonders if the thought she had was not really God but maybe it was just fear. She smiles and sits at the table. For hours, she and Cree engage in conversation and at the end of the date, she was relieved that Cree talked with her and took the time to get to know her a little. When the night ended, Jada was so full of joy and excitement that she thinks she may have finally found the one. She learned how much Cree liked children and that he was also hardworking and close to his mom. She thought that she really had hit the jackpot. She needed to tell someone. The only person she really wanted to tell was LD. It was odd to her that the first person she wanted to confide in was LD. She felt her friends wouldn't understand given what had happened to her a few months ago. They would judge her and make her feel bad for even dating again.

****

Lamar walked through the door from a hard day of work. Kelly was sitting on the sofa waiting for him. She had tears in her eyes. Lamar was exhausted and he did not want to talk about why Kelly was crying. He didn't do a very good job of

Chapter Four

hiding his feelings about not wanting to console her.

"What is it now Kelly? Everyday it's always something with you."

Lamar grunts and plops down in the chair next to the sofa. Kelly still crying shakes her head in disbelief.

"What did I do to deserve this from you?" Kelly asked.

"What are you talking about? I'm working," Lamar tries to explain.

"Yea I know. You are married to your work." Lamar puts his hands over his face out of frustration. He feels as if marrying Kelly was a mistake and he should have established his career first beforehand.

"I can't do this much longer," Kelly explained.

"Kell, what is it that was so important, that it brought you to tears?" Kelly stands up and wipes away her tears. She is wearing an apron with food stains from the dinner she had prepared all day. She was excited about having a night with her husband of five years. She waited for him to arrive for hours. She started to question the dynamics of their relationship and needed to feel loved and supported. She needed to be a top priority in their marriage but instead she was a second, third or maybe fourth thought to her husband. That night was the night she decided that she would no longer be alone in a loveless marriage. Kelly takes off the apron and exposes her designer dress that she slayed. Her curves hit every point in the dress as if the dress was made just for her. She then tosses the apron on the sofa and look to her husband.

"Happy anniversary Lamar."

Lamar's disposition suddenly changed and he instantly becomes apologetic. At the time, Kelly was so fed up, hearing another apology had no real meaning. They were only words that she became accustomed to. Kelly walked away and went to their bedroom leaving Lamar sitting in the chair with a contrite look on his face. He looked to the ceiling wondering how could he

He, Then Me, Comes You

have forgotten their anniversary. He felt so bad that he wanted to try and make it up to Kelly but knew that nothing could make up for what he had done. He got up and walked over to the dining room table where Kelly had laid out a very romantic spread. She made Lamar his favorite dinner. She bought the best wine and even purchased him a gift. The gift was sitting on the table with a silver bow and note attached to it. He picks up the box and opens it. In the box was a vintage Rolex watch with his initials engraved on it. As he reads the note he tears up, filled with regret. The note reads:

I knew you wanted this babe. I saw you light up when you saw it, maybe one day our son will light up too when you pass it down to him.

Lamar wakes up from his dream. He sits up in the dark filled room. For a while he just sits in silence. Moments later he opens his nightstand and pulls out the watch that Kelly gave him three years ago. He closes his eyes and thanks God for what he is doing in his life. Lamar asked to understand and see what he had done in his previous marriage. He needed to see what he had mastered at hiding. He felt ashamed and disgraceful. He thought that if he provided for his wife that it would be enough. He didn't consider Kelly's feeling at all. He thought since they had been together so long that dating her or showing her attention was not a top priority. He forgot that with women they always needed to feel important and top priority. If only he knew before he drove his wife into another man's arms. Tears begin to fall down Lamar's face as he realizes the type of man he was. He decided to pray.

"Father God, if you bless me with another mate. I promise You that I will be a better husband. I will love and cherish your fragile creation. Show me how to love her first. Show me what I need to do."

Lamar swore he would never marry again. He didn't want to be tied down or responsible for another person. He didn't even want

Chapter Four

kids. It was a typical response to a person going through a tough divorce but he didn't recognize his faults in the marriage. He didn't think that neglect was just as bad as adultery, if not worse. However since he began to get closer to God, the desire in his heart grew strong for another chance at love and marriage. He grabs his Bible and reads until he falls asleep, thanking God for answering is prayers.

****

It has been several weeks since Jada had seen LD. She didn't understand why. For days, she would see him sitting there and then suddenly he's nowhere to be found. She wondered if something had happened to him or if God told him he no longer needed to sit and wait. She missed him even though they only spoke a few times. She felt she needed him in a way. Jada and Cree's relationship has grown within weeks. However, during those weeks, they haven't been on one single date outside of Jada's home. She had never gone to his home or met any of his friends. This was a classic case of a hidden agenda, but Jada was so needy that she continued to ignore the red flags. All her friends were in relationships and she barely sees or speaks to them. All she knew was that she wanted what everyone else had. She often thought of her sister Mia. They were extremely close throughout their life. They hadn't spoken in a year. She couldn't get past the betrayal she thought had transpired between them. She didn't give Mia the time or respect to try to explain. She was preparing for Cree to come to her home again during late hours. She wanted to ask him why they haven't been on any dates but since they haven't slept together or made it official, she felt that asking him would be too presumptuous. She began to wonder if she chooses to sleep with Cree then maybe he would want to take their relationship to the next level. She clearly had self-esteem issues and was in no place to face them. She was swimming in the deep end of denial. She decided to speed things up so decides that she would greet Cree at the door with some sexy lingerie. As she waited on him to arrive the time gets away and

He, Then Me, Comes You

she falls asleep on the sofa. Jada suddenly becomes awaken by the sound of banging on her door. She jumps up to answer and Cree entered her home in a drunken state. Concerned by his appearance she looks to him for an explanation. Instead what she received was something else unexpected.

"What the hell you got on? Were you with another man?" Cree asked while screaming. He is clearly drunk.

Unaware of what was about to happen, Jada tries to calm him down but to no avail, he swiftly slaps her. He hits her so hard that she stumbles and hit the floor. As she sits in a state of confusion, the flashes of a previous abuse comes flooding to her mind. As Cree stands there he looks to her frail half-naked body. He drops to his knees and tries to apologize. Jada is now in tears and shaken by the encounter. She pleads for him to leave. Cree still on his knees begins to wipe away her tears. He hugs and tries to console her.

"No stop, just please... please leave."

"You want me to leave?" Cree asked.

"Yes, I need you to leave me alone."

"Why... so, you can be with that other man?"

"No, what are you talking about?"

"I got something for you. I know what you want."

Cree pushes Jada to the floor and pin her down. As she realizes that he is about to rape her, she screams with all her might and tries her best to push him off her. Cree grabs Jada big afro of hair and drags her across the room. He then turns her over without warning as Jada is squirming around crying out for God to help her. The thought of how this happened played in her mind. She felt helpless and foolish. She knew that Cree was not for her and that continuing to proceed with dating him was wrong. But she ignored what God was trying to warn her of. At that moment, instead of blaming God, she asked Him to forgive her. She then started calling out for Jesus.

"Cree in the name of Jesus I command you to stop! In the name of Jesus get off me! Stop! In the name of Jesus!"

Chapter Four

Suddenly Cree jumped up and looked to Jada. As she looked into Cree's eyes, she noticed his eyes changed and he was crying, scared at what had transpired. He shakes his head in disbelief and drops to his knees. He extends his shaky hands to Jada and pleads for her forgiveness. Confused by his demeanor, Jada still shaken up warns him to stay away from her. She immediately grabs the handgun she had used months earlier on herself and pointed it directly to Cree.

"Please forgive me, I don't know what came over me. I'm so sorry Jada."

She stands there ready and willing to protect herself. But what she notices is Cree clearly upset and aware of his wrong doings. Jada still holding the gun, tells Cree to leave her home and to get help. Upon his exit, Jada knew that God showed her grace and protected her from what was about to transpire. Grateful for his mercy, Jada drops to her knees and became thankful in prayer.

~ *Chapter Five* ~

It's not always the enemy, it's you….

The night came and went. Jada was left with the memory of Cree and what could have happened to her. She sat in silence, blaming herself for her own discretions. She thought how stupid she was to have accepted that into her life. What type of man did she think she could have, feeling like she deserved something less?

She knew the moment she accepted her responsibility at what happened, God heard her. She felt numb and cold. She wanted to have sex with Cree that night. She wanted to seduce Cree that night. She wanted to feel wanted and loved. She knew without a doubt that he was not for her and that he was hiding something. But she chose ignorance. She thought ignorance would save her, but instead it destroyed her. Jada wanted to understand why she needed to be loved by a man so much that she was willing to destroy herself in the process. Funny thing about ignorance is once you acknowledge it, it's no longer ignorance; it's a choice. When you have warnings, and have knowledge of what can transpire, you become a victim of your own choices. You are partly to blame in the events that come thereafter with your choices.

She could no longer blame anyone or anything else. Jada dropped to her knees again and thanked God over and over again. She yearned to be closer to Him. She needed to feel His presence in her life. She reflects back to her choices in life and asked God to show her how to repent and be a better person. She didn't ask why her or why would that happen to her, she didn't ask how could He

Chapter Five

let this happen? She only thanked Him. The truth was she knew why. Women who have been raped and abducted by a relative at a young age without knowledge of what's occurring are victims, but she was well aware of this situation. She understood. She was not a victim but a participant. Jada asks God again to forgive her and to forgive Cree. As she continued to pray, she felt this overwhelming sensation in her spirit and became filled with the Holy Spirit. She felt a calming and peaceful sense of serenity. She admitted her faults and asked God to help her. She told Him that she needed to be loved and that she wanted to be married one day and have a family. She asked Him to show her how to love herself and one day how to love a mate. During her prayer, she had a thought.

"Seek ye first the Kingdom of God and His righteousness and all these things shall be added unto you."

Jada begin to praise Him, shouting, thanking Him. Her journey with her relationship with God had truly begun. She praised well into the night; then she fell asleep with good intentions in her heart.

Jada opened her eyes, looking to the beautiful sky. She lifted her head as the sun smiled upon her. She thought how could she experience a tragedy one day and have peace about it a few days later? She rises and goes to take a shower. As she washes away the shamefulness of her choices, she remembers the night she almost lost her life. She remembers praying to God to save her and she would give her life to Him. She felt excited and nervous all at the same time. She thought about how God would help her and why He wanted to. She never felt worthy of being helped or even loved, especially from God. She decided to have breakfast. As she gets dressed, she receives several calls from her mother. It was funny, she thought, how when something happened, Claudia would have a sense and call her. She never knew how her mom could sense something wrong. She wanted to be that connected to someone, even if it were her mother, but the feelings of hate and regret consumed her, which prevented her from getting close or forgiving anyone.

He, Then Me, Comes You

Jada leaves her home and walks towards the restaurant down the street where she and LD had dined. To her surprise, she saw LD sitting at the booth sipping on coffee. She gets excited and approaches him.

"Hey LD. It's so great to see you." She leans down and hugs him.

"Well hello Ms. Jada. It's very nice to see you too. Please join me."

"How long have you been sitting here?"

"Just an hour," LD said.

"Why have you been sitting here for an hour?"

"I was led to come here, sit and wait." Jada smiles and looks up. LD gives off a coy smile as he notices her looking up. He knew what that gesture was.

"How have you been?" he asked.

"I've been stupid LD, but I'm so glad to see you. I really need to speak to someone of your caliber."

"Of my caliber? Of course and why have you been stupid, Jada?" LD inquired.

"I've continued to make bad decisions, especially with men."

"Well many of us have been stupid from time to time. How do you plan on changing your decision making?"

"Well, I decided to give my life to God and I have no idea how to do that."

"That's great Jada. I know that it may be confusing but I can help you. Don't be afraid, He's with you."

Jada looks to LD. Suddenly his voice becomes familiar to her. She recalls the night that she almost lost her life, when she heard those exact words. She looks puzzled as she continues to stare at him in silence. Could that have been LD who saved her and took her to the hospital that night? Is that the reason he has been sitting near her home for months? Who was he, she thought.

"Is there something wrong?" LD inquired.

Chapter Five

"Uh no, it's just that you have a very calming voice. My dad had a calming voice."

"Oh, where is your dad?"

"He died when I was eight."

"Oh, I'm so sorry to hear that. I know that was hard to deal with being so young."

"Nah it's ok, it was a very long time ago."

"Do you mind if I ask, why this decision to surrender to God?"

Jada looks away as she thinks about what happened a few nights before; she could feel bad about it but she is quickly comforted in her spirit. She takes a deep breath and begins to share her story with LD. As she tells what transpired, LD is certain that God has brought her in his life for a reason. He knew that he needed to help her. Her story amazed LD. Not because of God being there, but because she was at ease and so forgiving. Forgiveness is a hard task to accomplish. We think we forgive people but in a sense, we do not as easily as we would want to. To forgive someone means that you can help the very person who has wronged you. To pray for them and do not wish any harm against them or have a vengeful spirit against them can be hard. LD was impressed. Inspired by her story, he decided to share a bit of his story.

"Jada I'm so proud of you. Do you know how hard that was to do what you did?"

"Please do not praise me LD; I don't deserve it."

"Jada, if you want to be a servant of God, you will have to learn to be humble, sweet pea."

"Sweet pea? Why did you call me that?" Jada asked, stunned at how he knew what to say to her to calm her.

"I'm sorry; it just came to mind?"

"No, it's ok, it's just... my dad used to call me sweet pea," Jada said while smiling to LD.

"Oh, I didn't know, I won't say it again..."

He, Then Me, Comes You

"No it's ok, I like it." They share a smile and eat their breakfast. Jada enjoyed being around LD. She felt the presence of her dad. He didn't approach her with ill intent and she felt she could trust him, confide in him and be there for him. Jada didn't trust people very often. In fact her trust issues stemmed back from when she was a kid.

"LD, are you married? Do you have any children?" Jada inquires. LD smiles then pauses. She then regrets asking what is clearly a bad memory for him.

"I lost my family a long time ago. I was also stupid at several points in my life. I had something amazing and I messed over it. I was in a very bad space and I didn't think that I would ever come out of it. I remember lying down in the gutter somewhere, looking up to the sky ready to die. But at that moment, God told me to surrender to Him. He said that there was more for me to do here. I made a vow to give Him my life. When I surrendered, what happened over the next few years of my life transformed me in a way I never thought possible. You see, most times we must hit absolute rock bottom to get out of our own way. And at the bottom, there is God waiting with open arms."

Jada smiles as she listens to LD's soothing voice. She began to feel a tingle in her spirit again. She felt the Holy Spirit there. Excited by her newfound venture and friendship, she takes a deep breath and exhales. She was ready and willing to do whatever it took to make a change. She knew that doing the same thing over and over, expecting different results is insanity- she decided to leave her insanity behind.

"LD, will you please help me through this journey?"

"If it is God's will, Jada I will do my best."

"I'm so glad you are here with me. I've been looking for you on the corner. I was hoping we could become friends. Maybe become my confidant."

"Now you can call me. Hopefully, willing to join me at church."

"Yes, I may be nervous but I think I can handle that."

Chapter Five

"That's good," LD replied.

"Ok so I downloaded my first Bible on my Kindle. I've been reading it, but find it hard to understand."

"That's ok; take it one scripture at a time. No rush."

"Do I start at the beginning or in the middle during the new testament?"

"Start where God leads you to start. Before you read, pray about it and allow God to speak."

"Ok that sounds easy enough. I think. It's just you say to wait and hear God, but how do I know it's Him and not, you know, just me talking to myself."

"Usually he speaks where it coincides with the scripture. He may speak in a dream or through others. The more you read and get to know His word, the more you become accustomed with what his voice sounds like."

"What do you mean if it coincides with the scripture? How did you know He led you to the corner? I'm sure that wasn't in the Bible"

"Well it definitely wasn't me telling myself to go sit on the corner. But I know what you mean. Sometimes you can feel led to do something."

"Oh I get it; I was actually led to talk to you when I first saw you."

"Exactly, you may not know it's God at first, but when you get familiar then you would know that it's Him leading you."

LD takes Jada's hands into his. Jada looks up at LD. "I'm going to pray for you."

Jada nods in agreement. When he is done, Jada feels fear. She wondered what would happen and what she would discover walking down this path? Was she ready to discover and walk in her truth? Most people aren't. They continue to walk around like zombies, lifeless without meaning or purpose. After they finish their meals, they exchange numbers and Jada agrees to join LD for Bible study.

He, Then Me, Comes You

****

Jada decided to listen to LD and drop to her knees to hear from God. Not knowing what to say or do, she simply looked to the ceiling in hopes that He would start. But because Jada was unfamiliar with God's Word or Voice, she simply only heard herself speak and the words of the adversary telling her that what she was doing was stupid. However, she didn't give up; she continued to stay on her knees and then lay there waiting on God. While waiting, she fell asleep. During her slumber, she felt at ease and slept in peace. After a few hours, she woke up feeling refreshed and energetic. At that moment, she looked to her phone to see who had called. Claudia called of course, but then she thought about calling her sister, Mia. Mia and Jada are one year apart. They were extremely close as kids all the way up until a year ago, when Jada was dating Derrick. She and Derrick had begun dating and had gotten serious within two months. It was a time in their relationship where they met each other's family.

Everything was going well until Derrick met Mia. Mia is very beautiful and spunky. She was the kind of person that you just loved. She never had any enemies. She was one of those people who was so sweet and endearing; you couldn't help but love her. She and her sister always received compliments about their beauty. Jada never felt that she was in competition with Mia; it helped that they had different tastes in men. Mia loved a laid back man who read a lot and liked things like the museum and art shows. Jada found those things to be boring. But she felt she was getting older and needed to settle down with someone nice and grounded.

Their grandmother, Melinda, explained to Jada that she needed to be with someone other than the type of men she sought after. Jada loved a bad boy. Women find themselves attracted to bad boys because of their attitudes and because of the challenge. The challenge is to tame the bad boy. Ironically if women could tame them, then the men wouldn't be considered bad boys.

Some women have many misconceptions of what they think they

Chapter Five

need or want for that matter. Jada realized that her grandmother could have been right. Even though she wasn't attracted to Derrick, she decided to continue to date him anyway. She thought that she would grow to love him and she did in a way. She settled for Derrick.

When she introduced him to her sister Mia, it was as if a light switch had been turned on in them both. Derrick could not get enough of Mia. He couldn't stop smiling when he was around her and always found ways to bring her up in conversation. Mia didn't do a good job at hiding her feelings for Derrick either. Jada didn't notice how they felt for each other because she was so wrapped up in her own selfishness. She was focused on finally getting what she thought she wanted and that was settling down with someone, even if it meant doing it with someone she wasn't meant to be with. All that mattered to Jada was not having people look at her anymore thinking why she was still single at her age. That look that something was wrong with you because you haven't been able to find or keep someone to love you.

When Mia and Derrick came to Jada and told her that they were in love, Jada felt betrayed and angry. But her anger was toward the wrong person. She stopped talking to her sister and hadn't seen or spoken to her since. When she confided in her grandmother, to her dismay Melinda agreed with Mia. Jada was so disappointed with her grandmother's response that she didn't stick around to find out why she agreed and she stopped speaking to her as well. Months later, Melinda passed away. Jada was haunted by the way she treated her grandmother. She never had the opportunity to speak to her again or tell her that she was sorry. Jada knows that she has to make amends with her sister and didn't want to lose any more precious time. She didn't know what to say or what to do to begin to reconcile their friendship.

She knew she was being unreasonable and it had gone on too long but she was as stubborn as her mother. She never liked being wrong or apologizing for that matter. She decided to ask God for help. She would pick her phone up and stare at her sister's name

He, Then Me, Comes You

but never had the courage to call. She would chicken out or try to justify her reasoning for being stubborn.

So she decided it was time for a change and no longer desired to be this shell of a woman, walking around, feeling empty and hopeless. She wanted to trust in God. That's something she had a hard time doing but she asked God for his grace in helping her do so and she took a leap of faith.

****

Jada looks up to the sky as she stands next to her sister's grave. As she reads her sister's name on the headstone, she becomes filled with anger in her heart. She shouts out how much she hates God and that she knew He would disappoint her like He always has her whole life. She falls to her knees, weeping, looking for comfort, looking for answers but does not receive them. As she is bellowing out in pain, she continues to shout out remarks towards God, disregarding anyone around her. She doesn't notice the woman away down from her, visiting her husband's grave. The elderly woman walks up to her and offers comfort. Jada is so shaken up by her feelings of hopelessness and anger, that she rejects the offer. The woman remains there with the hope that she can be of some comfort.

"Young lady?"

"Please, leave me alone. I don't want you to tell me what everyone else has already told me."

"And what is that?" the elderly woman asks.

"That God is always in control and that it works out for the good."

"I wasn't going to tell you that," the elderly lady replies. Jada slows down her breathing and looks to the elderly woman. She notices the woman is wearing torn clothing and looks filthy.

"What is it then?" Jada asks.

"I was going to tell you that your pain is your own

Chapter Five

doing." Shocked by her comment, Jada pauses. She looks to her sister's grave and then looks back at the elderly woman. Jada boldly stands, now angry and appalled at the woman's accusation.

"Excuse me?"

"You stopped talking to her, did you not? And for what?"

"She betrayed me," Jada insisted.

"Do you yourself not need forgiveness? Are you a woman without flaw or sin? Is there no log in your eye?"

"No I have many flaws, but I didn't betray her."

"Of course you have. All sins are sin, no matter what the sin. Forgiveness is what we desire from God and he gives freely with grace, but you will not do the same for your sister and you yourself have sin?"

Jada looks to the elderly lady and suddenly her anger migrates from her heart and she is filled with feelings of regret and remorse. Jada puts her head down in shame. She didn't want to have anger towards her sister for this long; she wanted to forgive her but she was so filled with self-pity that she allowed darkness to consume her.

"What can I do? She's gone now." Jada asked.

"Pray, pray for forgiveness, pray for direction," the elderly woman says.

"What good is prayer? It does not help."

"Oh... that's where you are wrong, young lady, Prayer is indeed the answer. That's the misconception. God needs and wants us to pray. It is a powerful tool, a tool that many of us take for granted, and a tool that many of us try using to gain earthly possessions. You pray for homes, cars, and money but you do not pray for steadfastness, patience, courage, faith, humbleness, God's will and for your purpose. You do not pray for healing and believe it to be so. You expect God to help and be there but do you seek Him first?"

He, Then Me, Comes You

"I... I don't know if He wants me to seek Him."

"Of course, He does. Without faith, it is impossible to please Him, for he who comes to God must believe that He is and that He is a rewarder of those who seek Him."

"I don't have the strength or the understanding."

"Young lady, aren't you tired of lying to yourself?"

The phone rings loudly, waking Jada out of her slumber. She looks at her phone and sees that Mia is calling. She quickly jumps up, breathing heavily, and sweating from the dream that had occurred.

As Jada walks around the room that's filled with the ringing of her phone, she wondered how she could reconnect with her sister. She still felt betrayed by her and didn't know how to get past it. She answers the call and Mia answers with enthusiasm.

"Hello," Jada says in a slightly cold tone.

"Hello... Jada?"

"Hey Mia. It's been a long time; how are you?" Jada asks as her heart beats rapidly with each passing word. She soon realizes while speaking to her sister, that the anger she thought she had, had subsided. She doesn't feel it. Confused, she wondered where it went. Instead of feeling mad, she felt happy to hear from her sister. She felt happy that she is alive and well.

"Jada, I really need you. I need you to forgive me so we can go back to being sisters again."

"I would like that, Mia. I'm sorry for being stubborn and pigheaded."

"Well it wasn't entirely your fault. Can we talk in person? Is that ok with you?"

"Um yeah, that's sounds cool."

"Great... we can go to that place that we love so much," Mia suggested.

Chapter Five

"Sounds great. Meet you...um around 12:30." Jada said.

"Ok, see you then."

After ending her conversation with Mia, Jada decides to pray. She asks the Lord to help her with forgiving her sister. She wants to forgive her and she wants to forgive herself for being stubborn. Jada doesn't know if she could ever be as close as she was to her sister but it was a start. She falls back on her plush bed in shock that she could begin to heal over the feelings of betrayal from her sister. Her dreams became very clear that they were warnings for her and that she should take heed to them. It would be to her own dismay if she ignored them. She got out of bed and quickly prayed as best as she knew how for her sister and for wisdom and knowledge. She felt that she needed help while praying for guidance.

****

Mia and Jada are sitting in silence while sipping on some hot coffee. Jada looks around and notices that Mia is wearing an engagement ring.

"That looks like Grandma's ring."

"Uh yeah, well you haven't been talking to me and I told Mom not to say anything because I wanted to be the one to tell you that Derrick and I are engaged."

"Seriously? First you steal my man and now you're engaged to him?"

"Look Jada, we tried to be honest with you about our feelings, but you didn't want to hear it."

"Oh please, I never thought you would do that to me."

"Jada just stop it ok; you didn't love him."

"It doesn't matter," Jada replied.

"It does matter. Do you understand? Please try and see that you brought us together. You weren't meant to be with Derrick but I am. You know this. If it were the other way around I would've

He, Then Me, Comes You

been happy for you. Sometimes things work out that way."

"Mia, I don't know why I have these feelings. I really didn't love Derrick. I just felt rejected yet again. I thought that if I couldn't keep Derrick satisfied, then I couldn't keep any man. And for some reason that has been my situation ever since."

"Sissy, I get it. You know this... we used to tell each other everything."

Jada smiles and her feelings of anxiety and anger diminishes. She feels relieved. Having to carry anger around to that magnitude can weigh you down. She then feels silly and doesn't understand why she allowed it to be so long before speaking to her. Jada grabs her sister's hand and observes her ring.

"Grandma's ring does look beautiful on your hand."

"I know!"

"Ok then bighead, when is the wedding?" Jada asked excitedly.

"Well we decided to postpone the wedding."

"Why? Now that you have your sister back, we can go full speed ahead with this shindig."

Mia looks at her sister and into her eyes and tries to refrain from tearing up.

"What's wrong Mia?"

"Sissy... I have cancer. And with me going through chemo, Derrick and I decided to wait."

Jada suddenly turns pale. Her eyes widen and suddenly her heartbeat increases. As she sits there looking at her sister, she realizes that she may actually lose her. She can't believe that she could've lost her sister without knowing because of her petty ways. She begins to cry and soon her body trembles as she sits in silence looking at her sister. She gets an ill feeling in her gut and reflects back on the dream she had. Why is God punishing her, she thought. There are plenty of people who are evil but get away with murder and abuse, but because she had anger and was stubborn she deserved this? She thought as soon as she decided to give herself to God, He shows

Chapter Five

her that He can't be trusted. Why? Why would God allow someone like Mia to get cancer? Jada didn't have knowledge of God or His Word. She didn't understand that even the righteous would be tested and go through trials and tribulations for the greater good.

"I'm so sorry Mia. I should've been here for you."

"It's ok, Sissy."

"No, it's not. How long have you known?"

"Well ironically, when you were in the hospital, so was I," Mia said.

Jada gets up and pulls her sister close to her. She holds on tight to her while being apologetic. As she holds her sister tighter, she starts to hum to her the song she would always sing when she was in the wrong.

"I haven't heard this in so long."

"What do you need? What can I do to help?" Jada asked.

"Nothing right now; Derrick is treating me like I'm going to break into a million pieces. I just want to know about what's been going on with you."

"Nothing is more important than you right now; you can't tell me something like this and then not discuss it further."

"I know, I just get tired of thinking about it and always talking about it. I just need to be free from thinking about it for a moment."

"Well, I decided to give my life to God."

"You?" Mia asked.

"Yes, me."

"The same person who used to laugh in church and swear she would never be a religious stooge?" Mia asks laughing.

"Ok... ok; people change."

"I see," Mia says as she looks to her sister in admiration.

"I need all the help I can get with this change, not sure what I'm doing."

He, Then Me, Comes You

"Well you know Mom will be more than happy to help you in that area. I'm sure she's been dying to share her knowledge."

"I don't want Mom's help. I don't want anything from that woman."

Mia, concerned, grabs Jada's hand and holds it tight.

"One day, you will have to forgive her. She was young and…"

"No excuse for that, Mia. I know forgiveness is forgiveness but, I need time."

"Well Sissy, this process can be tough and having support will help you stay focused," Mia insisted.

"Just please don't tell her. I just need to go at my own pace and have a relationship with Him on my own."

"I get it," Mia says.

"I'm so heart broken right now," Jada says while tearing up.

"Don't be; the important thing is we are speaking again and you can go back to spoiling me."

They share a laugh and then hug each other tightly as if never wanting to let go. Jada felt a sense of relief in her heart. She felt regret for holding a grudge that had no meaning for so long and as she holds her little sister tightly, she fears she may also lose her. Cancer took their grandmother, aunt and two uncles and now it's after Mia. Jada remembered a scripture that LD said to her that reminded her of this situation.

"And the prayer of the faith shall save the sick, and the Lord shall raise him up; and if he has committed sins, they shall be forgiven him."

Jada knew then that she should and would pray non-stop to help her sister. Whatever Mia needed she was willing to do for the sake and health of her sister. At that very moment while embracing her, she had courage and began to pray for her little sister in silence. It flowed out of her like a never-ending river. She felt her spirit growing stronger as she prayed, pleading for God to heal her

Chapter Five

sister. As they part ways, Jada watches as her ill sister walks out of the restaurant. Jada wept hoping that God heard her prayers. She knew that she wasn't the best person and she had many flaws and needed healing herself, but suddenly what she needed wasn't so important. She didn't care that she desired to be married and have children. She thought what good would that be if her sister wasn't around to see her walk down the aisle or share in the joy of her nieces or nephews. Jada made up her mind that she would become this prayer warrior that LD had spoken of. She knew in her heart that if she had just a little faith that God would help her sister.

~ *Chapter Six* ~

No longer a babe in Christ...

Almost a year had passed since Lamar gave his life to God. He had become very familiar with the Word of God and every day he would take time to understand and apply the Word of God. He also looked over the journal that his father had sent him. He was amazed at the wisdom his father had and looked forward to meeting him. He dreamed of seeing his father and wondered if he shared the same likes, dislikes or if he had the same mannerisms.

While reading his father's journal, he learned that his father felt that being with his mother was the best decision he had ever made and creating him through the grace of God was an ultimate gift. His father gave advice about becoming a father but first learning how to be a husband. That stood out to Lamar. He was overcoming guilt he felt about his previous marriage and often wondered that if he had knowledge of being a husband, then things would have been better for him and Kelly. He even may have had children.

At this point Lamar wanted to learn how to be a better husband for his next wife and asked God for the tools to help him. While praying the thought to contact Kelly arose in his spirit. He had hopes that she was willing to talk to him. The divorce was not an amicable one and left a bad feeling in his spirit. He pulls out his phone, stares a moment in doubt but puts those feelings aside and texts Kelly. A few moments later to his surprise she responded and agreed to meet with him. He thought about what he needed to say

Chapter Six

to her or what he needed to hear from her. The relationship he had with God was so strong at this point in his life, that he always went to Him first before doing and making any big decisions. He even asks him about small things. Lamar was so in love with God that he allowed Him to lead him even on the smallest things. He got on his knees and prayed before meeting up with her. He wanted to be open to what she had to say and needed to receive whatever it was that was the truth. He desired to live and walk in truth and faith. For only the truth can set you free.

As Lamar entered the small, quaint restaurant he looked at Kelly as she sat there waiting. He stood there for a moment just watching as she was sitting patiently sipping on a glass of white wine looking to her phone. Her hair was naturally curly as she wore it halfway pinned up with loose hair in the back. It was just the way Lamar liked it. She was wearing a floral sundress that covered her legs. He continued to stand there admiring his ex-wife. He thought to himself how beautiful she was. He started to remember some of the things that attracted her to him and old feelings resurfaced. She looked over and she and Lamar locked eyes. He gave off a coy smile and walked towards her. She stood waiting and as Lamar got closer she extended her arms out to him ready to embrace him with a hug.

"Wow... I hardly recognized you," Kelly said.

"Really why is that?"

"You look different somehow, like a new man." Kelly said while smiling.

"Thank you; a lot has changed, but look at you- you look amazing as well. I missed that smile."

Lamar pulls out Kelly's chair and while sitting, she looks puzzled by his actions. He

"Thank you Mar, so what's new with you?"

They look to each other. The waiter interrupts their gaze and asks Lamar what he would like to drink and or if they are ready to order. He replies with water and he would need a minute to order. Stunned by the response, Kelly becomes confused.

"Now I know something is off, you didn't order a drink."

"I'm actually not drinking these days."

"Ok, what the hell is going on with you? Are you dying?" Kelly jokingly asks.

"Kell, I've given my life to God."

"Ok this is a joke, right? God? Since when do you believe in that?"

"I think I've always believed, I just never had the courage to learn who He was and why He is."

"Well there is definitely a change in you. But I never would have guessed that. Why have you invited me here?" Kelly said as she sipped on her wine.

"Well first, I wanted to ask you for your forgiveness."

Kelly takes another sip of her wine. She never thought, Lamar of all people, would be asking her for her forgiveness. She thought if anything, he needed to forgive her for her actions within their marriage. As she looks into the eyes of her ex-husband she noticed his sincerity, guilt and maybe regret. Unprepared for this exchange, she becomes uneasy. She was expecting some sort of disagreement about money, or possible breakup sex, but not peace and forgiveness.

"Why are you asking me to forgive you?"

"I've learned that I wasn't a very good husband to you and may have caused you to cheat on me."

"Are you serious right now?"

"Yes, Kelly I'm very serious. I'm ready to take on my part in the failure of our marriage. Please tell me what did I do besides ignore you and take you for granted."

"Wow, um ... well you weren't all that bad," Kelly said as she looks around the restaurant, wondering if she was on TV for a reality TV

Chapter Six

show or something.

"Kelly please, I need you to be truthful. I need for you to be honest with me and it's ok to tell me things you didn't think I could receive before."

"Ok then." Kelly grabs another sip of her wine. The waiter returns and asks for their order. They both order their meals and sit awkwardly in silence for a moment.

"Mar, listen I knew I was marrying a strong-willed man and that is what attracted me to you in the first place. But with that also came with you being close-minded and condescending. You made me feel like what I had to offer was insignificant and beneath you. Often, I felt stupid. You made me feel like I was only there to have sex with you, clean your house, and cook your meals. I mean sure, those are some duties of a wife but I didn't want it to feel like we were total cave people. I know I agreed to be the housewife, but that was to help support you in your vision and dreams. You didn't allow me to help you."

Lamar hangs his head down low and a tear falls from his face. Kelly notices his complexion and reverts to her nurturing character. Without realizing it she was holding Lamar's hand. He looks up to her and she lovingly looks at him. Kelly is impressed by who this man has become. Suddenly old feelings resurfaced for her as well. She thought, where was this man when they were married. She never witnessed Lamar cry before.

"I'm sorry; lately crying is like second nature to me now."

"I've never seen you cry. I always felt like you believed it made you weak."

"I did. But I learned it's quite the opposite," Lamar stated.

"Seems like you've been learning a lot this past year."

"Yea and through all of this I was contacted by my father."

"Really! Oh, wow that's great Mar! I know you've always wanted to contact him."

"Yes. Look Kell Bell, I want you to know that I think you are a beautiful, strong, and an intelligent woman. I forgive you for your behavior in our marriage and hope you can forgive me too."

"Yes, Mar, of course I forgive you," Kelly says as she adoringly looks at the man she once loved. Kelly suddenly wonders if she and Lamar could possibly reconcile and maybe remarry. But that thought soon passes.

"When I first saw you sitting over here... I started to regain some feelings for you but then I realized that you being the great woman that you are, may have not been the woman I was meant to be with."

"Really... why do you feel that way?" Kelly disappointedly asks.

"I was not my true self when we married. I didn't know my purpose. Now that I'm learning I now know what type of woman who bests suit me."

"And what type is that?"

"A woman that fits into my purpose."

"I see... your purpose, whatever that means. Well I think it's great you have found God but I'm not the religious type."

"Kelly, I hope that you take heed to what a wonderful person you are, forgive yourself and find your purpose."

"This has been so overwhelming. Thank you for this," Kelly replied.

For the first time since Lamar and Kelly met, they were at peace with one another. They ate their meals and smiled at one another in amazement at how amicable they were being. They continue to engage in conversation, knowing that it will be the last time they will be in each others' company. They become released from the soul tie that bonded them and Lamar felt renewed and embraces his new change.

****

Lamar lies in his bed restfully. The dark room remains silent.

Chapter Six

Suddenly he grabs his chest, rubbing his heart. He feels a sharp pain in his heart but he doesn't understand why. He worries he is having a stroke. As the pain increases, he becomes paralyzed and can't breathe. He struggles with fear trying to push through the pain.

As he continues to struggle, he drops and hits the floor waking him up from the dream. Lamar looks around the darkened room breathing heavy. Confused by the dream he rubs his chest. The pain had subsided but felt so real. Not sure what to do, he gets on his knees and pray. As he begins to pray, the pain he felt shifts to his spirit. His spirit feels heavy with pain and once again he can feel it in his chest. His heart is in pain.

"Lord what is this?" Lamar bellows out.

He begins to pray but is uncertain why he is feeling agony in his heart and spirit. As he begins to ask God why he feels this pain, God then shares an image of a woman crying. Lamar cannot see the face of the woman, but he sees her crying, screaming needing help.

"Lord who is she?" Lamar asks.

She is your wife, pray for her."

Unsure of how to pray for her, he then asks God for guidance and direction. Without hesitation, Lamar immediately begins to pray for the woman. He continues to pray until he no longer feels the pain in his heart. After he prays, he remains on the floor but sits back up against the bed. He remains distraught, wondering how he could literally feel the pain of the woman. It was as if God connected the two of them as one spirit. He felt saddened to know that the woman who is in pain is his future wife. He began to wonder why was she in pain and what else he needed to do to help her. When asked, God wouldn't reveal to him those answers. He would only feel in his spirit to pray for her vigorously. He then grabs the journal of his father and begins to look through it hoping to read anything about having this type of experience. In the journal, he read the importance of interceding prayer. He began to wonder if he should document his journey so one day he could share it with his future

He, Then Me, Comes You

wife and kids. He then grabs an old journal and began to enter what God has shown him and taken him through so far. Excited by what he has read back to himself, he thought how great God is for helping him to become a better man. A man of God to help do His will. He felt grateful and humbled.

~ *Chapter Seven* ~

God is not a genie...

Jada is at the hospital sitting with Mia while she gets her chemo treatment. Mia notices Jada strolling through her phone.

"What are you looking at?"

"Well, I decided that I wanted to get married and have kids, so I'm on this Christian single dating app."

"Ugh, seriously?"

"What's wrong with that?"

"Well for starters just because it says Christian, doesn't mean they are and you shouldn't look. Let God do the work."

"Right, like God has time to look for me a husband."

"I believe he already has him picked out."

"Really?"

"Yes, now don't get mad or anything, but with Derrick and I, we learned that we wouldn't have met if it wasn't for you, and Derrick told me that he was going to end things with you, before you two were going to introduce each other to your family."

"Yeah, I felt that. I remember that I suggested he meet you. Wow, that's funny. Now thinking back, I can see now how God used me. Immediately, you came to mind. Funny thing is I did think you two were perfect for each other. You two had more in common and agreed on a lot of things and views. I can't believe I stopped talking to you for so long because of that. I was selfish. I'm so messed up." Jada says as she slouches in her chair.

"You're not messed up. Well, sort of."

"Hey..."

"I'm just kidding," Mia said jokingly, as she tries to laugh it off

Chapter Seven

and refrain from vomiting.

"Right but it's ok, though," Jada said as she continues to flip through her phone.

"I say it will always be better to wait on God and let him lead you. It says a man who finds a wife, not a woman looking through the dating apps searching for creepy so called Christian dudes. Now don't get me wrong, in these days with technology a dating app may work. I won't put any limits on God, but I'm guessing he didn't lead *you* to a dating app."

Jada laughs with her sister and admires her sister's laugh that ends in a snort. She realizes how much she will miss that laugh as she looks at her sickly sister and thinks about God and if he was so good and just, then why He would allow her sister to become ill. Jada struggled with trust. When she lost her dad at a young age and then her best friend moved away, she doubted if God cared about her. After talking with LD, she was looking forward to getting to know God, but also feared what it entailed in doing so. She thought of God as a disciplinarian not really someone who cared or helped. Sure, she heard stories but didn't feel it held any truth.

"You may have a point, Mia."

"Why are you looking to get married now? You just decided to give your life to God. Focus on Him then the rest will come."

"I don't know, maybe he could help me with this God thing."

"This God thing? You really need to get to know Him."

"Yup that's what everyone keeps telling me. But there is no manual that comes with God."

"Uh, it's called the Bible, Jada."

"Oh... yeah... that thing. Which in a way is total bullshit. It doesn't make sense, is extremely contradictory and doesn't apply to today in any way."

"What's your goal? Is it to get to know God, or to fake your way to getting what you want?"

"Fake my way? As if God wouldn't know the difference."

Mia shakes her head at her sister. She is going through one of the biggest challenges in her life and still has faith to believe that all good things work through God. She feared at times that he would use her as a vessel for strengthening faith in people, including herself and her fiance. However, she wouldn't let this trial keep her from marrying the man of her dreams. As she looks to her sister she feels overwhelmed with hope. She believes that God brought her and her sister back together at this time for a reason. He gave Jada the strength to understand and forgive her. Mia thought if He could do that, He could most definitely heal her. Mia closes her eyes, as she feels ill due to the chemo. Several minutes pass and Derrick walks in.

"Hello... hello, ladies."

"Hey babe," Mia said. Derrick kisses Mia on the forehead and sits beside her. As he grabs her hand he notices Jada observing them.

"How are you, Jada?"

"Hey Derrick. I am ok... I think," Jada says as she looks him up and down, frowning.

"What? Why are you looking at me like that?" Derrick inquires.

"You look like you been working in a field or something," Jada explained.

"Oh I've planted a garden. I thought if Mia ate more fresh fruits and vegetable then it may help heal her."

"Oh good luck trying to pry bacon out of her hand. If she could she would eat bacon morning, noon and night."

"I know, right."

"Ok you two, you can shut up."

"Whatever," Jada says as she continues to go through the dating app.

"What are you doing?" Derrick asks as he takes Mia's cup and pours her some more water. He grabs one of her feet and begins to rub it, trying to make her feel at ease.

"Jada is looking at Christian dating sites."

"Why Christian?"

"Well she decided to give her life to God."

"That's amazing Jay, I remember I tried to get you to get to know God."

"Yes, I know. Well I'm going to do my best to learn."

"From a man's point of view, let God help you find a mate. Please do not look for one. Focus on your relationship with God, let Him lead," Derrick urged Jada.

"I wonder why everyone but me knows this and I've been stuck in

Chapter Seven

the dark."

"Well it just wasn't your time. Now you can focus."

Jada takes a deep breath and looks at how affectionate Derrick is towards Mia. She observes him and how he gingerly strokes her hair and looks into her eyes. He embraces and rubs her back while she tries to refrain from regurgitating. She feels saddened because she always wanted to have someone to love her that much. She wants someone to be by her side when she needed it the most. She wants someone who knew her, who wanted to know all her layers and to help peel them back. She smiles as she continues to observe her sister. She needed her to pray for her. Jada had made up her mind that she would focus on praying for her sister but has lacked in doing so. She prays every now and then when she feels like it. She felt guilty about not doing what she feels she should be doing; then she thinks that what she needed could wait until her sister was better.

"Ok you two, I'm going to leave and I will see you tomorrow. I can come over and cook for you."

"Since when do you know how to cook?" Mia asked.

"Well I can learn."

"Ok Jada, I'm already sick, I don't need to get worse."

"Oh... you trying to be funny?"

"I'm just kidding; that would be nice to see you. That's it... just come and visit. Do not bring anything," Mia says, while smiling.

"That's real subtle of you to say, bighead."

Jada kisses her sister and leaves the hospital room. As she walks through the halls of the sickly patients she thinks why Mia was the one who was ill. With all the dumb things that she has done in her life, She thought she should be the one with cancer. She felt that Mia didn't deserve to suffer the way that she has.

****

Jada walks into her silence filled home. "Honey I'm home!" She waits to hear back.

"Oh, yeah I live alone." She says as she flops on the sofa, sulking in her pity party. She remembers all that has transpired in this home and suddenly she becomes angry. She felt as if she was personally being attacked. Why was so much happening to her in her life? Jada was thirty-three years of age and never had a successful relationship and it seemed she couldn't get along with most people. While going over things in her mind, she suddenly blows up and begins to pick up things and throws them across the room. With each item she threw, she became angrier, as if it was fueling her. Again, over, and over she would grab something that she could destroy.

"God, I hate you! You say you want to help, but all You do is cause pain!"

While she was having her temper tantrum, she didn't notice that her mother Claudia had let herself in. Claudia stands and observes her daughter in her rage. Soon Jada notices her mother standing there.

"How long have you been there?" Jada inquired.

"Not long. I would ask if you were ok but that would be a stupid question. Do you feel better cursing at God? Did you get what you needed?"

"I just needed to let out some steam."

"And, did it help?" Claudia asked.

Jada flops back down on her sofa breathing heavily. "Why are you here?"

"You ignore my calls and you leave immediately when we cross paths at the hospital."

"Yeah, you couldn't get the hint that I don't want to see or talk to you?"

"Jada, we have to heal."

"I refuse to ease your conscience. Now get the hell out!"

"I told you about using that language and tone with me. I am still your mother!"

Jada looks to Claudia and laughs. She gets up and looks around the messy room and looks for a pack of cigarettes. When she finds them, she grabs one and throws down the pack. As she begins to light it, her mother approaches her and grabs it from her.

"Give it back."

"You are not smoking that with me here."

"Then leave!"

"Why Jada... Are you ever going to forgive me?"

Chapter Seven

Jada sits back on the sofa and leans back and covers her face. After a moment, she begins to cry. Claudia sits beside her but allows her daughter to go through her phase. She hopes it might be cathartic for her.

"I don't want to deal with our issues right now."

"Your sister told me about you trying to get a relationship with God and thought I could be of some assistance."

"I told her not to say anything."

"I have something for you," Claudia states. She hands her a new Bible with blue leather covering with her name engraved on it. Jada looking at it and admires the beauty of the presentation. When she opens it, she sees that her mother had written something inside. It reads:

I hope this will keep you in your walk of faith with your Savior and our Father, the living God. Be blessed my daughter.

Jada wipes away her tears and looks to her mother.

"I purchased it a few days after I learned you were in the hospital. I hoped and had faith that you would need this."

"Claudia, it's very beautiful, I would need help understanding it; I go to Bible study with a friend but it's hard to stay focused. Its boring."

"I gave you a version that is easier to read and understand. I ask that you pray before reading it to have God lead you."

Jada admires the Bible and flips through the pages and scans over some of the words. She takes a deep breath in hopes that her journey would lead to a better life, a peaceable one.

"I just don't understand God's way sometimes, I mean why Mia? Cancer? I just don't understand. We lost Gran, and now I may lose my sister. Why does God allow such things?"

"Well he didn't ask us to understand. Turn to Proverbs 3:5 in your new Bible."

Jada struggles with finding the scripture, but Claudia doesn't help. She wants her daughter to get used to finding the answers on her own. When Jada finally turns to the scripture and reads it, she closes her eyes and puts the Bible close to her chest.

"Jada, the answers are here for us for guidance and to give us

He, Then Me, Comes You

direction and peace."

"I get it."

"I know you do. I don't want you to think that I feel a certain type of way about Mia. But I must trust in God and His way. All things work out for the good through God."

"I would love to have that type of faith."

"Pray for faith and He will answer." Claudia leans in and tries to kiss her daughter but Jada rejects her yet again. Claudia doesn't force it but waits for God. When the time is right, Jada will be ready to receive her. As she gazes in her eyes she sees a desperate need of love and guidance and she feels that this is the place that Jada needs to be for her to change her way of thinking and her way of choices. Claudia leaves the mess of a home. When she exits, Jada sits in the mess that she has created. After awhile, she gets on her knees and begins to pray to the Most High, the Living God. At that moment, she begins the journey that will change her life in many ways she never thought possible. She gets up and begins to clean her home after realizing that throwing a tantrum and holding on to anger wont resolve anything, but will take away from what her sister really needs and that's for her to be strong.

****

Jada is standing in the midst of dark angels coming towards her. As she stands in her armor and holds her sword ready and prepared to fight, she becomes frightened and begins to shiver. Her knees are buckling as the angels become closer; she gets the strength in her spirit to swing her sword and strike each one headed towards her. As she slays the angels one by one, she becomes stronger in faith, giving her the strength to take on these spirits that are ready to devour her. She continues to swing her sword and when she hits the last one in her path she awakens from her slumber by a thump.

Jada fell to the floor, still swinging her Bible. She was holding it while she was reading before she fell asleep. She continues to lie on the floor still holding her Bible, slowing down her breathing and holding tight to her chest. Jada understood why the Word is so powerful in strength and protection. She keeps it close to her heart and begins to praise and thank God.

Chapter Seven

"Thank you, Father... please show me what I need to do. What can I do to help my sister?"

She sits up and prays for Mia. She became better at praying as she attended Bible study and prayer meetings with LD over the past month. At first, she was uncomfortable because they were all so experienced and grounded in the Lord. She thought that she would sound or look stupid if she worshiped aloud or prayed in the spirit. As she watched the other people, all she thought was how she wanted to be one of those women, so grounded in their faith; she wanted to learn to love and obey the Lord.

She became increasingly accustomed to praying and asking God for direction in her life. She was much calmer and went to every chemo session with her sister, reading and praying with her. Mia wasn't getting better. She was losing her hair and lost over 30 pounds. Jada didn't lose hope but she was feeling frustrated. She would spend most of her time dedicated to learning and reading, and praying but felt it was to no avail; she felt that God wasn't moving fast enough or at all. She began to feel frustrated and felt anger creeping back up in her. When she would feel that way she would call LD to confide in him. She finds herself calling LD more frequently as she watches her sister suffer. However, she doesn't cry or show her weakness in front of Mia because she wants to appear strong and faithful. She feels LD is the only person she can cry with.

LD and Jada are at their usual spot to meet for dinner. Jada eyes are swollen from crying and LD tries to console her.

"LD, I don't know what I will do if I lose her?"

"You will continue with your life and remember the times you had with her."

"I can't lose my baby sister."

"I need to ask, why are you praying? What is your intention with God?"

"What do you mean? I pray so He can save my sister, I mean that's what this is all about, right?"

"No Jada, what if Mia dies? Then what? Will you stop praying and pursuing God?"

Jada suddenly became pale as she stares at LD. She takes a sip of her watered-down soda and sits in silence. She didn't think about

He, Then Me, Comes You

Mia dying, she assumed that as long as she prayed that God would heal her.

"LD, why would God let her die? What good is He to let someone so beautiful die? I don't understand."

"Jada your faith cannot be based solely on the things you deem good that God does. Everything works out for the good through God even in death."

"What? What are you saying LD that prayer is useless? Then, why do it?"

"No that's not what I'm saying at all. Please don't misconstrue what I'm telling you. God chooses what is best. In the Bible, it talks about David and when he fasted and prayed to God for his son. He asked for His mercy and grace to heal and save his son. His son died. David didn't lose faith, he knew that he would see his son again and moved on with his life. I'm telling you this because you must understand, that God works in mysterious ways and your faith cannot be based on just the things *you* deem as good. Death is not the end."

"I don't want to hear this, this just made things worse. Why? Why so much suffering?"

"Jada, you know I don't like to sugar coat things because it doesn't spare you from the truth. God is wonderful in all His glory. You need to trust Him in all his ways. Have you read the story of Job?"

"Yes I have, and I can't believe he endured all of that."

"Right; I just want to inform you that you should desire a relationship with God solely for Him and His will, otherwise your faith will not be strong and will cease to uphold against life's trials and tribulations."

Jada sighs as she tries not to be frustrated. "I will try LD."

"There is no try, only do or do not."

"Are you quoting Yoda?"

"I love Star Wars." They both burst with laughter. LD was happy to see Jada laugh instead of grieving before there is something to grieve about. He constantly prays for her and her strength in faith.

"There's that smile!" LD says.

"I really don't like you sometimes," Jada says while laughing.

She didn't want to laugh. She wanted to stay in the frame of mind to be sad until her sister is better. She didn't think it was right to

Chapter Seven

be happy and joyful when her sister was suffering. However, God speaks to her through His word, reminding her.

"In this you greatly rejoice, though now for a little while you may have had to suffer grief in all kinds of trials..."

She thought about her faith and what she was really after. Did she only want to pray to God to heal her sister, or give her a husband and kids? She thought, *then what*? Will she resort back to doing things her way? What did her heart read? We could feed the poor, help a neighbor, or even give to charity, but at what cost? Do we do it because we expect things in return or are we that cheerful giver? Jada didn't want God to see her as a user. She truly craved his direction but she feels that with everything going on in her life, it could be misconstrued as her using God for some type of gain. What if Mia died? She thought, *what if I don't meet that right guy? What if I'm not meant to have children?* Will she give up her relationship with God? All these thoughts came flooding to her. She remembers a time when her mother used to drag her and Mia to church and she thought the people were so phony because they were there for show and not for a relationship with God. She did not want to be one of those phonies; she wanted an authentic relationship with God. She had had enough of her life decisions and desired Gods heart. She was determined to learn His heart and humble herself to His will.

****

"Hello Lamar, how are we doing today?"

"Oh... hey Tameka. I'm well, thanks for asking," Lamar replied while watching Tameka sashay across the pew wearing a fitted dress that showed off all her curves. Tameka was a very attractive woman. She was well educated and strong minded. She seemed committed to the church, but not really. It seemed she was more into church than the body of Christ. Her mindset was about appearances and playing Christian. There seemed to be a lot of those walking around, Lamar thought. Tameka is a faithful church going woman. She was raised in the church and very much desired to be married. Her ambition showed greatly, as she was known as a strong pursuer of men.

Tameka was so desperate to find a man in the church that would

He, Then Me, Comes You

give in to her seductive ways and her eyes were set on Lamar. He had been going to the church only for about a year now. He became accustomed to most of the women on the prowl there. He didn't pay too much attention, given his commitment to God and leaning on Him to direct him with whom he shall marry. None of the women in the church appealed to him. He kept himself busy with what God had called him to do. He learned that God wanted him to work with young men in fatherless homes as well as men getting out of destructive marriages. Most of his ministry is about uplifting men in the community, teaching them leadership and being the head of their household. Most are young men with no father in the home and many are full of anger and resentment towards their fathers. Lamar tries to direct them on what to do with their anger issues. He always wanted to work with men who dealt with his same issues. He felt if he could change and better himself as a Godly man then so could they. He decided that he was going to fund and build a large organization that will benefit them more. He needed donations to help on his vision. He's received some help but what God showed him needed much more prayer, fasting and more money. Lamar knew in his heart that God gave him that vision for a reason and he would steadfastly run after it. He didn't know when it would happen but he knew it would. He continued to prep and plan and hold on to faith.

"Lamar, some of us were going bowling tonight and was wondering if you wanted to join us? You're always working so hard and we never see you come out and enjoy yourself." Tameka insisted.

"I don't know. I have a lot of work to do."

"Oh, c'mon I really want to get to know you better," Tameka said, while smiling and trying to caress his hand.

Lamar politely pulled back. He felt the need to put Tameka's mind to rest; he wanted to make sure she knew they would not be together. He thought about it, but didn't proceed. He didn't think it was appropriate to put her in her place at that moment, but he did feel it coming.

"No, I'm good. You have fun and take care, ok." Lamar walks away from Tameka, leaving her feeling rejected.

~ Chapter Eight ~

God where are you? I can't do this…

Jada is lying in her unmade oversized bed as her wild mane covers the entirety of the pillow. She lays there and then tries to run her fingers through her mangled hair, but comes across some Cheetos she was eating earlier the day before. She removes the Cheetos from her fro and tosses them to the side. When she rises from the bed, food particles from her dinner falls from her white stained bra. She sits up on the edge of her bed and thinks to pray. She sits there tired and impatient, not knowing what to pray for. She felt that she was a robot and praying for something she wasn't sure she believed in. Sure, she wanted her sister to heal. She felt that nothing had changed in her life since she had given it to God. What was she looking for? She needed a sign, a complete 180 in all areas in her life but to no avail; it was just her sitting and stewing in her own filth. She gets up and grabs a pair of gray jogging pants, throws them on along with a hoodie that was stretched from the washer. She grabs her shoes and head out for coffee. As she walks down the busy streets, she notices people looking to her as her hair is in a large mangled fro and still contained food from her dinner the night before. As she enters the coffee shop and stands in line, she looks pale, with darken circles around her eyes. She stands there and ponders what her purpose was and what to do at this point in her life. Soon she reaches the front of the line and the young man looks to her in disgust.

"Um hello, what can I get you?"

Chapter Eight

Jada looks to the young man with vacant eyes and doesn't speak for a moment. She then looks to the other staff members behind the counter and then looks back at the young man.

"Give me a dark roast, please."

The young man tells her the price and as he takes the money from Jada's hand he has the urge to ask her if she was ok, but hesitates and decides not to.

She is sitting alone sipping on her coffee as she observes the customers talking and laughing and enjoying each other's company. She stares like a crazy person ready to end her life and theirs as well at that very moment. Soon a little girl walks up to her and she stops and looks to Jada.

"You have on mismatched shoes," the little girl says.

Jada looks down and sees that she has on two different shoes. She looks back at the little girl and then to the girl's mother, who comes to grab the little girl. The woman, who is wearing a white blouse and yellow cardigan, looks concerned at what was being discussed. She picks up her daughter and then lays down a ten-dollar bill in front of Jada, then walks away to another table across the shop. A few minutes later Jada walks up to the table where the woman and her daughter are sitting and lays the ten-dollar bill down.

"I'm not homeless. I just don't have the will to live anymore."

Shocked at what Jada said, the woman grabs her daughter to protect her from the crazy looking Jada.

"I'm sorry; I just thought I would help," the woman answered.

"Do I look like I need your help?"

The little girl nods and the woman, still holding her daughter, doesn't say anything but waits for Jada to leave. Jada looks around at the people looking to her. Moments later, she walks away leaving the coffee shop. As Jada approaches the home, she notices LD is waiting for her. She had been ignoring his calls and wasn't ready to talk about her present state of mind.

He, Then Me, Comes You

"Jada, are you ok?"

"I really don't want to talk right now; I have nothing good to say."

"What's going on with you? Why the sudden change. Why are you giving up?"

"What am I giving up, LD? I have nothing left to give."

"What have you done, but ask God to heal your sister? Trust me he's heard you, but you pray amiss. You are filled with determination to only pray for your sister that you haven't stopped to listen to what He has to say."

"Listen? What am I listening to? I've heard everything you've told me."

"Ok but have you been listening to God? Tell me, when you are done praying, do you wait to listen after? Or are you so wrapped up in your own selfish motives that you forget to listen?"

Jada throws her hands up and walks past LD in frustration. She walks up the stairs to her home and closes the door. She is not in a good space. She feels that this journey that she has taken has done nothing. Mia is still ill and nothing has changed much in her life. Where is this God everyone keeps bragging about, she thought? Where is this Savior that heals and blesses people? Jada still feeling hopeless, grabs her Bible. She stares at the pages, trying to read, but she's not able comprehend a word that she is reading.

"What do you want from me? What is it that I'm supposed to be doing with my life? What is my purpose God?" Jada ask desperately, hanging her head low with tears in her eyes.

"... *be quick to listen slow to speak and slow to anger.*"

Jada sits there in silence, crying until she feels the Holy Spirit calming her and giving her peace. She takes a deep breath and tries to gain a new perspective on what needs to be done in order to have a relationship with God. She has been going about it the wrong way. She didn't desire a relationship with Him but only what He can do for her.

Chapter Eight

"The Lord is not slow in keeping His promise, as some understand slowness. Instead He is patient with you…"

****

Jada is lying on her floor in her underwear with cartons of ice cream lying around her. She hasn't showered in days at this point. Her home reeks of foul odor, from not cleaning the dishes or taking out the trash. Her phone has many missed calls and is full of unanswered text messages and voicemails. As she lies on the floor she starts to get that feeling of despair. She asked God again desperately what her purpose was and has been waiting to hear from Him but she hasn't felt anything in her spirit. She hasn't had any direction in her life, she thought. She felt that at this point that trying to do it God's way was a joke.

"Grab the gun and end it," the injurious voice says.

Jada sits up and looks towards where her gun is. As she moves towards the gun, the Holy Spirit intervenes.

"…letting your sinful nature control your mind leads to death. But letting the Spirit control your mind leads to life and peace."

Jada stops dead in her tracks and stands still. She contemplates on using the gun on herself again. She looks and faces a mirror hanging on the wall. As she gazes at the woman looking back at her, she becomes confused - what is God leading her to do? She was so obsessed with praying for her sister that she began to lose herself and purpose in the process. She didn't feel God's presence at all. She felt ashamed of herself and what she has become. She's missed several days at the center and had not been there for any of the kids looking for her guidance. She decided it was time to let go of her pity and stand strong in her faith. She looked around and began to clean her place.

He, Then Me, Comes You

****

Jada is lying on the floor in a dark room. She hears voices but can't make out what is being said. She gets up and tries to get her eyes in focus. She feels light headed and weak. She struggles to rise and get in focus. When she looks around the room, she notices that the room is full of people walking; struggling as they hold on to what seems to be wooden crosses. She looks around confused at the people wondering where she was and who these people were. They were many people of all ethnicity and races. Men, women and, even children, walking past her, pulling crosses, carrying the cross and a small few had the cross strapped to their backs, walking as if it was a part of them. She looks down and beside her lies her own wooden cross. She gets up and tries to pick it up. She learns the wooden cross is heavy but bearable to carry. She struggles to get a grip on the cross due to her weakness; she feels frail. Jada continues to put the cross on her back so that she may move forward. She then looks to the others and notice one man dropping his cross. She looks concerned. The man shouts and screams at it.

"I can't do this! It's too hard. I just can't!" the man says. He abandons the cross and walks away from it. Jada looks around to see if anyone would stop him but they continue on with their crosses. Soon she notices more and more people abandoning their crosses, shouting at it as if it is holding them back. Some even run from it. As Jada contemplates on why anyone would want to carry his or her cross, she huffs and lies on the floor out of breath. She begins to give up and at that moment she notices a woman crawling towards the cross that she abandoned. Asking for forgiveness. The woman wipes her tears and picks her cross up and crawls with it on her back asking God to forgive her. Jada grunts and grabs hold of her cross. She struggles to get it up. When she finally gets a grip on it, she pushes it up and places it on her back. She begins to

Chapter Eight

walk forward leaning, due to the weight of it. It causes her to hunch while her knees buckle. When she looked over to her right, she saw a young woman, carrying her cross with ease it seemed. She wondered if her cross, weighed more, but it didn't seem to be. Jada takes a deep breath and hikes up the cross and moves forward. When she takes a few steps it drops and she stumbles. She tries again and over and over the cross falls and she stumbles. She doesn't give up but continues until she gets a good grip. She grabs hold of the cross once more and as she struggles to put it on her back, she can feel the Holy Spirit helping her.

"I am always with you."

At that point Jada realizes why the others were walking with ease bearing their cross. They asked God to help them. He is leading them as they follow in faith.

****

Jada wakes up with a pain in her back. She rubs it wondering how she can feel the pain from the cross. She gets up and then leans back down on her knees to pray. She knows why God showed her that powerful message and has been instructed to write it down. She grabs her booklet to write down her dream. As she writes she realizes that everyone has a cross to bear and it's up to us to trust in God to help with our cross. We all have different issues and personal circumstances we need to trust God with. Only he can help, no one has the power or the will to help us through our journey. We can give up but that cross will always be there to go and pick it back up to move forward and walk with God.

****

Lamar is fast asleep in his bed from reading the Bible. He has immersed himself in the Word of God so that his personal relationship may grow so that he may help others. He always desired to help those who were like him. As he has grown closer to God he

He, Then Me, Comes You

was revealed what his purpose was and prayed vigorously on God leading him. He thought God would lead him to teach young men in the church, but what God was leading and preparing him to do was much greater. Soon he is awakened by a loud noise. He jumps up and looks around, wondering if he may have been dreaming. As he gets up to look around he hears the noise again. Lamar grabs his gun and slowly creeps down the stairs. As he approaches the noise he notices a young man in his kitchen. He doesn't interrupt but only observes him. The young man is grabbing things from the refrigerator and eating like he hasn't eaten in days. Lamar doesn't interrupt but only continues to observe. He then says a quick prayer asking God what he should do. The Holy Spirit quickly answered.

"Whoever oppresses a poor man insults his Maker, but he who is generous to the needy honors Him."

Lamar flips the light switch on, immediately startling the young man. He jumps up and looks at Lamar. He stands there with his hands up, trying to put the young man at ease.

"Relax. I'm not going to hurt you. I'm not going to call the police. Just don't do anything rash."

"I'm sorry man, I can leave." The young man stated with fear in his voice.

"No, you can have as much food as you want if you would talk to me."

The young man is clearly homeless. His appearance is filthy, grimy and he is extremely frail from malnutrition.

"Ok My Lord, what is it you want me to say to him?" Lamar says to himself as he approaches the young man. He seems fearful of what Lamar may do. However, he slowly walks towards him with his hands in sight, assuring him that he is ok.

Lamar still observing, waits for direction. He feels the Holy Spirit tugging in his gut, leading him with action but has no words.

Chapter Eight

"I recognize you. You used to play ball at the rec center."

"Yeah, I used to," the young man confirmed.

"I'll make you a deal. You can have as much to eat as you want as long as you talk to me."

"Hey look, please don't call the police, I can just leave."

"I'm not tricking you so that I will call the police. I just want to converse."

"Converse?" The young man looks Lamar up and down and observes him.

"Yes, I just want to talk."

"I don't know if I feel comfortable," the young man states.

"Look I know usually in this circumstance someone would call the police, but I just want to help."

"Why?"

"Because I'm being led to."

The young man looks to Lamar as he continues to put him at ease. He drops the food that was in his hands and relaxes.

"Ok." The young man says.

"Ok; if you want I can make you something to eat."

"Ok, that would be ok I guess."

"Ok good, have a seat, young man."

Lamar begins to clean up the mess as he looks at the young man. He feels strongly about helping him. The young man sits looking around at Lamar's big home.

"What's your story?" Lamar asks.

"What do you mean?"

"Where is your family?"

"I don't have any family. My mother died and my friend's mom kicked me out."

"Your dad?"

He, Then Me, Comes You

"What's that? Do they exist?" The young man says sarcastically.

Lamar suddenly feels sympathy for him. When he looks to him he only sees himself. He sees strength and character.

"I know how you feel. I left home because of the abuse my mom was doing to me. She hated me because my dad left and she said I reminded her of him and she took her anger and frustration out on me."

"My mom was a strong woman, but she died of an overdose."

"I'm sorry to hear that. What's your name?"

"Kyle."

"I'm Lamar. Nice to meet you, young man."

"You seem to be doing ok for yourself now, how did you get through it?"

"Well my anger fueled my ambition. I swore I would become something to prove that I was nothing like my father so that my mom can love and respect me as I am."

"Did it work?"

"Nah, she passed away, a few years after I left."

"I'm sorry. My mom was a drug addict, but she was my best friend."

Lamar watches as Kyle devours his food. He didn't look like a person in need because of what he did; he was just in a bad situation and needed guidance.

"So, what are your plans?"

Kyle sits back in his chair and looks at Lamar. He didn't have an answer. In fact, Lamar was the only one who cared enough to ask.

"I don't know. I just turned 16. I tried getting a job but didn't have a place of residence to put down or a phone number."

"What about school?"

"I got kicked out for too many absences. I was embarrassed to go because I had no clothes. I couldn't bathe."

Chapter Eight

"Ok so if you are given a chance to have a place to stay and get things back in order, what would you do?" Lamar asks.

Kyle' ponders over Lamar's question. He takes a bite of his sandwich and sips on his soda. The question continues to hang over the table in an awkward silence. Kyle cleans his plate and sits back.

"Ok so what are you saying... that you want to help me? I mean seriously help me and not promise me some sad ass bullshit about setting me up and then nothing happening?"

"Yes, I feel led to help you."

"You keep saying that. Who is leading you?"

"God, and yes I sincerely want to help you, but you must help yourself as well. I can only do so much. You in turn will have to do the rest."

"What... you're going to set me up in some type of foster home? I don't feel comfortable doing that; I might as well stay on the streets."

"No, you can stay here with me."

"With you? Are you some sort of man looking for other men to stay with you?

"What do you mean?"

"Are you gay?"

"No, I'm not."

"And you're not afraid of me stealing your stuff?"

"No, they're only things, they can be replaced. But how many people have opportunities like these? You can take my offer, work hard and have a future, or you can choose to become a thief and possibly screw up your chances of a better life."

"What do I have to do?"

"One of the requirements is attending an all-boys retreat with me."

"And the others?"

He, Then Me, Comes You

"I will let you know all the details later."

"I don't know man, I don't know you."

"Do you believe in God, Kyle'?"

Kyle huffs and stops eating as he looks uneasy. He begins to look around in panic.

"You're one of those, huh?"

Not surprised by Kyle's question, Lamar is well prepared for a rebuttal and has become accustomed to the lack of faith and understanding people had. He was one of those people. He understands where they're coming from.

"And what is that?"

"You know, one of the 'holy sanctified, praise God all the time' people?"

"Well... Yeah, but not in the sense you think. I'm not one of those people who are going to preach at you and tell you to do the right thing. You know what the right thing is. Most people do. I'm going to help you learn to lean on God and allow Him to lead you."

Kyle was looking for Lamar to defend himself. He was waiting for him to say he wasn't and that he was different. But Lamar isn't ashamed of who he has become through the grace of God. He was proud to be "one of those people". He didn't care what people thought. He only cared what God thought of him.

"Were you waiting for me to say that I'm different? I am a worshiper of the Living God. The relationship I have with God is mine and mine alone. I'm willing to help you, but you will not degrade my relationship with Him."

"I didn't mean anything by it. I just want someone to be genuine and real for once. My friend's mom was someone who said she would help but when she couldn't get money any longer for me being there she said I had to go."

"Well it's a good thing she kicked you out. It led you here. Now you will have the help you need. All you have to do is humble yourself and allow God to bless you."

Chapter Eight

Kyle takes another bite of his sandwich and looks around again. He thought maybe this is a good idea and he can learn something from Lamar. Kyle was not a kid that was into neither drugs nor gangs. He simply needed guidance.

"Ok. I need help and you seem sincere."

"I'm happy to help Kyle. If I can change one person's life then I can leave this earth truly blessed."

"Do you have kids or are you married?"

"No, I'm divorced and no kids. Hope to have some one day."

"That's cool."

"Do you want another sandwich?

"Sure if you don't mind." Kyle said as he perks up and smiles. He sighs with relief. Sure, Lamar is a stranger but in Kyle's heart he feels he has nothing to lose.

****

Jada looks around her now clean and put together home. She looks over to where her Bible lays and grabs it. As she skims through it, she stops at one scripture and reads. She thinks to herself if only she can have this type of inspiration all the time. So she decides to write out some scriptures and put them on her walls. Like a crazy person, she begins to write and post them all over her walls. Hours pass and she looks to her home. As she admires the scriptures posted, she can feel the presence of the Lord. She can feel him in the room conversing with her through his Word. She lies on the floor looking to the wall and closes her eyes as she imagines God sitting next to her, massaging her head, telling her things will be ok and she can always count on Him. She has trust issues and has never trusted anyone fully. She didn't want to relinquish control to love someone that much. Fear consumed her and her soul. She wants to be better, become a better friend to God. She has the tools to be better but just needs the faith to step forward to be better.

He, Then Me, Comes You

"These words won't help you," the injurious voice whispers to her.

"This is a façade, merely a show to stop you from getting what you want. He doesn't love you. How could He? Your father died, your mother loves your sister more and he won't give you the desires of your heart like he promised."

Jada frowns in confusion, as she closes her eyes, hoping God speaks to her heart.

"Submit yourselves therefore to God. Resist the Devil and he will flee from you..."

Jada perks up in confusion. "Wait; if I tell him to go away he will?" Jada says to herself as she stands up and looks around her home. She grabs her Sword and sticks it out with authority.

"In the mighty name of Jesus, I command you to leave me alone and leave this home! You no longer belong here! I command you in the name of Jesus to leave this home now! Get out!"

After Jada tells the adverse spirit to leave her home she gets a sense of calmness and strength. She's heard of doing this but never believed it to be true. She knows without a doubt that she wants to get closer to God - not for her sister but because she feels she needs Him. She wants to build a sincere, genuine relationship with Him, even if that meant that her sister passed or she would be without a mate. She just wanted peace with God. She wanted and needed Him to be her any and everything.

****

Jada walks into the room where Mia is having her checkup with the doctor. Everyone looks up at Jada, hoping she was the doctor. When everyone sees it's just Jada, they all sigh with frustration and anticipation.

"Ugh, it's just Jada," Derrick says.

"Um, ok then..." Jada replies.

Chapter Eight

After months of chemo, Mia and her family are hoping for great news of recovery. As everyone sits in silence, not knowing what to say without sounding cliché, they all just pray silently to themselves in hopes that God will have mercy. Silence consumes the room. You can hear a pin drop as they patiently wait. A knock disturbs the room. Everyone perks up when they look to the physician. The physician, who stands at five foot five walks in with a clean white coat, holding a folder. Her face is graced with freckles all over. Her neatly waxed eyebrows are thick, and are the color of her brownish red hair.

"Hello everyone. I know you've all been waiting patiently for me. I appreciate that. This has been a battle and I'm glad through all of this, you all have been strong."

"Thank you, Dr. Reynolds," Claudia states.

Everyone hold hands as Dr. Reynolds opens her folder. Mia begins to tear up.

"As you all know Mia has suffered from aggressive cancerous cells in the right and left breast. With chemo, we hoped to help save her breast. The chemo has been successful. We have not detected any cancerous cells."

Everyone praises God for His mercy and grace. Jada amazed is shocked by the news Dr. Reynolds has shared. Could it be true that God has spared and given mercy to Mia, she wondered. Jada has gone deaf to the sound of praise as she watches her family rejoice from the grand news. Suddenly her sister grabs her and hugs her tightly.

"God is good!"

"Yes, yes He is." Jada says.

"I think we should celebrate. Let's all go out to dinner, my treat," Derrick says.

Everyone hurries along as they are still smiling rushing out of the building. Jada, walking behind, is skeptical of the results and wonders if this is the Will of God.

~ *Chapter Nine* ~

Finally, I'm starting to lean on you...

As Jada stands in front of the crowd, she feels the energy of the women pulling at her soul. She positions herself standing tall and ready to deliver a message, but is confused - what do they need? what are they looking to her for? She looks to one of the women in the crowd; she looks up at Jada desperately, with hope in her eyes. She is a young woman in her twenties. She has scars on her hands and left cheek as if she was burned. She has on a wig that is clearly too big for her head and frames her face in an awkward way. As Jada looks to the young woman, she feels in her spirit a sense of responsibility. She feels that it is her duty to help her the best way she can through the Holy Spirit. As she looks out into the crowd again, she notices more women looking to her for guidance. Feeling overwhelmed, with no answers, she begins to feel helpless. How can she help anyone when she can't help herself? As she continues to look over the room, the women begin to reach out to her, pulling at her clothes and her feet. Suddenly they all speak. "Help us; tell us how to gain strength."

The alarm disturbs Jada's slumber. She looks to the ceiling fan. She rolls her eyes at it for failing to do its job at cooling her off. The bed is moistened with sweat and tears. She then sits up and moves to the edge of the bed, reflecting back to the dream. Why is God showing her these things? She thinks God wants her to be this

Chapter Nine

leader, but feels that He may have chosen the wrong person. She is no leader, she thinks. How can she be, with the vain and stupid choices she's made in life? But then again, she thinks about the work she is already accomplishing at the children's center. Sure, Jada helps with the underprivileged kids but can she lead to help her peers? The thought of helping in that magnitude is terrifying to her. She doesn't want that type of responsibility. She then thinks if she doesn't have the courage to pursue what God is showing her, how many women will be lost or unsaved? She gets on her knees and prays for courage to do His will. She asks for God to allow her to recognize her flaws and to remind her that it's about His will and that she is simply a vessel being used. As she continues to pray she is reminded of a scripture she read recently.

Be strong and courageous, and do the work. Do not be afraid or discouraged, for the Lord God, my God is with you."

She begins to praise God and thanks him for his guidance and reassurance. She sighs and takes a deep breath, knowing what work is ahead of her. She's finally aware of her purpose. Now with this newfound understating, all she wants to do is study to be a better friend to Him. She wants to be a better servant to the Lord her God. She wants to be a better version of herself.

****

Jada is having dinner with LD; he notices something is off with her but waits for her to tell him how she is feeling. The silence continues as the clatter of the plate and fork collides. LD decides he is tired of waiting on Jada and jumps right in.

"What is on your mind, Jada?"

She looks to him. At first, she doesn't speak and then looks back down at her plate. He gives her a nudge under the table with his feet.

"I feel that God wants me to lead and help other women."

"And this upsets you because…?" LD says as he tries to

He, Then Me, Comes You

understand.

"How can I do that?"

"Well that's easy, through the Holy Spirit."

"None of this is easy, LD."

"I never said it would be easy, I said the answer was easy," LD said while wiping the crumbs from his mouth. He always seemed at ease, as if nothing bothered him and God was sitting with him. He's been through so much and has seen how God works so that his faith is greater than he imagined when he first walked with God.

"Why would anyone listen to me LD, given my history?"

"That's just it, because you have a history, you can teach others how to overcome it just as you have. No one wants help from someone who doesn't understand their plight or can't empathize with their situation. Would you go to a marriage counselor who's never been married? Or would a person with millions go to a financial advisor who doesn't have any money?"

"No. Well since you put it like that, I would be a great help to those who has been through what I've been through." Jada looks surprised and realizes that he's confirmed what she thought. She didn't understand at first, but is aware now of her journey. She hopes she can be a great vessel for God and a great help for those seeking God.

"God uses the weak and the overlooked. If he used someone to help you who hasn't been through anything, how can it come through as valid?"

"What do you mean?"

"I know that life seems so unfair, but when you think of the beautiful things about it, first comes suffering. A child being born, falling in love…"

"Falling in love? How do you suffer first?"

"Think about it, fear, putting yourself out there, pain of losing them."

Chapter Nine

"I can see that."

"You have come a long way Ms. Jada. I remember the first time I saw you. I felt so bad that someone with such a beautiful spirit would want to end her life. I wondered what you could have possibly been through to..."

"Wait what?"

"What?" LD asked.

"You said when you first saw me? How did you know I wanted to kill myself?" LD looks down and says a silent prayer and then decides to explain to Jada that he was the one who took her to the hospital that day she tried to end her life.

"How did you know I wanted to kill myself?" she repeats.

"Ok Jada, I was the one who found you and took you to the hospital that day."

Jada drops her fork as she gasps looking at LD's face. She shakes her head in disbelief - how did he know to look for her?

"How did you know what I did? I was alone."

"I heard the shot, as I walked down the street and as I was walking by, I saw a man pause and look up and said that you were crazy. I asked him if you were all right and he replied that you were not right in the head and needed help. I heard God speak to me and tell me to go and check on you and that's where I found you."

"LD, you saved my life."

"I didn't save your life, God did. It was through His grace that allowed me to help you and get you to the hospital."

Jada jumps up from the table and rushes to LD to hug him. She is now crying as she is holding him tighter. As she continues to hold him, everyone around them notices the compassion between them as they are consoling one another.

"I knew your voice sounded familiar. I remember what you told me that night. You said He is with me."

"Yes, I prayed for you and asked God if I can help you in any

He, Then Me, Comes You

way."

"That's why you stayed around?"

"Yes, that's why I stayed around. I felt in my spirit that I was supposed to help you but I'm not sure why yet. I asked God why you, but He hasn't answered that question yet."

"This is...just. I don't know why God loves me. I mean I know Jesus died for us because he loved us but sometimes I can't understand why. We are so messed up."

"That's just it, how can He have glory if we weren't in need of help?"

"LD, I love you, you have been the father figure I craved for, for so long." Jada kisses LD on the cheek as she hugs him tight. She appreciated God for sending her such an amazing person to help her through her messy life. His timing was impeccable. We may not understand what that entails fully but we can fully appreciate His timing and His glorious ways.

"Ok you are starting to make me blush," LD says.

"How is it going with the task that you won't tell me about?"

"I can feel the day is coming soon that I will be relieved from all of this waiting."

"Come on LD, what is it that you are so desperately waiting for God to do in your life? Is it another wife?"

"No, well yes, I would love to be a husband again but well, I told you I lost my family awhile back."

"Yes, you did."

"Well I'm hoping to be reunited with my child. I lost touch and hope the Father will help us come together."

"I will pray that He does. You are such a wonderful person and you deserve happiness."

****

Kyle looks around, admiring his new home. He walks through the

Chapter Nine

big home trying to familiarize himself. He walks around, looking amazed at all the books in Lamar's home. As he admires Lamar's accolades he gets a sense of relief and excitement that he may actually get the help he needs.

"What do you do for a living?" Kyle inquired.

"Well I own a few businesses. Nothing too big."

"Impressive."

Kyle looks around again at the books in Lamar's home. He picks one up to look at it more closely.

"That's a really good one."

Kyle smiles and looks to Lamar. "Is this really for real? It's just that not many people will let a complete stranger in their home; and to be willing to help them with no strings attached." Kyle states.

"Well then, there should be… that way when people need help they won't be so skeptical of the people who want to truly help."

Kyle nods in agreement and grabs his bag.

"Let me show you to your room." Kyle sighs with relief and follows Lamar to his room. He's never had his own room before and dreamed that one day he would. That dream was deferred when his mother died and he was left without a home or family to help. His heart begins to race with anxiety as he approaches it. They walk into a huge bedroom with a king sized bed, big screen TV, and a desk for studying. Kyle gasps as he looks to Lamar.

"This is my room?"

"Uh yeah, you have your own bathroom over in the corner there. All I ask is to keep your room and bathroom clean please."

"Hell yeah I'll keep it clean!"

Lamar laughs and gets an amazing feeling in his spirit. He watches Kyle who excitedly admires the room, looking through every nook and cranny. He knows without a doubt that he can help this young man and make a difference in his life.

"Well I let you settle in and then we can go get dinner later. You may want to rest or something." Lamar walks towards the door.

He, Then Me, Comes You

"Aye Lamar…"

Lamar turns and looks to Kyle. Kyle is tearing up.

"Thanks man, this means a lot to me."

"No problem Kyle. Just be great."

Kyle nods and plops down on his new bed. He lets out a loud sigh of relief. Lamar leaves the room.

****

"**Young men, you have a choice in life. It's not about where you come from or where you started in life. It's not even about how many times you may have fallen or failed at things. It's about choice. It's about making a choice to change your life and live for the better and becoming a better version of yourself.**"

As the crowd claps with agreement, a few men stand with smiles and tears in their eyes. Lamar stands proud to be able to deliver such a powerful message with men across the board. He feels privileged to be a servant and warrior of God. As he looks in the crowd he sees a man who resembles himself. The man begins to walk towards him. As he gets closer the man extends his arms out and Lamar realizes it's his father. Stunned, Lamar walks off the stage and towards his father.

A loud bang coming from another room interrupts Lamar's rest. He jumps up and grabs the gun he keeps locked up next to his nightstand. He casually paces himself, not realizing that Kyle is in the home. He walks downstairs and towards the kitchen - a soft glow comes the refrigerator light. As he approaches, he sees Kyle sitting grabbing things from the refrigerator. He doesn't notice Lamar as he is eating on a bowl of grapes.

"Hey." Lamar says.

"Hey… oh I'm sorry I woke you, I was…"

"No it's fine; I just forgot I had someone else in the house; not used to you yet."

Chapter Nine

"Did you want some?"

"What are you eating?"

"Anything I can find really, I'm really hungry."

"Why didn't you say anything at dinner?"

"I don't know, don't want to seem greedy or something."

"Listen to me Kyle, God has provided me with more than I need. Please feel free to eat whatever you want. Don't be afraid. This is your home now. I want you to feel comfortable and at ease. Matter of fact, make me a sandwich and I will have some grapes."

Kyle smiles as he prepares sandwiches for him and Lamar. They both sit at the table and talk for hours. The more Kyle gets to know Lamar, the more he realizes that he could really learn something from him and that he wants to get to know God as well. He has been angry with God for a while because he felt as most feel. He felt that God didn't love or care for him since his life has been an emotional hell ride. Lamar has shared that God has given us free will and does not interfere with our choices. Kyle asked a lot of questions pertaining to God and Lamar did his best at answering most of the questions. But with God, he found the hardest thing to comprehend was why God allows so much pain and suffering. Lamar himself has struggled with that question. As he got closer to God he found many answers to that question. He also learned that it was very simple and often wondered why many people couldn't accept the truth. Yet perspective can be a factor. Truth is debatable when it comes to God.

"Why do some suffer more than most?" Kyle asked.

"Well to my understanding a lot of that comes with lineage, our ancestors and family. So many of us have built false and faulty foundations for our families. We are not taught how to have a strong family fold. Most families do not have the one important thing that will stand firm."

"Let me guess - God."

"Well yes, we fear being wrong or believing in something that is not tangible."

He, Then Me, Comes You

"I can see that. But as we talk more, I realize that if I didn't go through the things I went though then I wouldn't have been led to you; which means I can the help I need in order to be the man I'm supposed to be. The choice was up to me and I could've said no. If I said no then my life could have been in the same turmoil or worse."

"Yeah! I learned that too. God will open doors, windows and even cracks and He will lead us to them and it's up to us to walk, or crawl through. Obedience is key."

"Lamar, now that I think of it, God talked to me that day."

"Oh yeah, what makes you say that?"

Kyle thinks hard back at the events that transpired that day.

"I had to beg. It's emasculating. I didn't want to beg for anything. I hadn't eaten in a week and I was so weak and scared and didn't know what to do. As I sat there for a while I felt the urge or more like a push for me to get up and walk to that store. I stood out there for hours; not much help. So I walked and stopped in front of your house. It was as if I wanted to be caught. I heard a voice tell me to go inside and get something to eat."

"Wow, you didn't think that you would get caught?"

"I did and maybe wanted to be caught. That way I would go to jail and at least I could have food and shelter."

"I'm sorry to hear that. I'm sure a lot of young homeless men think that way."

"Yea, but I know that the voice was God."

Lamar nods with a smile. They continue to engage in conversation and as the sun greets them they continue on.

****

Jada is lying in her bed thinking about Mia and how great it is that she is healed from her illness. It has been a few months since her last chemo session. They have been busy with the wedding plans and she feels extremely honored that she could be a part of it and

Chapter Nine

happy that her stubbornness didn't keep her from enjoying this joyous occasion. She thinks back to when Mia first started chemo and the effect it took on her and how strong she was. She admired her strength and faith and also admired the love Derrick showed her. She wondered if that type of love existed for her and if it did, when would she receive it? She was starting to lose patience and felt tempted to date random men. She needed to feel desired and at this point she didn't care with whom. She felt lust creeping up inside of her like a mischievous child ready to play. She began to toss and turn on the bed trying to get rid of that familiar feeling. She grabbed her plush pillow and put it over her head messing up her head full of curls.

She sighs hard and looks to the ceiling hoping God would send her a mate. She becomes frustrated and grabs her vibrator and stares at it for a moment. As she stares she feels convicted about pleasuring her flesh but only can think about her needs and that she needs to feel good even if it's only for a few minutes. The conviction of the Holy Spirit presses her and out of frustration she throws the vibrator across the room and plops back down on the bed.

"This is not working, God! You said You would give me the desires of my heart!"

The thought to read her Bible came to mind and as she reaches for it, her phone rings. She looks to see who's calling and it's Caleb. Jada suddenly perks up and fixes her hair. She wonders why all of sudden he decides to call her.

"Ok Jada, just relax girl," Jada says to herself. Her hands begin to shake and she presses down on the accept button.

"Hello." Jada says in a calm voice.

"Hey Jay, this is Caleb. How are you?"

"Caleb, hi! I'm good. How are you?" Jada replies nervously, hoping not to sound desperate.

"I know we haven't spoken in quite some time but I was doing some soul searching and wanted to apologize for how things ended with us."

He, Then Me, Comes You

"Oh wow, um well … I'm ok. You know it's been a year."

"Yeah I know that but I had heard what happened to you and felt guilty. "

"There's no need for guilt."

"I feel responsible for what could've happened. You could've died and I didn't do anything because I didn't believe you when you put the gun to your head."

"Well it all worked out. I'm doing better now. Much better in fact."

"That's great Jay, I'm happy you are better. Can I see you?"

Jada pauses for a moment. She looks to the phone wondering if God sent Caleb back to her? However the thought doesn't sit well in her spirit. She hesitates.

"Um I don't know..."

"I don't want anything just need to look at you and know for myself that you are ok."

"Um ok; I don't see the harm in that."

"Ok well are you busy now?"

"No not really."

"Is it ok if I come by and see you?"

Jada knew in her spirit if Caleb came by that old feelings will resurface and she may break her vow of celibacy with God and sleep with him. Her body is pulsating with just the thought of Caleb being near her again.

"It's just a friendly visit, nothing will happen." The injurious voice says.

Jada is still hesitant and she knows she should just break ties with this man here and now but she feels she needs closure. Her flesh needs answers to why he couldn't stay or commit to her. She needed to be desired and wanted by this man.

"That's cool, you can stop by."

"Ok I'll be there in twenty minutes, you need anything?"

Chapter Nine

"Uh no, I'm good."

"Ok see you soon," Caleb says.

Jada looks to her phone. She knows in her heart that she should call him back and tell him to stay away but her flesh and lack of trust in God is taking over. She then becomes frantic as she races to get ready. She checks her armpits to see if she smells ok. She then quickly undresses and hurries to the shower. As she rushes to the shower, thoughts flood her mind as to why she's getting ready only to say no. She thinks maybe she can sleep with him one last time to get closure or maybe they will get back together again and then another thought surfaces: that maybe God separated them in order for them both to grow and come back together. Soon she stops washing her privates and hops out of the shower. She panics and looks for something to wear. As she storms through her closet looking for something, she sits for a moment to think about what she is looking for from him. What did she need? Did she want to get back together with him or was she so lonely that she doesn't know what she wants? She asks God what she should do? She gets a tug in her spirit. The same feeling she got earlier that this is a mistake. She shakes it off and gets dressed. She puts on a casual dress that is modest enough but shows off her curves. She grabs a pair of her sneakers and puts them on so she doesn't give off the impression that she's trying too hard. She takes a deep breath and walks down the stairs to act as if she was busy doing other things. Moments pass and it seems like an hour has passed since Caleb said he was stopping by. She checks her phone and it has been an hour and a half. She looks to her phone, confused: why or what is taking Caleb so long. She thinks to text him but doesn't. She grabs the remote to the TV and turns it on. As she engages in a movie another hour passes. She grabs her phone and sends Caleb a text.

-Are you ok? Are you still coming by? -

She stares at the phone looking for an indication that he has read the text and is going to reply soon. Several minutes pass and nothing.

He, Then Me, Comes You

She tosses the phone to the other side of the sofa and continues to watch the movie. She can hear God speaking to her. He tells her that his intentions were bad. She wonders if she could just be doubting herself - is it really God's plan for her, or is she just fooling herself.

Another half an hour passes and there is still no response from Caleb. Jada sighs heavily and wonders why she allowed Caleb to seep back into her life. She was doing so well. As she gets up and heads to the kitchen, the doorbell rings. Jada looks to the door. When she opens the door she sees Caleb standing there with bags of food.

"Sorry I'm late; I figured you would be hungry so I stopped by the store so I could make you dinner."

Caleb barges his way into the home and heads to the kitchen and Jada soon follows him; he seems very comfortable in the home. He begins to unpack the bags and looks to Jada.

"What?"

"Um, you could've texted back..."

"I know but I wanted to surprise you."

Jada moves closer to Caleb and looks into the bags.

"No, get back."

"Why?"

"I told you, it's a surprise. You look amazing by the way. Look at you!"

He grabs Jada and hugs her tightly. She closes her eyes and takes in his smell. Is this the answer? Did God send Caleb to her? She wonders. Her spirit is in disarray and she feels uneasy about him being there.

"What made you contact me after all this time? I mean, it just seems odd you know."

"I wanted to reach out to you a long time ago but with everything that happened and then your sister being sick, I ..."

"Wait, how did you know about my sister?"

Chapter Nine

"I um... followed you one day. And I saw you go see her in chemo."

"Oh well that's creepy."

Caleb and Jada share a laugh as Caleb continues to prepare the meal. She smiles at him.

"Do you want to talk about it?" Caleb asks.

"Well she has cancer; well... had cancer."

"That's great, she beat cancer."

"Yeah, watching her suffer like that was so heartbreaking. All I could do is watch. But her fiancé was so amazing. He was her rock, her shield. I mean he was right there for worse."

"Is this the dude you used to date? The one you said she stole from you?"

"Uh yeah, Derrick, but I was wrong. So wrong to stop talking to my sister for all that time. I was foolish and selfish."

"Wow, you really have grown."

"I have?"

"Yeah, before you told me you would never speak to her again."

"Yeah I know. I can't believe how stupid I was. When I look back and think of the person I used to be, I think about how badly I wanted to talk to her. Tell her to stop being stubborn. Tell her life is so much more than what she perceived it to be." Jada says as she looks into the eyes of the man who abandoned her when she needed him the most. The same man who didn't care enough to check on her to see if she was still alive when she texted him from the hospital. Jada thought that this was a time to get her closure and forgive Caleb.

"You shouldn't be hard on yourself. We all have things we want to tell our younger selves. I was selfish as well. I have many things I regret. I should've been there for you. I was not the man you needed me to be."

"Thank you for saying that. I forgive you by the way."

He, Then Me, Comes You

Jada and Caleb share a look.

"Let's let this chicken bake and we can talk some more."

"Oh sure, let's go in the living room. Grab the wine you brought."

"Oh yeah I figured you would need a glass."

"I do, I haven't had wine in a while though."

Jada and Caleb make themselves comfortable on the sofa. Jada kicks off her shoes and sits back as she engages with Caleb. He looks at the walls and reads scriptures Jada had put up.

"So Jay, what else is new with you?"

"Um... I gave my life to God."

Caleb spits out some of his wine. "You what?"

"I gave my life to God."

"You?"

"Yes me."

"Jada Renee Clemens?"

"Yes." Jada says as she sips on her wine.

"Wow..."

"What? What's the big deal? People find God all the time."

"Nothing, but I didn't think you would be someone who would want to be that type of person."

"What type of person is that?"

"You know; someone who looks for God to solve all of their problems, I mean God is not always the answer, I know you had a near death experience, but it's over."

"Well a lot has transpired and getting to know Him has really helped me."

"I can see that."

Caleb moves in and kisses Jada on the lips. Surprised by his gesture, she pulls back. She pauses and contemplates what this will lead to. She then leans in and kisses Caleb again. As they

Chapter Nine

continue to kiss, he caresses her soft hair and tenderly embraces her. She felt in her spirit that this is wrong and happening too fast but she ignores it. She needed to feel wanted. She needed to feel loved even if it was only for a few hours. God promised the type of love that she didn't believe feasible. She only saw what was in front her. She lacked faith. She didn't trust God enough to help her through her loneliness. She didn't think God understood. I mean, how could He? He wasn't human. He didn't understand the needs of women. He didn't understand what it meant for a woman to be rescued by a man. As these thoughts crossed her mind, she knew how ignorant she sounded in her head. But she couldn't think or feel past her own selfish desires. She couldn't think past her flesh.

"I want to make love to you," Caleb whispered.

Jada was shocked at his boldness. She thought *why now?* What gave him the impression that she would want him again? Caleb grabs Jada by the hand and leads her upstairs to the bedroom. She begins to shake with doubt. Usually she wouldn't care if she was disappointing anyone, but she felt guilty. She thought what would LD and Mia think of her? What would God think of her? The feeling of her flesh overclouded her spirit and her judgment.

"What if he's the man God sent? He could be your husband, the man you've been waiting for." The injurious voice insisted.

Jada thought again: what if this is the man God sent to her? She's been praying for a husband. This is it! God has answered her prayers. She allows Caleb to lead her to her bedroom.

He lays her on the bed and begins kissing her from her head down to her neck. She then closes her eyes and thoughts run through her mind. She knows this is wrong. Wrong because of why it is happening, not the actual physical act. She became so careless with her body. LD helped her understand the importance of keeping her body clean from impurities. She ignores those teachings. She allows Caleb to continue to kiss and caress her. He then undresses her and he admires her naked body. At that moment Jada does something unusual and covers herself. She's ashamed of Caleb looking at her. Her breathing becomes heavy and she thinks maybe

He, Then Me, Comes You

this is not the right thing to do. Confused by her reaction Caleb looks to her.

"I've seen you naked plenty of times Jada, why are you embarrassed?"

"I...I don't know, something doesn't feel right. I don't think we should do this."

"Do you still love me?" Caleb asks.

"Yes, I do, well I think I do. I'm not sure anymore."

"Well I love you."

"You do?" Jada asks.

"Let me show you."

Caleb removes Jada's arms from covering herself and begins kissing her naked body. Jada cringes as he continues. But after awhile she talks herself into enjoying it and let it happen.

Jada is lying on the bed as she looks over to see Caleb cleaning his genitals. She frowns and wonders if she made a mistake and wonders if this is the man God has sent and that's the reason they came back together. She shakes her head and tries to be happy; that's she maybe next to get married. She gets a little excited, wondering if this will happen soon and she and Mia could start having babies together. With each thought she gets more and more excited. Caleb walks back into the bedroom and begins to get dressed. Jada admires him and wonders what their children would look like.

"You don't have to go, you can spend the night."

"Oh no Jada, I have to go."

"But why? Tomorrow is Sunday, you don't have to work."

"I know, but I have to get home or she would think something is going on."

"I'm sorry, she?" Jada asks in confusion.

"Yeah, Jada - I'm engaged."

Chapter Nine

Jada jumps up and suddenly her heart sinks deep down in her stomach. Her breathing becomes heavy and she looks confused. She shakes her head in confusion and denial.

"Wait, engaged? You can't be engaged. Since when and why did you sleep with me?"

"Jada, calm down. I thought we both wanted it. You know, like a way to give each other closure."

"What the hell are you talking about, closure? I thought we were getting back together?"

"Back together? No I don't want to get back together."

"So you used me?" Jada says with tears in her eyes.

"Oh don't start crying. Jada, you knew what this was."

"And how could I have known that? Wait, that's the real reason you were late isn't it?"

"Look I don't have to answer to you."

"I was perfectly happy without you interfering in my life! You didn't have to come over and destroy me once again."

"When are you going to start taking responsibility for your own demise, Jada? I asked if it was ok to come by. You could have easily said no. You wanted to have sex."

"No, no, no I didn't want this."

"Sure you did. You purposely put on the dress that I love. You basically encouraged it."

Jada looks around, thinking how Caleb is absolutely right. She jumped in the shower in hopes that they would be intimate. She wanted it. She convinced herself that she needed it. Her conviction hits her hard. She knew better and accepted what had transpired. She thought how stupid she was for doing what she knew felt wrong. God warned her in every way. He initially told her to tell him no, He encouraged her to call him back and tell him it wasn't a good idea. He even told her when he was two hours late. He also told her again before the act of sex happened. All of those warnings and Jada still ignored God and his direction.

He, Then Me, Comes You

"I have to go, Jada."

"Yeah go and do me a favor, lose my number, don't ever call me again. Let's just part ways and never speak again."

"The chicken is done. Enjoy your meal." He says as he shakes his head and grabs his things and leaves. Jada falls back on the bed and begins to cry harder than she ever cried. She was crying because she felt she disappointed God. She has come a long way in her walk of faith and was warned of the adversary deceiving her and steering her away from God. Her heart becomes heavy with regret and pain. As she sobs for forgiveness from Him, she grabs her Bible and holds it close to her heart.

"I'm so sorry God. Please forgive me!" Jada screams out as she continues to sob.

****

Lamar walks into the house, excited about news he just received.

"Kyle! Hey Kyle, where are you?"

Kyle rushes into the living room, wondering what was going on.

"Hey what's wrong?" Kyle asks.

"Nothing; I have great news?"

"Wow what is it?"

"God put on my heart to plan a boys' retreat and I planned and prayed about where we should go."

"Oh that's what up! You' re going to Jamaica!! "

"Uh nah. We are going to Africa!"

"Oh shit!"

Lamar looks at him and smiles, shaking his head.

"Sorry it's just that this is great. How long are you going to be gone?"

"You mean how long are *we* going to be gone?"

Chapter Nine

Kyle eyes widen as he looks to Lamar. He steps back as he holds his head with excitement.

"Are you serious? I get to go to Africa with you?"

"Of course, this is your trip as well. We are going to help and educate many young boys about God, amongst other things."

"This is crazy! I'm going to Africa! I can't believe this. I never would've thought I could have a chance to go to the motherland."

"This will be a great experience for all of us."

"This is so dope! I can't believe it."

Lamar stops and looks to Kyle with a blank stare.

"Oh no, no, no, no..."

"What?" Kyle asks.

"I just remembered I'm going to miss a big event."

"Why?"

"We are going to be in Africa for a few months and ..."

"Oh shit, we are going to be in Africa for months!"

"Yea, watch your language. It's a pretty important event. One of my friends is getting married. I'm sure he would understand; still I really wanted to be there."

"I'm sorry man."

"Ah no, its fine. I need to call him. Go get dressed, we are going to get our shots."

"Wait, shots?"

Lamar gestures for Kyle to leave the room. He jumps with excitement and goes to his room. Lamar takes out his phone to call his friend.

****

Lamar and Kyle are waiting in the doctor's lobby. Kyle is taking pictures of himself.

He, Then Me, Comes You

"What are you doing?"

"Oh I'm taking pics of me getting ready for my shots. This girl I like at the church is digging a young brother, so she has to know I care and what not."

"Oh, that's what it is. What young lady is this?"

"Oh, that girl Kara."

"Kara… Kara. Doesn't ring a bell."

"The girl who is in the dance group with the long hair. She wears it in locs."

"Oh ok. Oh she's a nice young lady. When I started going there, she used to offer me gum. I thought my breath stunk all the time."

Kyle laughs and Lamar joins him and the other people waiting in the office looks to them.

"What? Does my breath stink?"

"Well…"

"Whoa really!"

"Nah I'm just messing with you." Kyle says, while laughing at Lamar.

Kyle has become comfortable with Lamar as he now thinks of him as father. Lamar has become a positive influence on Kyle and his decision-making. He is back in school, earning his diploma and he also has been helping Lamar on some of his business ventures. Lamar is teaching him how to be a better man and how taking responsibility for his actions is vital. He taught him that mistakes are a part of life and we learn from them, and in turn it's where we get our growth. Kyle has even started his own journal as Lamar encouraged him to put his feelings, aspirations and dreams down on paper. He also taught him how to pray and what praying entails. How it's a huge communication tool with the Living God. Kyle grabbed on to the concept of praying and also about being honest with God. While doing so, he has gotten many things off his heart and spirit. Lamar can see how Kyle has evolved from the time when he took him into his home. He has become the father figured

Chapter Nine

he dreamed he could have.

"Lamar Daniels, Kyle Stevens." The nurse called out into the lobby.

"You ready, my man?" Lamar asked.

Kyle nods and puts his phone away.

****

Lamar jumps out of his slumber in severe pain. He grabs hold of his chest and drops to the floor. The loud thump startles Kyle as he comes racing in the room.

"What was that? Are you ok?"

Lamar extends his hand out gesturing to Kyle that he is ok as he holds on to his chest.

"Are you sure? You're not having a heart attack are you?"

"No, I promise you, it's not a heart attack, I'll be fine, just go back to bed."

Kyle exits the room, still suspicious of Lamar. He doesn't go far. Lamar still is in pain. He gets on his knees to pray. He knows the pain and why he is in pain and quickly grabs his Bible and begins to pray for his future wife. He asks God to help direct him on what he should pray for. As he prays his chest worsens, and he yells out for God to release him from this pain. Moments later Kyle returns and gets on his knees next to Lamar. Lamar doesn't say anything but continues to pray. Kyle also prays for Lamar. Kyle doesn't know what is going on with Lamar, but doesn't care. He just follows his instinct and prays with him. Soon the pain in Lamar's chest subsides and he grabs Kyle's hand. He doesn't stop praying, but slows down his breathing. Several minutes pass again. Lamar gets up and sits on the edge of his bed as Kyle looks to him, confused. He sits next to him and Lamar looks to Kyle and can see the devastation and concern in his eyes.

"Are you ok? I just got you in my life, I'm not ready to lose you."

Lamar smiles and hugs Kyle.

He, Then Me, Comes You

"I'm fine."

"That didn't look fine. That looked pretty intense."

"Let me explain. Several months ago, God revealed to me that my future wife was in pain and I needed to pray for her."

"He does that?"

"What?" Kyle asked.

"God tells you who your wife is?"

"If you allow Him to, yes. He's God. He can do anything."

"Whoa, so what does this have to do with your heart and the pain you were in?"

"Nothing except I can literally feel her pain. He showed me that she is in pain, her heart is in despair and I need to pray vigorously for her. I have been praying for her every day, but there are times when she needs it most that God will show me."

"Dude, that's pretty intense. I mean I heard of twins feeling each other's pain, but this type of connection is powerful."

"I think so too. I'm so fearful for her. I can't help her. I can't hold her. I can't be there for her and let her know that everything is going to be ok. I just want to hold her in my arms. She must feel so alone to be in this much pain."

"But she's not alone, and she does have you. You are helping her by praying for her. I mean, that has to be the best thing you can do for her right now, right?"

Lamar looks to Kyle smiling, proud that he has faith in God. He was so grateful for the opportunity of helping this young man and leading him. He hopes that he can also lead his own children with a life with God one day. He grabs onto Kyle and hugs him again.

"Thanks."

~ *Chapter Ten* ~

Regret comes swift and there is no one to blame…

"What do you think about these arrangements for the centerpiece?" Mia asks.

Jada is looking and staring out the window, spaced out, not hearing what Mia has asked. Mia doesn't ask again but just observes Jada. She gets closer and puts her hand on Jada's.

"Huh? What? What I miss?" Jada asks.

"What's going on, Sissy?"

"Huh, nothing. Why you ask?" Jada says as she tries not to look into Mia's eyes.

"That's what we're doing now? We're lying to each other."

Jada sighs and shakes her head, hanging it low. She begins to tear up and then looks to Mia.

"Sissy what is it?"

"I can't believe what I did."

"What? What happened?" Mia asked concerned as she wipes Jada's tears.

"I slept with Caleb."

"What? When?" Mia asked while in shock.

"It was about a month ago and now I'm late."

"Wait - you're late? Meaning you're having his baby?"

Chapter Ten

"Yes; what am I going to do Mia? I can't have this man's baby. He's engaged and…"

"Oh no Sissy, he's engaged? Did you know that when you slept with him?"

"No, I didn't. I swear. I thought it was God bringing me a husband. I thought the timing was just right. He came back in my life right when I wanted a husband."

"Wanting a husband and being ready for *your* husband are two different things."

"I'm so heartbroken. I put myself in this situation. I did this to my baby. He or she will grow up without their father in the home." Jada says as she gets up from the table and gazes out the window, thinking how disappointed she is. She was doing so well in her faith.

"Don't be so hard on yourself."

"I have to be, Mia. I have to take full responsibility for this error."

Mia grabs Jada and hugs her tightly. She cries with her sister, letting her know that she will get through this with a strong support system.

"Please don't tell anyone. I'm not ready to deal with it all yet."

"I understand Sissy; I would never betray your trust. You can count on me to be there for you."

"Thanks Mia. Ok let's just focus on your wedding stuff."

"Are you sure? You don't want to talk about it, or maybe just do this another day?"

"No, what good would that do? I will still be pregnant tomorrow."

"Do you mind if I ask - why did you think he was your husband? I mean what led you to believe that? Have you two been dating again?"

"Well, ok; before I tell you, promise me you will not give me that look."

"What look?"

He, Then Me, Comes You

"You know that look that you and Mom share. The 'how can you be stupid' look."

"Ok, I will try my best."

"Ok try hard." Jada adamantly says, while staring in her eyes.

"Ok."

She looks at Mia as she hesitates to explain what transpired that day. As she begins to tell her, she stops and looks away. She tries again but stops once more.

"Oh please just tell me!"

"Well he called me out of the blue and asked to come and see me. He came two hours late and made me dinner. I was so happy to be looked at and desired, so I felt that God might have brought us back together. Well within an hour, we had sex."

Mia gives Jada the stupid look and Jada frowns. "I told you not to look at me like that!"

"I'm sorry. I said I would try but in this case, it's well deserved."

"Yeah, ok."

"Sissy, I'm sorry but that was very careless of you. You haven't seen Caleb in - what?"

"A year."

"A year! And you thought God sent him to you, so you felt so comfortable that you would break your vow of celibacy with God and have sex with him?"

"No I didn't feel comfortable. In fact He warned me several times. I was being my usual selfish self. I can't say I can't believe this is happening to me because I knew what the consequences were. I just didn't care. Like you said, I was being careless."

"Ok I need a drink."

"Oh now you want a drink, the one time when I can't have a drink with you?"

"Yes, sit there and watch me nurse a glass of wine."

"No, we might as well have dinner then."

Chapter Ten

"Ok just let me call Derrick and tell him."

"Only about dinner!"

"Ok, I said I wouldn't tell anyone."

****

Jada and Mia are enjoying dinner when she gets a text from Derrick.

"Oh no."

"What?" Jada asks.

"Derrick is having a hard time replacing his best man."

"I thought his best man was going to be his friend, which is weird that you haven't met by the way."

"Yeah - he has been extremely busy and he has to be out of the country."

"Oh wow, that sucks."

"Yeah; so now Derrick's cousins are fighting over who should be the best man."

"Oh boohoo."

Mia looks at Jada, irritated that she dismissed her. "Leave that up to the baby."

"That's not funny."

"It kind of is."

"Whatever. This is the worst."

"Things could be worse."

"Oh yeah - like what?"

"You could have cancer." Mia says with a serious look.

"Now that's really not funny." Jada says.

Mia laughs and finishes off her glass of wine. Jada breaks off a

He, Then Me, Comes You

piece of bread and throws it at Mia. They both laugh at one another as Mia lets out a loud snort. People at the other table hear them and start laughing amongst themselves.

"I love that snort of a laugh you do."

"Oh whatever, you used to make fun of me all the time."

"Yeah but now I can't get enough. It's a beautiful sound."

****

Lamar is going through the house as he is checking off things. He looks to his bags that he has packed.

"Kyle!"

Kyle hurries in the room struggling with a bag as he tries to carry it down the stairs.

"What's in there?"

"My PlayStation and other things."

"What? You're not taking your PlayStation."

"Why not? I can play with it wherever we stay."

"No sir, no gaming systems on this trip."

"But we are going for several months. By the time we get back I would have wasted hours of playing 2K. Soon the next year will be out".

"I'm sorry but we will have plenty of things to do and playing video games is not one of them."

"I mean we will have downtime right?"

"Yeah."

"What will I do then?"

"You can mingle with other people there. Make new friends get to know their lifestyle and traditions."

"What? That's not fun. I need my PlayStation. It's like being

Chapter Ten

without an arm."

"I just purchased you that only a few months ago."

"Yeah well, I've grown very attached to it."

"Go take it back to your room."

Kyle huffs and opens the suitcase and grabs his PlayStation out. He pulls out the controllers and cords that go with the games.

"Look at all that mess."

"I'm putting it back. By the way, who's going to keep an eye on our place while we're away?"

"A close friend of mine will do it; you know Brother Mathews?"

"Oh yeah, his lady is nice."

"Hey."

"What? She is. And friendly. She gives really nice hugs."

"C'mon teenager with the hormones. Cool down."

"What?"

"Take that mess upstairs and bring back down the things we need. We are packing light. You need to hurry up. My boy will be here to drop us off soon."

Kyle sighs and grabs the gaming system, almost tripping over the cords. He looks back at Lamar and heads up the stairs to put his things back. Lamar continues to go through his checklist. He checks and rechecks the things he and Kyle will need. Moments later Kyle comes back downstairs.

"You good?"

"Yeah. I'm just nervous. I've never been anywhere outside the state, let alone the country."

"Well I'm glad you can share in this experience with me."

"Me too. I want to help build schools and help restore clean water to the villages. I feel like I'm making a difference in other people's lives. I feel important, like I matter."

"Of course you do, Kyle. You made a huge difference in my life;

He, Then Me, Comes You

I know that."

"Aye man, we don't need to get mushy right before we leave. In fact, living here with you has made me soft. I need to get tougher."

"Oh really, you think opening up about your feelings and being there for others is soft?"

"No but the other day when I was walking the neighbor's dog, I like, cared that the dog was constipated. I talked to him and helped him ease into it."

"Really?" Lamar said while laughing.

"Oh you think that's funny?"

"No, not at all." Lamar said still laughing.

"Then after I walked her dog, Mrs. Doubtfire had me watching her soap operas with her."

"Mrs. Doubtfire?"

"Yeah you know that movie."

Lamar looked confused, then realized what Kyle was referring to. He immediately laughed because the neighbor Mrs. Kennel did resemble Robin Williams. He laughed so hard that he had to take a break from checking his list.

"I don't see why me watching soap operas and helping her dog poop is funny."

"Oh, that's because it's happening to you."

"Whatever man. Is everything here?" Kyle asked.

"Um yeah, everything seems about right." Lamar says as he looks over his checklist one last time. There are five suitcases for both Lamar and Kyle. He figures he will only need a few things, and the other case has things to help their plans for the people who welcome them into their home. Lamar was led to help young men in Africa years ago. He never knew it was going to be through the grace of God that he got the opportunity to follow through and he didn't anticipate having the responsibility of a young man living with him - teaching him to be a better man and person. He thought

~153

Chapter Ten

back on his life and how it has transpired over the past year. He has gained a strong relationship with the Living God, reconnected with his father and is now looking forward to seeing him. He also has taken on the responsibility of helping a young man and had the pleasure of interceding in prayer for his future wife. Lamar felt extremely blessed and highly favored. He only wanted to grow stronger in his faith. By doing so he knew it would take more faith and patience. Suddenly Lamar hears someone blowing a loud car horn. His friend is there to take them to the airport.

"You ready?"

"Oh yeah!" Kyle expressed.

"Alright, then let's go."

****

Jada stands, looking in the tall oversized mirror. She lifts her shirt and admires her belly, thinking about the beautiful life growing inside her. Even though the baby was conceived in error, she gets excited about bringing life into the world. There were plenty of single mothers raising children every day and Jada thought she would be no different. She smiles a coy smile and continues to admire her belly. She begins to rub it. She then sits on her bed still in sight of the tall mirror, looking down to her belly.

"Hello little baby. I'm your mommy. I'm going to be taking care of you for the next nine months. Well more like eighteen years. I hope one day you can forgive me for allowing your conception to be in error. I want you to have your daddy but I'm not sure if having him in our lives will be the best thing. I don't know, baby. What I do know is everything will work out for the good through the will of God. I love you very much."

Jada leans back and falls on her plush oversized pillows. As she lies there, she begins to imagine what the baby would look like, what characteristics it will have and portray. What type of gifts it will have. She then leans over and grabs her phone, contemplating

He, Then Me, Comes You

on whether or not she should inform Caleb. She knew that Caleb would not be happy about this. In fact, he may not believe her or tell her to get an abortion. She looks to the phone several times until she decides that she won't inform him at this time. Moments later the doorbell rings. Jada jumps up in confusion since she wasn't expecting anyone. As she races down the stairs to see who is at the door, she notices the tip of LD's head.

"Hey LD! How are you?"

"Hey Miss Jada, I'm sorry to come by unannounced, but I haven't seen you a while and wanted to see how you were."

"Oh no worries. Come in, please."

LD enters the home and sits on the sofa. Jada sits next to him.

"So how have you been? What's been going on? I know you've been busy with your sister's wedding plans but how is your walk of faith going?"

"LD, I don't know what it is but you have a way with your timing. It's quite impeccable actually."

"Why, what do you mean?"

"Well I messed up."

"How, what happened?"

"I was in my feelings about a month ago and my ex came by and we slept together." Jada explained.

"That's just a setback Jada. Forgive yourself, ask God to forgive you and try not to put yourself in that position again."

"Yes I've tried but it's just that... well I'm pregnant."

LD leans back and looks to Jada. He shakes his head disappointed, but assures her he will be there for her by taking her hands into his.

"And he is engaged to another woman. I didn't know until after, but still..."

"It will be ok, Jada. I am here for you."

"LD, you have always been so kind to me. I don't deserve your

Chapter Ten

kindness and mercy."

"Nonsense; of course you do," LD states as he kisses Jada on the forehead.

"I feel extremely stupid. But I'm happy and in love with my baby already."

"That's not a bad thing to love what you've created," LD says.

"I'm sorry, would you like something to drink?"

"Um yes, a cup of tea would be nice."

Jada gets up from the sofa and heads to the kitchen. She fills the teapot with water and puts it on the stove. Before she leaves, she notices the bottle of wine sitting near the trash on the floor. It's the same bottle she had drank the night Caleb came over. She grabs it and stares at it for a moment. She then wonders why she kept the bottle. Why didn't she get rid of it? She then returns to the living room where she finds LD admiring the awards hanging on the walls.

"These awards are for your writing?"

"Yeah."

"Wow, impressive. I haven't been in your home long enough to actually look at them or read it."

"Would you like to read some of my work, LD?"

"I would love to."

"Great I will email you a few."

He sits back down on the sofa. Jada then sits.

"I also see you have been talking to God. His word is all around you."

"I thought that would help."

"And does it help?"

"Yes. I can feel his presence and hear him all the time. The problem is that I don't listen to Him.

"Why aren't you listening to him?"

He, Then Me, Comes You

"I'm not sure, could be I'm being foolish?"

"Could be?"

LD smiles as he messes with Jada. Jada playfully pushes him.

"Has there been any news about your kid? Have you decided to meet him?"

"I have actually. It will be soon. And I would love it if you would be there, Jada."

"Me? You want me to be there? But why would you want me there?" Jada asks, in shock of the sentiment.

"Well you and I have become very close and I would like to think of you as a daughter."

"Oh wow LD, that is great. You are like a father to me as well and I would be honored to be there with you."

"That would be great."

Soon the whistle of the teapot interrupts their conversation. Jada immediately gets up and heads into the kitchen to fix them both a cup of tea. Moments later she enters back into the living area and hands LD his cup of tea.

"So when will this happen?"

"Well after praying I have decided that it will be a year."

"Whoa a year is a long time? Why so long?"

"That's the time God has given me. I've always trusted his time, why not now. I put it on my calendar and decided that would be plenty of time to prepare."

"Yeah it will. Well, we will be with you.'

"Oh yeah that's right, you will have a bundle of joy joining us. I get to be a grandfather!"

"You better be. You must be there and go through this journey with me."

"I wouldn't miss it for the world."

"I also think it's time for you to meet my family, you know my

Chapter Ten

sister and her soon to be husband."

"I think that its time too. I would be honored to meet your family, but why not your mother?"

"Oh I still have unresolved issues with her."

"Why? Isn't it time to have it resolved? You are a woman of God. What is it that your mother did to you that you deem is unforgivable?"

Jada moves around in her seat uncomfortable at the thought of Claudia. She hasn't talked about what had transpired between her and Claudia to anyone except of course Mia. But that's only because Mia was involved. When Jada and Mia were young, Claudia was a different person. She was not a Godly woman at all, only a woman portraying to be. In fact she was a prostitute. She felt she did what she needed to do in order to feed her children. Like most single mothers, doing what is necessary to survive is rarely judged amongst the group of women. They all understood the struggle and knew whatever was done to survive was accepted, in all categories. When Jada became of age, she noticed the change in Claudia. She had promised the girls that she would never bring her work home or that she would expose them in any way to the business. However Claudia fell in love with one of her tricks. It wasn't wise at all but yet it happened. At that point Claudia would allow the man to come by and even spend the night. Soon he got comfortable with coming by and before you know it, he lived there and even pimped Claudia out. During one night when Claudia was gone, he decided to take advantage of Jada.

He raped her and beat her every day for a year. Claudia knew what was going on and ignored what was happening to her daughter. Many stories like this one happen more than it should, but Jada being young, just wanted it to stop. When she noticed he was looking at Mia, she decided to take things into her own hands. She told her mother that if she didn't kick the man out that she would call the police.

Claudia didn't take threats very well at that time from anyone. She

He, Then Me, Comes You

told Jada that if she called the police that she would lie and deny any accusations against the man she loved. Jada was so devastated that she couldn't believe that her mother would lie to protect someone like him. All Jada knew was that she had to get out and take her sister with her. She succeeded with the cost of putting her mother in jail, which meant she and her sister had to go to a foster home. Her grandmother was not around to take care of them. There she met Lamar.

"LD. she allowed a man she claimed she loved, rape me several times. Now I know that I have to forgive her. I pray one day God will do me a kindness and remove the memories from my mind, but they still haunt me."

"Jada I'm sorry that happened to you. It happens too many times within families."

"Yes I know. I hope one day I can help many abused women get through something like that, but the pain of the memories won't allow you to heal. I want to forgive my mom. I know she is a different person now and she didn't want that to happen to me, but it happened. Those scars will be with me until death and when I see her, I see him."

"What happened to the man?"

"He died. Someone shot and killed him."

LD looks to Jada, wondering if she was the one to have shot and killed him.

"No it wasn't me. I do want to shake the hand of the person that did."

"I hate to say this to you now, but I feel led to tell you."

"What's that?"

"You have to forgive the man that raped you."

"Say what! He doesn't deserve forgiveness. Why would I ever forgive a man that would do that to a little girl? I can't forgive my own mother, let alone forgive him. And what difference does it make; he's dead."

Chapter Ten

"I know, but you have to forgive them both, Jada. Not for them but for your own salvation."

"LD, how can I begin to muster up the thought to forgive him?"

"I can help you. Or you can speak to others who been though what you've been through."

"I hate him. He will never receive my forgiveness."

~ *Chapter Eleven* ~

It's time to grow up and walk in your purpose...

Jada has come a long way from when she tried to take her own life. She knew that this life that she chose with God would not be easy and she was ready to be that vessel that God needed her to be. During her prayer she felt a tug in her spirit to fast. Jada wasn't very familiar with the process nor why it was needed or why it was important. Scriptures came to mind as she continued to pray. She felt God speaking to her heart.

"If ye have faith as a grain of mustard seed, ye shall say unto this mountain, Remove hence to yonder place; and it shall remove; nothing shall be impossible unto you.... this kind goeth not out but by prayer and fasting."

Jada didn't quite understand what God wanted.

****

"Jada this is great." LD commented as he learned Jada was going to fast for a breakthrough.

"I'm not sure why or what I'm doing it for. Help me understand."

"Fasting has been a part of God's children for centuries. It's a way to deny your flesh to strengthen your spirit man to get closer to God."

"Spirit man?"

Chapter Eleven

"Yes the spirit within you to be connected to God in spirit."

"It sounds great, so I wouldn't eat?"

"Well there are many fasts. What did God lead you to do? Is it a absolute fast?"

"What type is that?" Jada inquires.

"Where you abstain from all food and liquid."

"Whoa, for how long?"

"Well that's between you and Him."

Jada plays in her hair, twirling it around looking worried about what to expect and wondering if she can accomplish the task. LD grabs her hand to assure her that it will be ok.

"You can do this. I have faith in you. He is calling on you to get closer to Him."

"I know and I want to, all I can think of is Him and pleasing Him. I want Him to be proud of me, LD."

"I understand, go, pray and ask Him how long he wants you to fast and what type he wants you to do. Listen Jada."

"Ok LD; thank you."

Jada is on her knees, holding her hands, ready to speak with God. She doesn't know the words to say or what to expect from fasting. She's read several scriptures on the matter but has not really understood the purpose.

"God please help me so that I may get closer to you. I want to lean on you and have more faith in you and your word. I need a breakthrough and would like to fast. I'm not sure if this will be good to do while pregnant, or if You will help me with the reminder of what I did. I'm praying to ask how long do you want me to fast and during this fast, would you like me to eat any meals or no meals and just juice or no juice and just water? Help me to get closer to you. In Jesus name I pray, amen."

Jada stays on her knees waiting to hear from the Holy Spirit.

He, Then Me, Comes You

She doesn't hear from Him, only doubt that she won't be able to accomplish this. She fears she will disappoint God again. She begins to praise Him and remains on her knees until she hears from the Holy Spirit. An hour passes and Jada is faint. She shakes her head and decides she was done waiting to hear from God. When she gets up, she suddenly feels the Holy Spirit speaking to her. She receives the answer on how long and what type of fast she should do. Her eyes widen when she learns that she will fast for 4 days with only water. She thinks maybe she didn't hear correctly so she shakes her head in disbelief and walks towards the kitchen. She hears the Holy Spirit again telling her when to start. She huffs and walks back to the living area and plops back down on the sofa. She knows without a doubt that it is God speaking to her. It was so clear and concise. She will fast starting in 3 days for 4 days with absolutely no food. Jada grabs her Bible to feed her spirit so that she may prepare for the fast.

****

It's the third day of Jada's fast. Jada is trying to pray but finds it hard to concentrate. The adversary is pushing her to break her fast and commitment to God. She closes her eyes as she tries to pray for strength. The first two days were extremely difficult but Jada fought through it with the grace of God. She tries to do some writing to keep her mind off eating but all she can do is think about food. Everywhere she looks she wants what she sees. She looks out the window and sees a kid with a hot dog and her mouth begins to water. She then realizes that's she's vegan and would not be able to eat it anyway. She doesn't care about what food she eats as long as its food. She tries to focus on the computer screen but the words are dancing off of the page. She writes the same sentence over and over again. She gets frustrated and irate and plops down on her sofa. She takes one of the pillows and places it over her head and screams into it.

"God please this is so hard! I need you to help me through this. I

Chapter Eleven

can't do another day. I'm so weak, I can't concentrate!" Jada says as she lies down on the floor with her arms spread out, begging God to give her the strength and courage to get through the fast. She continues to lie there weak and frail. Moments later her phone rings. She looks towards the phone but is too weak to get up and answer it. She asks God to give her the strength and faith she needs to get through this. The adversary is all in her head telling her she can't.

".... I can do all this through him who gives me strength."

"My soul is weary with sorrow, strengthen me according to your word."

Jada acknowledges the words being spoken to her as she repeats it, asking God for power and strength. She rises up and thanks God for his grace and mercy. She takes out her computer and begins to write again.

****

"I think these chair covers are ugly. What do you think, Sissy?"

"Yeah they are too girly. I would go with the basic satin white covers."

"Yeah, I think so too." Mia says as she and Mia are going through wedding plans. Jada has completed her fast and is excited about being closer to God. She's learned a lot about herself and what she needs to do to repent and live a Holy life. She no longer desires to be with someone because she's lonely. She now goes to God when she is feeling that way. He instills in her peace and joy. She is more laid back and at ease. As Mia is talking about the chairs, Jada stares in a peaceful daze.

"Sissy... Sissy, are you listening to me?" Mia asks as Jada continues to stay in her daze. Mia pinches her to snap her out of her daze.

"Ouch; why you do that?"

"What's up with you? Are you high?"

He, Then Me, Comes You

"Of course not." Jada says as she points to her belly.

Derrick enters the room. Jada and Mia are sitting at the dining room table at their newly purchased home. Derrick kisses Mia on the cheek and looks down at the mess covering the table. The home is full of unpacked boxes.

"What?" Mia asked.

"Nothing, I'm just looking. I have no opinion."

"Babe, you can give your opinion."

"Why, so you can tell me what I think is stupid?"

"I'm sorry babe, but what you've said is stupid." Mia said while laughing. Jada looks away, trying not to look at Derrick's facial expression.

"Ok... you see, I'm good with just showing up, dressed and ready to eat."

"Uh that's so cliche. I want you to give your opinion."

Derrick looks to Jada. He observes her face. He stares for a moment.

"What?" Jada asks.

"Nothing, it's just that you're radiant, like you're glowing."

Jada and Mia look to each other as their eyes widen. Derrick notices Mia's face. He knows when she is keeping something from him. He stares at Mia. Mia casually tries to look away, avoiding eye contact.

"How do you know if someone is glowing?" Mia asks.

"Babe, you get that glowing look after you throw up when you were in chemo."

"Oh well then, she may be sick or something."

"What's going on?" Derrick asks.

"What do you mean, babe?"

"You know that you stink at lying, right, Mia?"

Derrick looks back at Jada. She gives off a coy smile and then he

Chapter Eleven

looks down at her breasts. She gets offended and tries to cover them. Her breasts have gotten larger.

"Jada, are you pregnant?"

She sighs and rolls her eyes at Derrick. She gets up from the table and goes into the other room.

"How can she be pregnant? I thought she vowed a time of celibacy with God?"

"She did but she slipped, babe. She already feels really bad about this."

"What is she going to do? Is she going to be with the father?"

"No, he's engaged to another woman."

"Engaged to another woman..."

"Mia! You said you wouldn't say anything!" Jada yells from the other room.

Jada reenters the room and sits back down at the table. She looks up at Mia and Derrick. Her eyes are red from crying.

"Look Jay, we all make mistakes, some greater than others, but we will help you through this, ok?"

"Thanks brother in law. I'm glad you are here to help. I really need people in my corner."

"Well, you have it." Derrick said as he gets up and kisses Jada on the cheek. She feels better knowing her family has her back and she doesn't have to endure this pregnancy alone.

"Oh and that satin chair cover is ugly." Derrick said as he leaves the room.

"Well at least we all agree on that."

****

Jada is lying in the bed at the hospital. She is in pain waiting for her son to be born. Mia helps her sister as she is wiping away her sweat. She tries her best at comforting her, trying to make her feel at ease.

He, Then Me, Comes You

"I can't do this, Mia."

"Yes you can. You can do this."

"Ok Jada I need you to breathe, ok, don't hold your breath," the nurse says, encouragingly.

"It hurts so bad."

"I know it does but you have to breathe. Like this..." the nurse says as she instructs Jada on her breathing methods.

The nurse is a young woman in her thirties. She is a dark skinned, very beautiful woman with Bantu knots gracing her mane. She smiles at Jada as she tries to calm her down so that she may focus.

"Jada, look at me," the nurse insisted.

"Ok."

"That's good. Like that. Continue to slow your breathing down. Another contraction will be coming soon. Just remember to breathe."

Jada looks to Mia. She is smiling and reassuring her that she can do this. Jada looks exhausted as she tries to relax before the next contraction. She closes her eyes, hoping that Caleb would want to be a part of their son's life. Her eyes are filled with tears.

"Are you ok, Sissy?"

"No, I just really messed up this time."

Jada weeps when she gets another contraction. She tightens and holds her breath, with her eyes closed tight.

"Jada, stop holding your breath. Jada listen to my voice, you have to breathe." The nurse says.

The nurse grabs Jada's hand to console her. "Ok, Jada I'm going to check you again."

"Ok."

The Nurse spreads Jada's legs and checks to see how far dilated she has become since the contractions have become closer

Chapter Eleven

together. She looks up to Jada and smiles.

"Ok Jada its time to push, are you ready for your baby boy?"

'I'm ready. I'm so scared." Jada expressed.

"You will be ok. Just focus on me and slow down your breathing ok."

Jada nods in agreement and pushes as the nurse instructs her to. Soon the doctor enters the room. She is an older man with short brown hair and glasses.

"How we doing?" the Doctor asks.

"She's ready to push."

"C'mon Sissy you can do this, just push."

Jada continues to do as the nurse and doctor states and pushes when the time comes, and rests when she can. The nurse then instructs her to do one final push.

"Here he comes." The doctor says.

Exhausted, Jada looks down to see her baby boy. When she looks to him she sees nothing but darkness. It's a blob of nothingness. She looks to Mia. Mia is smiling with glee, excited to see her nephew. Jada looks confused – why doesn't Mia see the blob of darkness? She begins to panic as the nurse brings the blob closer to her.

Jada's heart is beating so fast that it's wakened her. She is breathing heavy and her pillows are drenched with sweat. As she wipes away the sweat from her face, she then looks to her hands and notices that they are covered in blood. She sits up and panics as she looks down at her blood stained sheets. Scared as to what she may see, she hesitates before pulling back the rest of the covers. She then leans back and begins to cry, wondering why this has happened to her. She doesn't quite understand God's will and reasoning for things but questioning them is never helpful. Jada pulls her duvet covers back and looks down to her unborn fetus lying there. She is now crying harder as she looks at the image of her baby. She grabs

He, Then Me, Comes You

the phone and calls Mia.

"Hello, Sissy are you ok?" Mia asked given the late hour.

"No, can you please come over, I need you." Jada says as she is sniffling in the phone.

"I'm on my way."

****

"Jada, you need to go to the hospital so they can check on you, make sure everything is ok."

"I don't understand. Am I being punished?" Jada asks with tears in her eyes, confused as to why so much pain was going on in her life.

"No Jada. It just wasn't God's will for you to give birth to that baby." Derrick stated.

"God's will? God's will? Was it God's will to have me go through rape for almost a year? Was it God's will for me to grow up without my parents? I'm so sick and tired of hearing about God's will. You know I'm starting to think that God is full of shit. I can't endure anymore of God's will. I might as well do what I want to do, because you know what? There is pain either way, so why not be happy doing whatever I want to do?"

"Jay, I know you are hurt right now and you don't mean what you are saying."

"Yes I do, I'm tired Derrick. I'm so sick and tired of His will and His plan for me. I just want to die. I have no life left in me, do you understand! No life left!"

Derrick grabs hold of Jada bringing her close to his chest. He holds her as tightly as he can. Mia also holds her. She sobs hard as Mia and Derrick hold her close. Derrick begins to pray aloud hoping God would give grace and mercy to Jada for her anger. God understands us and doesn't hold what we say or do against us sometimes. He reads our hearts. If God looks to our thoughts or our actions, we would all be in trouble. However God is a loving

Chapter Eleven

and patient parent. He allows us to grow and develop in our way of thinking and actions.

Jada is in grave pain and soon she will realize that some pains are not our own, but most are. We choose a path and put ourselves in situations and circumstances due to fear. Even when we think there is no way out... Fear can hold us hostage. Fear of the unknown also pushes us to make bad decisions in the moment.

"I'm going to stay the night with you, if you're not going to go to the hospital. You don't need to be by yourself right now," Mia suggested.

"I'm tired."

"Ok let me remove your sheets and make your bed so you can get some rest."

"Wait, just hold me a little longer, please Mia. Don't let me go. I need you. Please, just don't let me go." Jada pleaded.

Mia heart begins to feel heavy as she sees how vulnerable her sister has become. She has never witnessed Jada this low in spirit. She feared that her faith would stagger. She needs God to help her through this. Mia silently prays for Jada as she continues to hold her.

"I can clean this up," Derrick insists.

Derrick grabs the sheets off the bed and begins to clean the stains. Jada continues to cry on her sister's shoulder as many thoughts go through Jada's mind and she tries to understand the ways of God. Many have tried and failed to understand for he is a mysterious God, a God that is beyond our understanding, wonderful in all his ways. Jada begins to calm her breathing and peace fills her heart.

"Thank you God." Mia whispers.

~ Chapter Twelve ~

Remember God knows all, He is the same...

Jada is sitting on the edge of her bed. She reflects back to when God showed her men lined up in front of her bed and the death of her unborn child. She decided that she would not indulge in pity or feelings of worthlessness. Instead she decides it's time to make a real change. She knew that she was half committed to God and his will. She was making bad decisions based on what she thought God would want her to do so that she could get her way. She gets on her knees and prays for forgiveness, asking God to help her heal and forgive those who have been hurt. She needed the strength to understand why she should forgive the man that raped her and the strength to find it in her heart to genuinely do so.

"Heavenly Father, I need you to forgive me and my ways. I have tried to mislead you to think I was really after your heart but instead was only after my own selfish desires." Jada says it with all her heart with sincerity.

As she continues to ask for forgiveness, a peace comes over her whole body. She begins to bellow out with a gnawing scream. As she continues to scream she cries out to God asking Him to help her. She sits in silence as she waits to hear from Him. She has her eyes closed with head hanging low, crying, hoping He heard her plea. Minutes pass and nothing. Jada falls asleep as she waits to hear from God.

****

Chapter Twelve

"No, go away! Stop! Please stop." Jada yells out.

"If you say anything to anyone, I will take Mia and she will be mine too."

Jada looks over to her little sister. Mia stands there gripping her doll. Jada immediately calms herself.

"Mia its ok, go play in your room. Ok."

Mia continues to stand there, but soon Jada gives her their special signal letting Mia know that everything will be all right. Mia smiles and nods as she leaves and go into the bedroom.

"Good girl. Now lie down."

Jada does as the man says and closes her eyes. She asks God to make the man stop. But he doesn't. She continues to pray with her eyes closed, asking God to make him stop. After the torment stops, he gets up and walks out of the room. Jada is now shaking, asking why this happened to her. As she asked God for answers, she hears a still voice telling her to not to be silent. The Voice encourages her to tell someone she could trust. Jada is so scared that she ignores the Voice. For months this continued on and Jada prayed and prayed, asking God to help her. And again she hears the Voice encouraging her to tell someone she trusts. Jada heard the Voice encouraging her to tell her teacher. But over and over again, Jada ignores the Voice out of fear.

The next day Jada is sitting at the coffee shop reading her Bible. The dream she had was running in her mind like a bad horror film. She was led to read Deuteronomy 31:6. She then realized that God did speak to her and that he in fact was trying to help her. When she was younger, she thought that with children, God should rescue them. But she was misinformed on the heart of God. He doesn't swoop down from the heavens and save us from every terrible thing. He directs and guides us. She now realizes that she didn't have to endure being raped and molested for so long; if only she listened and told someone, she and her sister would

He, Then Me, Comes You

have been saved. Eventually they were put in foster care but it could've happened a lot sooner if only Jada had been obedient. She looks around the coffee shop with new eyes. She wondered - how much pain and suffering she could have avoided if only she had a relationship with God before. She sighs with the relief that now, with the wisdom that she has attained, He will guide her in her decision-making and it will significantly improve. She looks through the window. She observes the people going on with their lives, laughing and talking. She noticed this one little girl and how she was pulling away from her mother. Her mother was holding her hand very tightly, as she was screaming to stop. Jada realizes that *we* are that little girl with God and how He tries to help and comfort and teach us ways that will help and protect us. But we are the little girl pulling away, thinking we know what's best because we want what we want. Jada smiles to herself. She thinks how foolish we all are. She shakes her head. Moments later a very handsome young man approaches her.

"Hello." The young man says.

"Hey." Jada says.

"May I join you? I see you're reading the Bible."

"Uh yeah I am but right now, it's just me and God, so no thank you."

The young man smiles and nods. He walks away rejected. Jada frowns and wonders why she didn't have the strength to do this before. She figured people will get there when they get there and everyone's journey is different and will have meaning to others.

****

Jada decided it was time to heal and move on from the pain that has caused her to continue on with bad decisions and unforgiveness. She called Claudia to come by for lunch. As Jada waits for her mom to come by, she says a prayer to help her forgive her mom and hear what she has to say. She hopes that her anger will subside

Chapter Twelve

and she hopes that she can accept the truth no matter how difficult it will be to hear. A few minutes pass and Jada gets nervous.

"God please be with me. I need you."

Claudia rings the doorbell. Jada rises and answers the door. As she looks to Claudia, a sense of love rises up in her.

"Hey you." Claudia says.

"Hey," Jada says as she hugs Claudia. Claudia is shocked and holds on to her first born. She begins to tear up. She hasn't felt a hug from her daughter since she was ten years old.

"Come in, have a seat. Lunch is ready."

"Did you cook it?"

Jada gives her a look. They both smile and Jada leads her mom to the dining room table where she has the table beautifully decorated with her best china.

"Wow, Baby, what is this?"

"I thought we can have a lunch in style. This is a very big moment for us."

"I think so too."

Jada and Claudia nervously look to each other. Claudia grabs Jada's hand to try and calm her nerves.

"Baby, I know this is difficult for you. I'm ready to answer any questions you may have. I know that you have dealt with this pain for several years."

"I don't want to sound cliche, but why did you allow him to hurt me?"

"Its not cliche at all and I was expecting that question. I have no excuses and I want to be honest with you. I pray that you accept the answers."

"Ok," Jada says, as she takes a deep breath.

"I loved myself more and figured you wouldn't remember it and you would get over it eventually."

He, Then Me, Comes You

Jada looked at her mom for a moment. She looks confused because she assumed that the answers would be different; somehow she had expected her mother to say "I didn't know." Jada had a rebuttal for that. She wasn't ready for the actual truth.

"Are you ok?" Claudia asks.

"Yea, um. I'm going to need a glass of wine." Jada says as she gets up and heads to the kitchen. She returns with two glasses and bottle of an old red. She sits back down and takes a bite of her food.

"I'm ok."

"Can I ask you a question - did he ever touch Mia?"

"No, he said he wouldn't as long as I continued."

Claudia swallows hard and also takes a sip of wine.

"When they took us away, did you feel relieved? Happy that you didn't have to care for us anymore?"

Claudia nods for a moment, trying her best not to cry. "Yes." She says. As hard as it is to hear the truth, telling it is just as hard. In order to heal an infected wound, you need to get the infection out which may cause a great deal of pain. This is what they both needed to heal and move forward. Jada prays to God to keep her and Claudia strong to continue.

"When did you feel you made a mistake?"

"During rehab. We had to face ourselves and I had asked God to help me. When I started going to church, I felt so much conviction. I couldn't stand to look at myself. I relapsed and started binge drinking until a friend from the church found me unconscious in my own spew. I wanted to die. I felt I deserved to die for what I allowed to go on in my home. I should have …"

Claudia paused as she breaks down and cries. Instead of the cold look Jada usually has for her mother, this time she actually grabs her hand and consoles her. As Claudia looks into her daughter's eyes, she regains the strength to continue.

"I should have done right by you girls. I don't want to give excuses because there are plenty of single moms who have done it with

Chapter Twelve

less and with more children. I only ask that you can forgive me. I mean truly forgive me, where we can build a relationship and we can get to know each other. You have done great for yourself and I had nothing to do with it. I was never a part of it. I've read all of the books you've written and poems, and I framed some of them. I just want to be there for you when you get married and have your children."

"I want that too. I thought I would have a lot more questions, but they seem unimportant. They don't matter anymore. I don't need to know why or what could have been. Right now I just want to learn about who you've become as a woman now and learn how to develop a healthy relationship with you, so my children will have their grandmother in their lives. I forgive you Mom. I promise to work on it and not use the past against you. With God we will start fresh today."

Claudia smiles and grabs Jada's hand.

"You called me Mom."

"Yea I guess I did." Jada says as she smiles.

"This chicken is not half bad."

"Yeah, I took a few cooking classes. God has led me to learn how to cook and keep my house cleaner."

"Wow."

"What?" Jada asks.

"You know what's going on, don't you?"

"No, what?"

"You are being prepared for your mate."

Jada eyes widen, as she is amazed and confused. She wonders why now? Why does God feel she's ready now to prepare for a husband? She worries she will mess up and displease Him. She worries that the man she meets will judge her and look at her like she is filthy from all the men she's been with.

"I didn't think I would be ready for that for years."

He, Then Me, Comes You

"God is mysterious. He is wonderful in all His glory. His timing is perfect. Do not try to understand it. Only accept it."

"I'm afraid Mom, what if he sees the damaged me?"

"Then you would be one of the luckiest people. Having someone loving you through your battle scars is an amazing feeling."

"Ha, battle scars. That's a great way to see it."

"I'm glad we're able to talk and move forward. I've missed you so much."

"I've missed you too Mom."

"Say it again."

"What?"

"Mom - say Mom again."

"Mom." Jada says as she smiles.

Claudia and Jada get closer as they begin to hug and hold each other for a long while.

"I'm going to need your help with something else." Jada says.

She takes a deep breath and repeats a little prayer in her head. She was ready to forgive all parties involved in her despair. As Claudia waits for Jada to finish her request, she also says a prayer to herself.

"Do you know where Michael Saxton is buried?"

Claudia is shocked by Jada's question. She wasn't quite ready for her to deal with everything. She never thought Jada could say his name without feeling anger or resentment towards her. She was wondering why she needed to know why the man who raped her for months was buried? Was she going to take a deuce on his grave? Was she going to have his grave dug up and removed? She didn't know what to expect.

"Um, yes I do, but why do you need to know that, Jada?"

"I want to visit it. It's part of my healing. I wrote him a letter and I want to read it at his grave. It will give me closure and help me forgive me."

Chapter Twelve

"I'm not sure that's a good idea."

"Please, I need to move past this. I have prayed about this and have been led to write down what I wanted to say to him, go to his resting place, read it and then burn it."

Claudia is still concerned about her daughter's request but is willing to allow her to heal in a way she feels is best through the grace of God.

"Ok, only if you let me and your sister come along."

Jada nods. She gets up from the table and begins to clean up. Moments later Mia walks in.

"Now that's what I like to see!"

"Hey how'd you get in here?"

"Um... my key; you said you and Mom were having lunch for only a couple hours, and I need help picking out these flower arrangements and I need help with the parting gifts."

"Ok I'm here for you, Mia."

"I'm glad to see that the lunch went well. Did you two resolve anything?"

"We actually resolved a lot. We are moving past the hurt and starting fresh with faith."

"That's so wonderful! I'm so happy right now, can I get some of those hugs?"

****

Jada gets out of the shower and plops on her bed. She sighs with relief. Today is the day that she will go to the grave of the man who raped her. Many things race in her head and she fears when she reads his name on the grave that she would break down. She fears that God will not be there to support her. She grabs the letter that she has written to the man who raped her. As she begins to read over it, her heart gets heavy.

He, Then Me, Comes You

"Jesus please, I need you to be with me through this. I know he's deceased but the thought of being any where near him makes my skin crawl."

"Who you talking to?" Mia says.

"So now I have to be ok with you just coming in here anytime you want, huh?"

"Yes... and nice booty. What are you doing, squats?" Mia asked as she tries to touch it.

"Hey! Get off my butt."

"Oh please, you know you don't care."

"No not really, probably the most intimacy I will be getting for a long time." Jada says as she and Mia begin to laugh.

"Well in that case..." Mia grabs on to her other body parts and they are playing and giggling. Then Mia begins to throw pillows at her.

"Ok, now you need to put some clothes on. Your boob just smacked me in the face."

"I know what you're doing and thank you."

"What? I don't know what you are talking about?" Mia says while winking at her. She goes into Jada's closet to help her find something to wear. As she looks through her clothes she puts things up to her to see how they look.

"Um... I thought you were helping me?" Jada asked.

"I am helping you, by helping myself."

"You are such a pain."

"Yup, we got time missed and I need to make up for it.'

"Girl, I'm paying for most of your wedding expense - if you don't get out of my stuff and help me."

"Ok fine but I'm taking this dress!"

"Oh no not my Dolce."

"My Dolce now."

Chapter Twelve

Jada rolls her eyes at Mia. She could have the whole closet of clothes if she wanted and Mia knew it. Jada didn't care much about those things, she was just happy to have her baby sister back in her life. As Jada begins to get dressed and tries to keep her sister from cleaning her out, she feels the presence of God. She feels joy and happiness. She feels him all around her and begins to smile knowing that things will be ok, even if it doesn't appear to be so. Jada is knocked out of her trance by a pillow to face.

"Mia!" Jada screams, as Mia laughs hysterically.

Not another soul in at the cemetery. The air has a crisp breeze. Jada, Claudia, and Mia stand in front of the headstone that reads "Michael Saxton". No words are said as they stand. Jada grips the piece of paper tightly as she fights tears. Mia and Claudia just wait with her patiently. They do not rush her. They wait for her to move. Jada closes her eyes. When she closes her eyes she sees an image of God. She feels as if He is standing along side of her holding her and helping her through this. She opens up the letter and begins to read.

This isn't the hardest thing I've had to do. Forgiving myself was. Over the years there were many things I thought I wanted to say to you but as time passed, those things seemed insignificant. I remember you. I remember your eyes and how they were sunken in from all the spirits you took in before raping me. I remember how you acted as if nothing happened for hours later. I remember you trying to play with me and my sister like a father would. I used to think that you would stop and eventually become a decent man. But no, you disappointed me over and over again. I want you to know that I forgive you. I'm sorry that your father beat you when you were a kid; I'm sorry that you were also abandoned by your father and your mother. I pray that God forgives you for your indiscretions. You no longer hold any power in my life. Rest in peace.

He, Then Me, Comes You

Mia grabs Jada's hand as Jada takes a deep breath. Claudia hands Jada a lighter so that she may burn the piece of paper. As the paper fizzles away, Jada releases it and begins to cry. She felt a huge weight lifted from her spirit. She felt light and relaxed. She grabs her mother and sister's hand as they begin to walk towards the car.

"I'm so proud of you, baby." Claudia states.

"Me too Sissy, that took real courage and faith."

"Thanks for being here with me."

****

The restaurant is quiet with sweet whispers. Jada remembers the time when she and LD sat in the very spot when they first met. LD had become the father figure she always craved. She thought about how his voice always calmed her; how his strong presence represented the grace of God. She loved LD. She loved him like a daughter should love a father and he loved her. She was so excited about going with him to meet his son. She wondered if he possessed the same zeal for God as he had.

"This is a nice little quaint place. Do you come here a lot?" Claudia asked, while looking around the cozy restaurant.

"Um yeah, this is the spot LD and I go to."

"LD?"

"Uh yeah... LD is the man who I recently found out saved my life. He's the one who called 911 and got me to the hospital."

"Say what!" Mia said.

Mia and Claudia eyes widen as they await Jada's response. They are in shock with suspense as Jada informs them of her testimony.

"Yeah he found me and then we became friends."

"Like lover friends or…" Mia asked.

"Oh no not at all, he is this older gentleman, very sweet and very committed to God."

"Oh is he married?" Claudia asked, excited of a potential mate.

Chapter Twelve

"Ugh, mom. Leave my friend alone."

"What? If he's single and I'm single, what's the problem?"

"I don't know."

Mia smiles and nods in agreement with Claudia. Jada frowns as she sips on her glass of water. She didn't want to combine her relationship with her family; having LD separate was her coping mechanism. She had so much anger for her mother that it never crossed her mind. She looked at her mother and wondered if she was lonely and that she spent most her days at the church and with Mia. She didn't have many friends. Jada then thought about LD and if he too was lonely? She thought maybe it wouldn't be such a bad idea for them to be together.

"So why all of a sudden you are not eating meat?" Mia asked.

"Well I decided to become a vegan. I read a lot about the benefits of living a life without meat and thought I would like it, and I do."

"I don't know - meat is so yummy."

"Yeah but with our history of cancer, I learned that a lot of meat carries cancerous cells when we consume them."

"Whoa really? Wish I would've known that! Maybe I can become a vegetarian." Mia says as she stuffs her face with bacon.

"Yeah, I'm sure you can." Jada says sarcastically.

"What? Bacon isn't meat. It's a piece of heaven." Mia says with with no doubt whatsoever.

"Whatever, you silly person."

"I'm so happy that you are changing your lifestyle and becoming a woman of God, Jada. I can see Him shining in you."

"Thanks Mom."

~ *Chapter Thirteen* ~

Life is funny, you know… who can understand it?

"Mia, you are so small. You can wear any of these dresses," a bridesmaid said, while sipping on complimentary champagne.

"I know, I need a butt or some curves. These gowns are falling off of me," Mia replies.

"I think you should wear the Vera Wang vintage."

"It's a ten-thousand-dollar dress, Jada!"

"So what. I told you I was going to spoil you and I meant it. Um... who else would I spend my money on?"

Mia tries to hold up the gown she is wearing, exposing her breast.

"Thank you Sissy, you are the best."

The boutique clerk comes back over to assist with more drinks.

"Um excuse me; please let my sister try on the Vera Wang."

The boutique clerk looks to Jada as she waves her Amex Black Card. The clerk then smiles and exits to get the dress. Everyone raises their wine glasses to salute Jada. She is feeling great about doing this for her sister and smiles uncontrollably. Life was getting better for Jada and she couldn't be happier. She felt great for truly turning her life over to God and wondered why everyone didn't do this. She then thought about the part about relinquishing control. As the thought crossed her mind, she thought about the time she had dinner with LD and how he explained that choosing God would

Chapter Thirteen

consist of being under attack and that she would have to be strong. She endured so much within the last year and she didn't think she would've ever gotten through it. But with the help of her family and friends, she crawled her way through.

"Oh wow! Look at you Mia in that dress! It's perfect! That's the one!" Claudia yelled.

The rest of the women completely agreed, judging by their reactions and smiles of amazement. As Mia stands there, happy and excited about her big day, Jada looks to her in admiration. She was so proud of Mia and how she conquered her fears. Mia is dancing in her dress then suddenly an eerie feeling comes in Jada's spirit; confused by the feeling, she looks to Mia and at that moment, Mia faints and falls to the ground.

"Mia!"

****

Flashing lights staggers in Jada's peripheral. Silence overcomes her; she cannot hear the commotion going on. She looks to her right and sees her sister going into an ambulance as their mother is crying and panicking. Claudia is signaling for Jada to join them in the ambulance, but Jada doesn't move. Soon everyone is gone and all that's left is Jada still sitting in shock as her phone continues to ring and vibrate. An hour has past and Jada then decides to head down to the hospital. When she arrives, and walks through the halls of sickly people, she feels nothing - nothing in her heart, nothing in her spirit. Her shocked state has her numb. When she arrives at Mia's room, she stands there for a moment to prepare. She hopes its just stress from planning the wedding but having this relationship with God has her in tune and she has been given the gift of discernment; she is fully aware of why Mia is here. Jada walks into the room and Claudia and Derrick are surrounding Mia. Derrick is crying, as he is holding her hand with his head down. Claudia sits silently in the chair beside her bed. Mia looks to Jada with tears and swollen eyes. She says nothing as their eyes meet. Jada walks over to Mia and kisses her cheek.

He, Then Me, Comes You

"Maybe I shouldn't have eaten that bacon." Mia says.

Jada smiles and shakes her head in amusement at how strong Mia is being. She rubs her head and kisses her again.

"I love you, my Mia," Jada says and then exits the room.

Jada sits quietly in the hospital cafeteria, sipping on a cup of coffee. As she stares off into space, trying to not think or feel, she decides to sing a song in her head, giving thanks to God. She hears God speaking to her, but tries to ignore Him. Her disposition exudes sadness and confusion. She just wants to continue to think of Mia as healthy and happy. Moments later Derrick enters the cafeteria and notices Jada. He sits down next to her.

"How are you holding up?" Derrick asks.

"I'm not... you know, holding up. I'm not sure why this is happening to her. They said it was gone but now... now what? What did they say?" Jada asks as she stares into Derrick's bloodshot eyes.

"They said her cancer is back, and not only is it in her breast but has spread to her ovaries."

"I don't understand, I don't... I..."

Jada rises from her chair with an attitude. Derrick tries to console her. He didn't want her to cause any commotions in the cafeteria.

"He said pray, pray and have faith. We did that, right? I mean I prayed constantly and I had faith. You did too right.... and mom, she prayed. Hell, there were many prayer groups praying for this, they had faith right?"

"Jada calm yourself, please." Derrick said while trying to console her.

"No, this isn't right, she was just cancer free, just six months ago and now, it's back, vigorously! No, no I can't accept this." Jada runs out of the cafeteria leaving Derrick sitting in despair.

****

Chapter Thirteen

Derrick walks into the room with Mia, still resting and Claudia praying over her daughter. Claudia stops and looks to Derrick.

"Did you see Jada? Did you talk to her?"

"Yea, she's not in a good space right now."

"I know her; she needs time to process things," Mia says.

Derrick looks to Mia; he kisses her and begins to rub her head. Mia smiles through her pain. Derrick observes the love through Mia's eyes and his heart gets heavy.

"Ms. Claudia, can you give us a minute please," Derrick requests. Claudia gets up, touches Mia's hand, and exits the room, closing the door behind her.

"Did you talk to her?"

"I tried, she... she's not good right now."

"I can only imagine. She is very passionate and stubborn," Mia says.

"Did you decide if you are going to start chemo after the wedding or before?"

"Um, babe I..." Mia looks to Derrick. She begins to cry and Derrick looks worrisome.

"What, what is it, Mia?"

"Um well I've decided not to go through chemo again."

"Are you giving up?"

"Babe, no. I'm listening."

"Listening? He told you not to go through chemo? Didn't He?"

"Yes, He told me to be brave and to live life in peace as best as I can."

Derrick rises and puts his hands on his head in frustration. He starts to pace around the room. Derrick thought. *why would God want to take the love of my life? Why would He give me such a wonderful gift and then take it away*? However, Derrick was no babe in the faith, he knew why. Mia was being used for the greater good of the

He, Then Me, Comes You

Will of God.

"Babe, please tell me what you are thinking?" Mia inquired.

"I'm thinking how wonderful and brave you are to listen and obey our Father. I'm thinking that it makes me love you more and then it makes me mad and sad that I'm going to lose you and I won't be able to grow old with you. I don't know what to do with these feelings."

"You are the greatest man I've known and I can't imagine leaving you. But you have to be brave. Don't you know that's why God chose you for me? He chose you because you understand and you will help me through this."

"Yes, Mia. I know. I can still have my feelings."

"I know it hurts," Mia says.

Derrick leans down and connects his head to Mia's. They pray God will allow them to marry and spend a little more time together. They begin to cry together in pain and in joy. They are joyful because they know what this will do for those involved. God has the master plan. We are simply pieces on the chessboard. Some are pawns. Yes, the pawns are usually considered unimportant and usually the first to go but they are highly important. A pawn can be a barrier, a covering, and they can also be any piece on the board when they reach the end of the path that they're on. Mia was happy to be a pawn in Gods great plan. She knew it was more than her and her time on earth will soon pass.

"When did He tell you?"

"On the way to the hospital, when I prayed to him about it, He told me it was time to let go. He said to enjoy my time left with you in peace."

Derrick started to cry uncontrollably as Mia caresses his face. Derrick shakes his head in disappointment as he continues. Mia being strong for her future husband continues to console him.

"Please don't leave me Mia. Mia, I need you. I can't..."

"You can. And you will. He will help you through this. God is

Chapter Thirteen

and will always be the only thing you can't be without. Do you understand me, my king?"

"Yes."

"Don't fret. His plan will serve you well also." As Derrick lies on Mia's chest crying, they pray in silence to strengthen each other for what's about to transpire. Soon you hear Derrick praying for his future bride and Mia then begins to cry. The nurse comes to the door, but sees them consoling each other and stands for a moment as her heart becomes heavy. She doesn't disturb them but only watches and observes the grace of God.

****

Jada storms into her home and paces back and forth as her heart beats faster and faster. She grabs hold of her hair, pulling it frantically, not sure of how to calm herself. As she paces back and forth, she looks to the scriptures written and placed all over the walls; with each grunt of disappointment, she reads another scripture and another. She closes her eyes and holds her head, as she tries to get God's Word out of her mind. With each pace, she grows hotter with anger and frustration. She can now hear and see the Word of God in her mind. She knows now she's not able to escape His word. She drops to her knees and lets out this gnawing scream and tears start to pour from her swollen, tired eyes.

"I hate this! I can't take this anymore! Where are you! Why God.... Please answer me! Why?"

Jada stands and looks to the scriptures with rage, feeling defeated. She starts to tear down the scriptures. She reads each one before she tears it down, one by one, mocking the Word. Interrupting her childish behavior is Derrick as he walks into the home. He stands there and Jada looks to him. They lock eyes with no words. All you can see is Jada's chest moving faster from being in a rage. She pants as she stares at Derrick. Moments pass and they both stand, and still no words are said.

"Why?" Jada asks as she begins to cry again with a gnawing

scream.

Jada becomes weak at the knees and falls to the floor sobbing and asking God why over and over. Derrick comes closer to her and tries to console her.

"She's so good and wonderful and kind. Why her? Why Derrick? Why is this happening again?"

"Jada, our understanding is not His understanding."

Jada is now puzzled by Derrick's answer. She looks up at Derrick. How can she believe that dying is God's will? Jada wasn't very familiar with the ways of God but she had hoped she would learn from this experience.

"I know my sister. She's not going through chemo again, is she?"

"No, she's not. She feels God instructed her to be at peace. And to live her life as best as she can in peace, free form chemicals destroying her body. ."

"Are you ok with this? I know it's a stupid question considering but..." Jada says.

"It's not a stupid question. I will be ok."

"Are you going to try and talk her out of this?" Jada asks. Derrick hangs his head down and sighs.

"No Jay, I'm not going to talk her into getting more chemo. It's hard to watch someone you love go through the agony of putting that poison in their body. God showed me what would transpire. I chose to love your sister. I knew she needed me and if God willing to keep her or release her is solely for the good of us all."

"Why did you come to talk to me? Why didn't my mother come?"

"I volunteered because I have a word to give to you."

"And what is that?"

"Death is not the end."

Jada shakes her head. "I want to believe that. My heart hopes for that."

Chapter Thirteen

"It's not the end, Jada. Be encouraged and have faith, for you will see your sister again."

"How long did they say she had if she doesn't take the chemo?"

"Six months maybe a year. The cancer came back now in her cervix, breasts and lungs."

Jada tries to refrain from crying again. She is nodding in disbelief, trying her best to hold her composure.

"Thank you... for coming by to check on me and for being there for her. I mean I know she's your wife and that is your duty, but you know what I mean."

"Enjoy her on this earth now and be joyful that she will be with our Father and have faith that you will be united with her again," Derrick says.

Jada stands and looks to her mess. She nods in agreement as she begins to clean up.

"I need a moment, Derrick."

Derrick kisses Jada on the forehead and exits the home. She lies on her sofa and gingerly cries to herself, asking God to forgive her.

"Father, I was wrong to question your purpose with your daughter, my sister. I'm happy she will no longer be in pain and I ask you to be with Derrick, for he needs the Holy Spirit to strengthen him."

"Come now, let us settle the matter... though your sins are like scarlet red, they shall be as white as snow..."

"Thank you, Father."

****

Jada stands at Derrick's and Mia's door. She stands there for a moment, trying to compose herself. Wondering what to say or even how to behave to avoid any discomfort for Mia. Jada rings the doorbell and is greeted by Derrick. Derrick appears to have been crying and hugs Jada. Jada then steps back and looks at him. She gives a sincere look of compassion for his heart. She hugs him again and walks into the back room where Mia is resting. As she gets closer to her sister, she smells the wonderful scent of apple pie baking in the background. Its Mia's favorite. Jada kisses Mia and she wakes from her nap.

"Hey big head."

"Hey, I didn't mean to wake you."

"Well then you shouldn't have put your hot breath on me." Mia says jokingly as she makes Jada smile. She is going to miss how incredibly strong Mia is. Mia's spirit just lights up a room. She tries not to think of the time she didn't speak to her. She was such a hardheaded foolish person.

"I smell apple pie," Mia states.

"Yeah I think Derrick made you one. He's such a good man. I was so wrong. He is so perfect for you."

"I know. I'm going to miss him."

"Ok from now on, we are just going to focus on you being happy and healthy so you can get down the aisle in a few months."

"I'm so excited!"

"Um so have you and Derrick ever… "

"What?"

"You know done the wild monkey dance?"

"The wild monkey dance? What are you talking about, fool? Just ask if we had sex?"

"Well I was trying to be a lady about it."

"By saying wild monkey dance? But no we haven't."

"Whoa! Seriously?"

"We wanted our wedding night to be special." Mia said.

"I decided to do the same and rekindle my celibacy vow and wait when I meet my husband."

Chapter Thirteen

"Oh wow, that is great! But you need some hot panties."

Jada playfully hits Mia in the arm and they share a laugh. Jada leans in and hugs her so tightly not wanting to let her go. Moments later Derrick comes in with two plates of apple pie and ice cream. Mia eyes lights up with excitement like a kid in a candy store.

"Oh this smells so good babe, thank you for my treat."

"Yeah this looks really good, it smells and tastes just like Grand's apple pie. Hmmm so good."

"This is Grand's recipe."

"Say what? Oh wow, from now on every occasion soon to be brother, I want apple pie."

"No problem."

Derrick leaves the room and all you can hear is the sound of the fork hitting the plate and smacking from Jada eating.

"I hope the dude you marry can tolerate your smacking."

"Shut up, Mia. He's going to love me."

"Eh, maybe a strong like, not love."

Jada takes some of her ice cream, puts it on her finger and puts it on Mia's face.

"Ugh no you didn't, you bum."

"Stop talking about me, then," Jada says.

Mia playfully tosses some pieces of apple pie from her spoon at Jada's face.

"Uh ok now you're about to get it!"

Jada jumps on Mia as they continue to playfully wrestle. Mia is screaming and laughing at the same time. Derrick comes in the room and watches his fiancé and soon to be sister in law laugh and play. The sound of Mia's laugh makes his heart happy. He just wants to take her all in. He grabs his phone and begins to record. He wants to capture these memories. He smiles adoringly at his beautiful fiancé. As he continues to watch, suddenly a piece of apple pie to his face snaps him out of his trance.

He, Then Me, Comes You

"What the! What was that?"

"What you looking at, fool?" Jada asked.

"Ok you think you're funny? I got you." Derrick leaves the room. Mia jumps up and tries to take cover.

"What are you doing?" Jada asked.

"He's coming back with the tub of ice cream."

"Huh? Why?"

Derrick enters the room with the tub of ice cream and starts flicking it at Jada and Mia.

"What the hell! Derrick, this is cashmere."

"So what!" Derrick says.

Derrick, Jada and Mia start a mini food fight. They are laughing and hiding within the furniture in the room. All you can hear is the high pitches of Mia and Jada screaming as they slip and fall on the ice cream on the floor. Derrick tries to help Mia but gets slapped in the face with a handful of ice cream. Several minutes pass and they all are lying on the floor and their clothes stained with ice cream. They are all out of breath.

"Wow, I haven't had this much fun in years."

"I know right. I really needed this." Mia said.

"Jada you thought you were slick, thinking no one saw you eating the ice cream off the floor."

"What are you talking about? I did no such thing!" Jada says as she wipes her mouth off and giggles.

"Ok, I have to clean this mess up."

"Oh would you look at the time." Jada says as she looks to her watch and tries to get up and leave.

"Wow really Jay? You're not going to help clean this mess?" Derrick asks.

"You got this. C'mon, what did you expect, I pay people to clean my own house."

Chapter Thirteen

Mia shakes her head and shrugs looking to Derrick. He waves her off and helps Mia.

"Love you guys!"

****

A few months has passed since Mia has relapsed. Jada had been spending a large amount of time with God. She knew that Mia was going to die soon. She didn't know if it was going to be a year or less. She knew God is the only person Who can help her understand and get through this. She tried to fast for Mia's recovery but failed at fasting many times. She didn't prepare herself. As she broke ties with the men she's been with, she came to an understanding of why she would fail. With each day, she committed to spending more time with God and getting to know His Heart. She learned that God would never hurt us or tempt us. That's not what He does. He wants us to succeed but will allow us to undergo test and trials to strengthen us. She didn't understand that we are in a war, a war with the adversary trying to mislead and deceive us. God has shown Jada that she was under attack when she was very small. The adversary saw the strength and endurance in her. Because her parents failed at preparing her for the fight, the enemy had a grip on her. She and other people couldn't understand why God would allow a child to be raped, or what we perceive as bad, to happen to a young person when they had no control over what happened to them.

Many people lost faith in a God that seemed to be absent, a God that didn't care for His children. What many people have failed to realize is that with free will comes the outcome from our ancestor's choices. We suffer from what decisions were made from our parents and from their parents and so forth. It can be a generational curse at times. Jada was raped because of the poor choices her mother made. Claudia's poor choices came from her mother. We often think God should protect children from our choices, but then free will would be irrelevant. He promises to be there through your suffering and deliver you from the bad choices of your parents. With Mia and her suffering also came a choice. Jada had been led to become vegan because of her family's risk of cancer. Having a plant-based diet would decrease her chances of having cancer like Mia and her grandmother and many others in her family. God never said there wouldn't be suffering and trials. He said during the storms he would help us. He can give us an umbrella. He can provide us with rain boots and even a raincoat. Jada has received her umbrella and soon she will learn to get her boots and raincoat. As long as she allows God to lead her, she will be prepared for trials and can have joy through any situation. Jada had become accustomed to praying and listening for direction from God. She would date Him. She would get dressed and prepare meals with Him. She would ask for intimacy and the Holy Spirit will provide that. With each date, her need to be held by a man or loved by a man subsided. She still desired a husband, but decided to wait for her anointed husband. By waiting she can truly be sure that what God provided will be nothing less of what she needs and deserves.

****

Jada is walking through a desert with her cross, strapped to her back as she pants for water.

"Drop that cross and leave this desert. I will provide you with plenty of water and a man that will love you and make you feel good." **The injurious voice said.**

Jada looks over to her left and sees water glistening like a mirage. She stops as the weight of the cross becomes heavier. It almost appears as if someone is sitting on top of it weighing it down. She drops to her knees while staring at the water. She can almost taste the water on her lips. She closes her eyes and prays that the Holy Spirit will give her strength.

"You can't do this, Give up now. I can help you. I will be there for you where you won't have to suffer." **The voice insisted.**

Jada rises and with all her strength and might she screams and pushes forward through the desert.

Chapter Thirteen

"Get away from me! Leave me alone in the name of Jesus!"

****

"You are really looking great, Jada. This vegan lifestyle is doing great for you," Mia stated.

"I know. I feel incredible. I have so much energy. I started exercising and can play with the kids at the center I volunteer at, without having to rest and catch my breath."

"I felt God leading me to do the same but didn't listen. I'm glad you are allowing Him to lead you, Sissy."

"Why didn't you want to have a big blowout bachelorette party?"

"Honestly Sissy, I don't have the strength today. I just want to spend time with you. I want us to bond as sisters before I spend most of my time with Derrick."

"Yeah, I need this too. I forget that when you get married, Derrick is going to want most of your time, seeing how you may not have a lot of it."

"Yeah, we are going to travel. I'm so excited to see these many different places."

Jada smiles at Mia. She remembers a time when they were younger and Mia was so lost and confused. After their mother was sent to prison and they had to live in foster care for a while, Mia wasn't herself. She wasn't the fun loving, bubbly little girl. She fell into a depressed state for a year and Jada was afraid that if she didn't find a way to contact her family, that Mia would have fallen into a life like Claudia had - drugs and prostitution. Jada recalled a time when they were sleeping and she was praying over her. She forgot that time she relied on God to help her and her sister. Jada had suppressed so much of her childhood that she forgot the fact that she was a warrior and servant of God then, she just didn't know it.

"So what do you want to do? You want to watch a bunch of love sick movies while eating some vegan pizza?"

He, Then Me, Comes You

"Ugh vegan pizza? I'm already dying, I don't need to eat vegan pizza."

"Mia! Really?"

"What? I'm just accepting my current situation. I've made my peace with it and I hope by me being out right blunt about it, it will help you too."

"It's still a sensitive subject. You will not have to live without me, but I have to live without you."

"True. I get it. I will pray for you. I will pray that your heart will be at peace when I go and after."

"There can still be a recovery, Mia."

"Sissy. I'm not going to heal from this. Not this time. God has told me I will soon be with Him."

"Well this is supposed to be a happy occasion, let's just stop talking about it. Do you want me to order you a pizza full of bacon?'

"Oh yeah, now you're talking."

"Fine, I will order you a pizza full of crap."

"Oh thank you, Sissy."

Jada pulls out her phone to order the pizzas online. Mia grabs a blanket and puts her feet under Jada's leg as she gets comfortable.

"You have the coldest feet ever. It could be 90 degrees outside and you would still have cold feet."

"Yeah I know."

"Hey I have a question for you. How are you feeling about the wedding night? Do you need some pointers from your big sis?"

"Ugh no. It's bad enough you slept with my soon to be husband and now you want to give me pointers on how to please him? I'll pass."

"Mia, we never had sex."

"What?" Mia says as she perks up.

"Derrick and I never had sex. Wait - he didn't tell you?"

Chapter Thirteen

"I never asked because I didn't want to know." Mia says.

"Derrick told you he was celibate for years."

"I know but you know how you are and…"

"Really? You are going to go there?"

"Sorry."

Mia raises her hands with joy. She yells out a resounding "yes!" and closes her eyes thankfully.

"Ok, tell me how you really feel."

"You have no idea how relieved I am."

"Well I have some clue," Jada says as she gets up to the table to pour a glass of wine. She drinks it all and then pours herself another glass.

"Um... ok are you going to pour me some?"

"Huh? Oh yeah."

"What's up with you? Why do you seem uneasy because I'm happy you didn't sleep with Derrick?" Mia asked.

"No, it's just you think I'm nasty."

"What! No I don't.

"You think I slept with every man I came in contact with."

Mia looks away from Jada trying to hold her tongue. "Well you have been with a lot of men."

"See I knew it!"

"Sissy I do not think you're nasty."

"What do you think then? What do you think of me?"

"Jada you…"

"Oh no! You called me by my government. You always call me Jada when you about to crush my dreams or my heart!" Jada says as she grabs hold of the bottle of wine and begins to drink from it.

"Will you stop being so dramatic! You always do this. I don't think less of you because of the choices you've made. Those are your choices. I think you are a wonderful woman. Who you chose to give your body to is your business."

"How did you do it Mia? How did you remain pure and abstinent?"

"Through prayer. I asked God to keep me until I was married. Oh trust me it was a battle, but He helped me with my chastity."

"You are pure and I've had more men then I can count on my fingers."

Mia bursts with laughter as she looks at Jada. Jada frowns and continues to drink the wine. As Mia continues to laugh and snort, it breaks the tension in the room causing Jada to laugh as well. Mia is laughing so hard that she leans over and falls on the floor.

"Why is this so funny?"

"Because you are so nasty!"

"See I knew it!"

Jada grabs Mia's pillow and hits her with it. Mia, still laughing, can't fight back but takes the hits from the pillow.

"Ok I'm sorry Sissy. I love you so much but the important thing is that you are a better person now. And well... maybe you can give me a few pointers. I do want to please my husband."

"I don't know if I want to help you now."

"Oh just tell me nasty," Mia says as she bursts with laughter again. Jada gets up and heads to the bathroom.

"Come back Sissy. I was partly playing."

"I hate you!" Jada yells from the other room.

~ Chapter Fourteen ~

How beautiful and graceful God is…

The green leafy tall trees are filled with beautiful linen graciously swaying from the low hanging trees. Their leaves waves with the wind as the sun kisses their heads. It is a beautiful perfect 78 degrees of bliss. It was as if God made this day perfect just for Mia. His blessings were shown that day. Everything was lined up perfectly with His timing. The lawn was sunken in and was covered in beautiful polished white flooring. The chairs are lined up and decorated with lavender linen and a festoon of white lilies. The runway leads to a wooden dance floor with tall carved stands holding the lighted lanterns. There are many white candles surrounding the area, creating a lovely ambiance. Round tables are set up, with a decor fit for a Queen and King. The wedding planner, who is a lanky woman dressed in a black Prada pantsuit, barks at the men putting creating the wedding atmosphere. She looks around frantically making sure everything is in perfect order.

"No those flowers are to be set up over there. Get it together!"

****

Mia is lying on the floor in her under garments. She has her hair pinned up and makeup half way done; however, it is ruined and smudged all over her face because she is crying and wiping her

Chapter Fourteen

nervous tears away. Her friends, who are also her bridesmaids, are standing over her, looking concerned. One of the bridesmaids tries to help her up but Mia is fighting her off, telling her to leave her be.

"Mia are you okay? Do you need me to get Derrick?"

"No, he can't see me like this!" Mia shouted.

Moments later Jada walks in carrying Mia's dress, covered by white satin. *Why is she on the floor*, Jada wonders, confused. She immediately panics, thinking the worst.

"Mia - are you okay!" Jada asks, as she puts her things down. She tries to reach out to Mia.

"Yeah I'm ok; well I'm freaking out a little."

Jada shoves the ladies out the way trying to make way. She gestures impatiently for them to move.

"Why what's wrong? You have been waiting for this for a long time. I know because you wouldn't shut up about it," Jada says as she helps Mia sit up. Mia sighs and looks around.

"I'm really nervous, I mean Derrick is so wonderful, Sissy; why is he marrying a dying woman? Am I ruining his life?"

"What? Why would you say something like that? Derrick loves you and he doesn't care if he could only share one minute married to you. He would consider that a honor."

Mia smiles and gets up from the floor. She wipes her eyes again and now has her makeup smudged over her lips. Jada frowns at her.

"Do I look ok?" Mia asks, still wiping her face.

Jada grabs a mirror and shows Mia; Mia's eyes widen as she looks to Jada, worried about her makeup.

"Don't worry, Sam can redo your makeup. You need to stop this. This is supposed to be a great joyous occasion today. What do you think our Father would say to you right now? Have you spoken to Him?

He, Then Me, Comes You

"Yes earlier. He told me to breathe. He said that He is with me and that everything will be ok. But you know I may have misunderstood."

Mia smiles and Jada shakes her head. She grabs Mia's face and kisses her when she pulls back to look at her; the makeup that was on Mia is now on Jada's cheeks and lips. Mia burst out in laughter as she falls back. Jada hurriedly looks in the mirror and bursts out laughting as well. Soon the other bridesmaids join them. The laughter within the room is so loud that the workers putting the flower arrangements together stop and look around to see where the noise is coming from; as they realize who is laughing, they chuckle a little themselves.

"So Mom is going to be here shortly and I have something special to give you."

"It's not any of your recipes is it? Because I'm already sick..."

"Ok that joke is getting real old now... my cooking is getting better."

"If you say so, Sissy. What do you have for me?" Mia asks while holding her hand out, smiling like a little girl showing all her teeth.

Jada pulls out a box of old letters she wrote to Mia while they were not speaking. She hands them to her and she opens her eyes.

"What's this?" Mia asks.

"These are letters I wrote you when we weren't speaking; it was my way of still talking to you when I was being selfish."

Mia looks up at Jada in tears and shakes her head in disbelief. She looks through the letters and is amazed how many there are. She opens one up and reads it to herself. She smiles at the funny parts mentioned in the letter. When she's done with the letter, she looks up at Jada and instantly hugs her tightly.

"This is wonderful, it will be like I never missed anything in your life at that time and when I read it as if I was there. You have amazing writing skills, by the way. The way you capture the essence of the moment is incredible. I can just imagine you when

Chapter Fourteen

you describe the moments in this letter."

"Thanks Mia, I hope you can forgive me for being an idiot."

"Of course I can."

"And you don't think I'm an idiot?"

"Of course I can forgive you." Mia says smiling, extending her hands out for another hug.

"Do you think I was an idiot?" Jada asks more sternly.

"I love you."

"I really don't like you," Jada says laughing, slapping her arms away.

Jada rises, grabs and looks in the mirror, trying to remove her makeup so she can get it redone. Mia takes a deep breath and gets excited again.

"Okay I'm over my pity party. I'm going to marry the man of my dreams and enjoy the rest of my life with him, whether it's a day or six months."

"That's great, Mia!" one of the bridesmaids exclaims.

"Okay where is Sam?" Mia asks while looking for her. She steps out from the crowd of women and waves. Mia sits and allows Sam to redo her makeup. She closes her eyes and remains at peace knowing God is with her always. She feels silly for thinking that she is ruining Derrick's life and is happy to have him until she is with God and Jesus.

****

Mia is standing in all white, glowing as she waits to be Mrs. Cox. Her dress is covered in Italian lace, hugging her curves, so elegantly draped with admiration; pieces from her grandmother's wedding dress has also been added. What a lovely touch of family this adds to the dress! Her shoulders are gracefully exposed while glistening with a hint of gold shimmer. Her hair is pulled back, sleek with a part on the right side; a large red roses graces the

He, Then Me, Comes You

area close to her bun. Around her throat is a diamond necklace originally owned by her grandmother, to pass down. It has been in the family for generations and is only worn on the wedding day. Mia's face is glowing with the perfect shade to match her flawless skin. She grabs hold of her stomach because of the fear of this day. She's been waiting for this day all her life and can't wait to spend years with her anointed husband. She thinks of how she will never be able to bear his children and watch her grandchildren grow and come to her for Godly wisdom. As she thinks of the things she'll be missing, a wave of peace and reassurance comforts her. She smiles and politely thanks the Holy Spirit. She looks upon her mother and sister's faces, feeling thankful that they are there to help, supporting her through this very tough transition. She begins to chant to herself that this is going to be an epic day. She lets out a sigh of relief and reaches out for her bouquet of red roses that are beautifully gathered together with white satin strings.

"You ready?" Jada asks while smiling. Jada is also wearing a white gown requested by Mia so she may stand out from the rest of the ladies. The white satin dress is draped over her body, covering her from neck to toe, exposing only her back to show off her tattoo of an old English writing pen. The bride-maids are wearing yellow dresses altered to match their unique personalities. They all grab their bouquets and line up, ready to stand their positions. The wedding planner barges in, gesturing for everyone's attention.

"Okay ladies, positions please." The wedding planner barked as the women complied and lined up with Mia standing in the back. She began to tremble as she holds on to her bed of roses. She closes her eyes and asks God to give her strength to walk down the aisle and state her vows to her ordained husband. She also thanked Him for knowing her needs before she did and asked Him to give Derrick strength. The music starts and the women begin to walk. Mia clenches as she waits and takes a deep breath. She stands proud with the mercy and strength that God has blessed her with and waits for her cue. Moments pass and soon the song that signaled Mia to walk graced the audience. Mia walks out of the home and steps onto the walkway. The standing crowd gasps as the beautiful

Chapter Fourteen

Mia pauses. Her family and friends are delighted with glee as they see Mia standing tall, stunning in her white dress. As she begins to walk down the aisle, she smiles, showing off her beautiful teeth, trying to refrain from crying. As she looks towards Derrick she notices his demeanor. Derrick, dressed in all black, looks to Mia with love in his eyes. His mouth is slightly open, as he looks to Mia walking slowly down the aisle. Tears are falling down his face and he begins to tremble with excitement. He licks his lips, cleaning them from the tears running down his face. Mia sees his tears and frowns. She also begins to cry as she slows down. Derrick is not able to wait for his bride. He walks off the podium and walks down the aisle to meet Mia. She smiles as he approaches her. He grabs her hand and they walk back to the podium together. Mia hands over her flowers to Jada and holds on to Derrick. He adoringly looks to her and wipes her tears from her face, carefully trying not to ruin her makeup.

"Hello beautiful," Derrick says.

"Hello my King." Mia says as Derrick leans in to kiss her. He grabs and holds her tightly. He whispers sweet things in her ear as she giggles. Their family and friends are laughing and showing love while admiring them. The pastor clears his throat interrupting them.

"Can we get started?"

"I'm sorry Pastor, I just love this woman."

"I understand, that's why we're here." The pastor states as laughter follows from the crowd.

"Ladies and gentlemen we are gathered here today to join this man and this woman in holy matrimony. Derrick and Mia both have written their own vows. Derrick, if you please."

Derrick kisses Mia's hand and caresses her face. He looks into her eyes and tells her how he feels.

"Mia, my sweet Mia. You have been and will always be a miracle in my life. I am so grateful that God has trusted me to carry your heart in my spirit and soul. It will always reside in that place no matter if

He, Then Me, Comes You

you are present with me in the flesh or otherwise. Thank you, my queen, for allowing me to love you. Thank you for allowing me the privilege to know you as a woman, a follower of Christ, and a friend. I love you not only with my whole heart, but also with my mind and spirit. I promise to cherish and love you as your husband as long as God will allow."

There is silence after Derrick states his vows. Everyone is wiping tears from their faces, emotional with the sincerity in Derrick's voice. His love exudes and radiates all over his body and it is very apparent. Even the pastor has wiped a tear or two.

"Ok then… that was… um …ok, Mia your vows please," the pastor finally states.

"I should've gone first," Mia states while smiling, and again laughter comes from the crowd.

"I'm going to try and get this out without breaking down. Ok so… Derrick, my king, where do I begin? These words that I will say to you come from a place where only God resides. I've heard of women speak about men who are God like and are extraordinary, but I didn't expect to receive one. I thought 'what makes me special to have such a wonderful person in my life?' When I look at you, all I see is God. And I know without a doubt that He exists. My king, I will do my best to love you and make sure you know everyday that you are loved because you deserve to be loved with all the strength I possess in my body. I promise I will honor you as a husband as king should be honored."

"The rings please."

Derrick places the ring on Mia's finger and kisses her hand. Mia also places the ring on Derrick's finger. They smile at one another.

"…. I now pronounce you as ordained husband and wife, please salute your bride."

With cheers of joy in the background, Mia and Derrick engage in a long passionate kiss. Jada is delighted as she watches her little sister filled with happiness.

Chapter Fourteen

****

The dance floor is filled with well-dressed people dancing and having a great time. Mia and Derrick are in the background, walking together through the crowd, speaking and laughing with family and friends. Jada admires her sister and new brother from afar. She is so filled with joy, knowing how happy Mia is on this day. She never understood what it meant to wait for your God anointed mate. We all have free will to choose whom we can love and if we want to marry that individual, things will work out, but there is a reason why divorce statistics are so high and people are miserable in marriages. When you wait on God to bring you and your mate together, He will provide you with everything you need and ever wanted. He knows you better than you know yourself, so why wouldn't you allow Him to bring you two together?

After seeing how God works with Mia and Derrick, Jada is now convinced that waiting for God is the best thing to do. He will lead her to her very best. As Jada smiles still adoringly at her new husband, looking to her sister, Mia looks back and they connect eyes. Mia blows a kiss, signaling Jada to join them. Jada gets up and heads over but is soon interrupted by one of her relatives. Her aunt Jessie is obviously drunk.

"Jada hey baby, how are you doing?" Jessie asked.

"I'm ok Aunt Jessie," Jada says, frowning. She's disgusted at her aunt's behavior at such a special occasion; she looks at her while she talks. Jada steps back as her aunt continues to talk, now spitting on her.

"Oh I'm so sorry baby, I didn't mean to..." Jessie stops in the middle of her sentence and looks at Jada. Jada looks concerned and before she could ask if Jessie is ok, she regurgitates all over Jada's shoes. Jada closes her eyes in frustration and pushes her aunt from her personal space to keep her from getting vomit on her dress. Jada walks away, upset. Mia witnesses this unfortunate event and

He, Then Me, Comes You

worries if Jada will be ok.

"What's wrong babe?" Derrick asks Mia.

"Oh it's Jada; drunk Aunt Jess just threw up and I think some of it may have gotten on Jada."

"Oh that's bad." Derrick says as he kisses on Mia. Mia smiles as Derrick continues to gush over her and shows affection. As they are kissing and loving on one another, Lamar walks over to them.

"Ugh enough all ready," Lamar says.

"Hey man, what's good? I thought you were in Africa and couldn't make it?"

"Yeah I'm sorry I tried to make it back in time so I could be here for you."

"Oh its no worries, I'm glad you can finally meet my wife. Mia this is Lamar, Lamar, this is my amazingly beautiful wife Mia." Derrick says as he brags and begins kissing her and holding her tight. Lamar clears his throat trying to interrupt them from their marital bliss. He gets louder. Mia pulls back, smiles and looks at Lamar.

"I know you're all in love and everything but you have plenty of time later for all of that." Lamar says.

"I'm sorry, I just can't get enough of him." Mia says while caressing Derrick.

Mia then pauses and looks at Lamar oddly for a moment. Lamar eyebrow rises as she is looking at him.

"You know you look really familiar. I feel like I know you."

"I'm not sure how." Lamar states.

"Hmm its this real familiar feeling I'm getting with you. Are you married?"

"No, divorced."

"Oh I'm sorry, are you courting anyone?"

"Mia?" Derrick says.

"What I'm just wondering you know for …"

Chapter Fourteen

"She would kill you. Leave it alone, ok my new wife."

"You're right. Lamar would you like a drink or…"

"No I actually have to get home, I can't stay. I just wanted to be here even if just for a moment.

"Oh no, you sure you cant stay at least just for 15 minutes?"

"We can have dinner sometime but I really have to get home."

"Ok man, I will call you later. Thanks again for stopping by."

Lamar gives Derrick and Mia a hug and then leaves as the women watches admiring him and smiling as he walks by them. Lamar doesn't notice ignoring each woman gushing over him. Mia looks up to find Jada, and as she comes up to her, Mia has this look on her face.

"That damn Jessie threw up on me, of course it had to be me. I mean really, what the hell!"

Mia doesn't say anything but smiles as Derrick observes shaking his head.

"Ok why are you looking at me like that?" Jada asks while looking confused.

"I just met a great man for you!"

"Mia!" Derrick yells.

"What - he is perfect!"

"If he's perfect then he's not for me, I'm a complete mess."

"I agree." Derrick says.

"Derrick!"

"What? She said it. I just agreed."

"Whatever Jada you are not a mess, well you are God's mess and He is working on you. You deserve happiness." Mia states. She looks at Jada and caresses her face. She hugs her tightly and then they begin to dance. Derrick holds on to both of them and dances with them. Everyone looks to them with admiration. Claudia is also looking to them with tears in her eyes. She grabs her chest as

He, Then Me, Comes You

if her heart is filled with complete joy. Jada then stops and hands Mia to Derrick.

"May I have this dance my beautiful wife?"

"Of course my husband."

Derrick escorts Mia to the dance floor. The band begins to play the song that they first danced to. He is holding her closely to his body as if the two are one. Mia is holding tight to Derrick as he is leading her across the dance floor. She feels as if she is floating as Derrick grips her. She places her head on his chest closing her eyes as she thanks God for this memorable day. Derrick whispers in her ear.

"This is the best day of my life. You have made me the happiest man alive. If I could I would marry you over and over again."

Mia smiles as a single tear falls down her face. She kisses Derrick as they continue to dance until the song ends.

****

Jada is lying in her bed. Mia soon wakes her up. She is staring at her and watching her sleep.

"What the! Were you just watching me sleep?" Jada says she jumps up. She looks around wondering if she was still asleep or dreaming. She covers her eyes and tries to calm her nerves.

"Yeah, you looked so peaceful. I didn't want to wake you."

"That's so creepy Mia."

Mia is looking at Jada, smiling, not able to contain her excitement. She just returned from her three week long honeymoon in the Caribbean's. Her skin is graced with a nice golden tan. Her face is also glowing. Jada sits up and rubs her eyes from the sleep.

"You look like an experienced woman." Jada says while smiling.

"It was amazing Sissy. The weather was perfect and we couldn't keep our hands off of each other the whole time."

"I bet."

Chapter Fourteen

"Your expertise helped too. He was very satisfied. It was like we were literally in heaven."

"Oh yeah! Glad to hear you had a wonderful experience your first time. Wish I would've waited." Jada says as she gets up and heads to the bathroom leaving the door opened. She sits on the commode and relieves herself.

"So you're just going to use the bathroom with the door is open?"

"Uh yeah. You've seen my butt plenty of times. Don't act brand new."

Mia leans back and falls on the plush bed. She closes her eyes and speaks to God for a moment. Jada is still talking but Mia doesn't hear what she is saying.

"Mia… Mia, earth to Mia!"

Mia jumps up and looks to Jada confused.

"Huh?"

"Seriously? You didn't hear anything I said?"

"No Sissy, I'm sorry. I was…"

"… in La La land? You finally got you some and is crazy now?"

"Whatever." Mia says as she lies back down on the bed. Jada leaves the bathroom and reenters the bedroom and lies next to Mia. They both lie and look to the ceiling.

"Are you ok? Did you get sick?"

"Not even once. God was really looking out for Derrick and I. He allowed us to enjoy our honeymoon without any issues."

"How do you feel now?"

"Scared." Mia says softly. Jada looks to her. She sees a tear on Mia's face. She doesn't say anything. Jada grabs her hand.

"I'm not angry with God. I'm grateful He has given me this time. I just want more time."

"How do you know you wont have a few years?"

"I can feel it Sissy. I can feel my spirit getting stronger because my

He, Then Me, Comes You

flesh is dying. I don't have much time."

Jada lifts her head and looks down at Mia. She can see the fear in Mia's eyes, the type of fear that she will be forgotten or missed only for a season. She looks away and closes her eyes. Mia then looks back at Jada.

"You are the most courageous person I know Mia. I have cried for days thinking about how much I will miss you and how I could've lost you if I was still in my stubborn state of mind."

"Stop Sissy. We have moved past that."

"I know. I'm sorry. You said you know you don't have much time. How long do you think you have?"

"Sissy. I have a matter of weeks, maybe a month."

"Really? How could you know that?"

"I prayed about it. God is preparing me. He has shown me. I had a dream about it. Derrick was so devastated."

"I hope he will be able to get passed it."

Mia leans over and looks in Jada's eyes. She moves her wild hair from her face. Jada looks concerned.

"Will you do something for me?"

"Anything."

"Will you promise me to not let Derrick stay depressed too long? Remind him of God's mercy and grace. Don't let him fall into a state where he will not be able to live his life. And after three years if God permits, tell him its time to move on and look for another wife where he can have children with."

"Whoa Mia, I don't want to see him with another woman."

"I know but he cant live the rest of his life alone. He has too much to offer someone."

Jada buries her head in one of her pillows. For a moment she screams into it. She shakes her hand in disbelief that she is having this conversation with her sister who is giving her last wishes before she dies. Her heart gets heavy. She tries to hold back from

Chapter Fourteen

crying.

"I promise. This is just too much."

"No its not. Its life Sissy." Mia says. She frowns and then grabs Jada's hand.

"What?" Jada asks.

"I'm sad I will miss your wedding day."

"My wedding day? I don't see that anytime soon. I may be on God's do not disturb list for years." Jada says. Mia smiles.

"He's revealed to me who your husband is."

"Say what? Really?"

"Yes."

"Why would He tell you and not me?"

"He will."

"When was this?"

"Does it matter? Just know that you will have your day. But I wont be there to see it. So I want to tell you now what I would've said on that day."

"Oh please don't do this now Mia. My heart can't take it."

"Sissy, it's going to happen. I need you to ask our Father for strength."

"Where's Derrick right now?"

"He's at the church. He had some things to take care of."

"Can we at least have breakfast before you give me your death speech?" Jada says sarcastically. Mia looks at her then she smiles. She shakes her head at Jada knowing that she is trying to hide her feelings by being difficult.

"I will cook us some strawberry pancakes, ok?"

"Ok, make sure their vegan pancakes please."

"Of course Sissy."

He, Then Me, Comes You

Mia and Jada are sitting at the dining room table. The house is silent with just the sound of a fork hitting the plate. Mia is chewing on slices of bacon. She is staring at Jada as she is devouring her pancakes. Every time Mia tries to talk to her she changes the subject about something else. Mia is now just staring at her. Jada looks away.

"Sissy."

"Nope."

"C'mon Jada. Will you please listen to me?"

"Fine. I'm full now so tell me what you want to tell me."

"I love you Sissy. This is hard enough."

"I know. My belly is full and I'm less irritated. I know this is difficult for you. I'm sorry I'm being difficult. I just need you Mia. I need you."

"I need you too. I just need you to know that you have been the greatest sister. "

"Mia please, I can't." Jada says. She gets up and tries to walk away. Mia gets up and follows her. She grabs her hand to stop her from leaving.

"Sissy stop! Please."

Jada stops in her tracks and looks down. She is shaking and doesn't want to look at Mia.

"Jay please look at me and let me get this out."

Jada turns to look at her and sits down on the couch. She wipes her eyes and looks to her sister.

"God was kind enough to bless me with a sister that was amazing and protective as you. I know that we haven't always seen eye to eye. But you need to know that you are special. You will do great things in the name of God and I hope you understand and know how important you are. I need you to stay strong and fight Sissy. No matter what life brings you, go to God first and be prepared. Don't ever give up. God will always be with you. Thank you for loving me and being the other half of me."

Chapter Fourteen

"That was beautiful Mia. Thank you for those words."

"Promise me you will never try to take your life again. Promise me you will live life to the fullest and help anyone that you can."

"I promise." Jada leans in and kisses Mia. They hold on to each other for a moment, crying and caressing each others hair.

"I love you Sissy."

"I love you more Mia."

~ *Chapter Fifteen* ~

Death is not the end, Be joyous…

"Jada! Jada! Please help me!"

"Mia! Mia, where are you?" Jada calls out to her. She is now frantic trying to search for her sister. Jada is exhausted from running and searching desperately for her sister, to no avail; she drops to her knees and pray.

Jada's slumber is interrupted by the sound of her device ringing in her ear. As she realizes that she has been dreaming, she takes a deep breath and exhales with relief. Her dreams are becoming more vivid and detailed; she is confused with fear and anxiety. She feels guilty and full of doubt after she awakens. Both feelings are not of God. She sits up at the edge of her bed and looks to her phone. Her heart feels heavy. She knows what had transpired. Her sister has passed. She has several missed calls and texts encouraging her to call back. Jada hangs her head, waiting for all the hurt and pain to resurrect in her heart. Instead she is filled with comfort, peace and joy. Jada leans back on her bed and lets out a sigh of relief. She thought she would be angry, scared and confused on why this has happened. Instead she has knowledge and is filled with gratitude for being able to prepare for her sister's departure into heaven. Moments later she gets another call from Claudia. She reaches to answer.

Chapter Fifteen

"Hey..."

"Jada, did you get my calls?" Claudia asks.

"No I'm sorry I was asleep." There is a silence on the line for a moment.

"I know, Mom," Jada whispers.

"I can't breathe," Claudia says.

"I can only imagine what it's like to lose a child. I'm here for you, Mom. Do you need me to come over?"

"No, I need some time. Are you okay?"

"Yes, I am.... surprisingly."

"Can you please go and check on Derrick? He's not answering any of my calls."

"Okay, I will just go over."

"Thank you, Jada. I will meet up with you later." Jada remains in silence as she prepares herself for what's to come. She knows that she has to be there for Derrick; he is her brother now and will always be family.

****

Jada is banging on the door where Derrick resides. She looks through the window and sees the house is in disarray. She takes out her keys and lets herself in.

"Derrick! Derrick, are you here?"

"Go away, Jay."

Jada looks around the messy house and finds Derrick in the master bedroom curled up holding the blanket Mia made. She gets in the bed and sits up beside him. She looks over to him but doesn't say anything.

"Please leave me alone Jay. Let me have this time alone."

He, Then Me, Comes You

"I just needed to know that you are ok."

"I'm ok, now leave."

"I can't leave you like this. You are my brother who has lost the love of his life," Jada says, while holding on to Derrick's arm.

"I can't breathe without her, Jay. I know God has her now. But I just can't breathe. I needed more time - oh God why couldn't I have more time!" Derrick says, as he yells while crying his heart out. Jada is moved and can't help but cry alongside of him. She sinks into the bed holding on to Derrick as he continues to grieve. She doesn't say anything, but holds him and let him cry.

****

Jada walks into her home feeling sad but encouraged. She knows that Mia is in a better place and not in pain. She walks around her home trying to feel the presence of her sister. As she looks around she notices a box with a note on it. It was tucked away under a cabinet. Jada pulls it out and notices it is from Mia. Confused by the box, she grabs the card and reads it. The note reads:

Hey Sissy, I hid this from you because I didn't want you to open it. I bought you a wedding gift. You will be meeting him soon. I hope you listen to God and trust Him with your whole heart. Remember He knows you better than you know yourself. Open it on your wedding day. I know it will be hard for you, but I hope you honor my wishes and open it on that day. Be happy my love.

P.S. DO NOT OPEN THE BOX!

Jada picks the box up and shakes it. Nothing moves in the box as she looks to it, wondering what it is. She smiles to herself as she thinks of the face she may have had when she was hiding it. Jada sits on the floor and leans back against the wall holding the box to her chest as she begins to cry. As she begins to thank God for the opportunity for having her sister, a wave of comfort comes over her. The Holy Spirit is calming her soul. She feels comforted and at ease.

Chapter Fifteen

"Thank you Father."

****

A calm quietness befalls the room as Jada sits in silence staring at her sister's casket. She doesn't quite understand how to proceed. No tears are freed from her tear ducts. She expected to be full of anger and ready to have certain feelings towards God. However, because of God's grace she could prepare for this event that allowed her to be at peace with losing her sister. She continues to sit in silence. Moments pass and then she stands and walk towards the casket and stares at Mia lying there, looking so peaceful, free from cancer and pain. She smiles at her. She embraces her hair, then her face. As she continues to gaze upon the rested Mia, she recalls all the times they played together as kids and how she would always want to make her proud. Jada felt blessed. Not too many people can enjoy having the love and closeness of a sister so close in age. It was like an extension of herself. She turns back to sit down and looks up to ask God for strength to help her through this day. She sits in the chair and tries to think of how she will respond to people who will soon be there, trying to show her consolation. She can't hide and be aloof. She had to endure the many sad looks and apologies from family and friends that she hasn't seen or spoken to in years. Jada sighs and then closes her eyes hoping God will answer her prayers where she is at peace. Moments later Claudia enters the funeral home and sits down next to Jada. They continue to sit in silence. Claudia then grabs Jada's hand and holds it tightly.

"Are you ok?" Claudia asked.

"I am, Mom. I was able to prepare for this and I'm grateful."

"I'm so proud of you Jada, you have really amazed me."

Jada turns to look at her mother. As tears form in her eyes she feels the need to be strong. She needs to be strong for her mother and Derrick. It's one thing to lose a sister or even your parent, but for a parent to bury their child is a burden and pain that some are not able to handle because it's not part of the cycle. A parent should never have to bury their child, but it happens every day.

He, Then Me, Comes You

Jada's heart becomes heavy as she hugs her mother tightly. She felt guilty for being so full of pain and resentment with her family. She thought, *how could I have been so stubborn and selfish.* Sure, Jada asked for forgiveness from God but the hardest thing to do is forgive yourself and forgiving yourself is what we so desperately need God to help us with.

"Mom, I want you to know that I truly forgive you. I know raising us with no money was hard and you choosing to do what you felt you had to do to feed us and so forth. I know anyone can fall into the deceit and destruction of the adversary and I no longer judge you for your choices. I pray that you can truly forgive yourself."

"That means a lot to me, Baby. I'm so grateful God has answered my prayers and brought you back to me. I really missed you and I look forward to getting to know you."

Jada begins to cry as she hugs and consoles her mother. She feels peace and love and joy all at the same time. Jada thought how awesome God is. Now she knew what it meant to have joy when going through such hard times in life. She knew that without God that she wouldn't be able to undergo such pain or disappointments. His Holy Spirit is there when you call upon Him and trust in His power. She felt humbled and ready to move forward with what God had planned for her. As she continues to hold her mother, she knows that she will see her sister again and regains the strength to lay her in her resting place.

There are many people gathered, conversing and observing Mia's body. Derrick is sitting alone in the corner with his eyes swollen from crying for days. He sits, holding his wife's ring. As people approach him to show their condolences, he nods and looks down at the ring. He knows he has to give it back to the family because it's a family heirloom. Jada notices the pain that Derrick is trying to conceal. She wants to be there for him, but is not sure what to do. She can only do so much. Only God and time will heal his heart. As Jada observes Derrick, she notices a man approaching him. She is not able to see his face because of the crowd but she notices his

Chapter Fifteen

demeanor and is captivated by his presence. As she stares for a moment to get a good look at him she soon realizes its Lamar. Jada immediately perks up and becomes giddy with excitement. She's not sure how to act. Her body becomes paralyzed as she gazes upon him. *How does Lamar know Derrick*, she thought? Suddenly the room becomes quiet and the only thing she sees is Lamar. Her hands become sweaty and her breathing heavy as she continues to stare. Lamar stands next to Derrick, holding his hand, praying for his friend. Jada's feelings for Lamar ignite at that very moment. She remembers when they were kids and how big his heart was. She would often become upset when kids used to pick on him. She felt helpless and didn't know how to help him. The feelings she had for Lamar when they were children was more than puppy love. She didn't know what it was but she knew it was more than a childhood crush. She knew that it was an unconditional love that would last a lifetime. She wanted to pray for him. She wanted to be the rock he could lean on when he was in need. She wanted to help him. As she continued to stare, she doesn't notice her mother watching her as she watches Lamar. Claudia approaches Jada and places her hand on her elbow.

"Are you ok?" Claudia asks.

"Uh yea... I'm fine."

"What are you gawking at?"

"The man I will marry." Jada stated with confidence.

"Oh wow, you're kidding me," Claudia said.

"Nope."

"Go and speak to him."

Lamar continues to pray for his friend while others bowed their heads also praying to give Derrick strength. As Lamar continues to pray, Derrick cries and places his head near Lamar's shoulders. Lamar also begins to cry because of the pain he could only imagine feeling. Jada, still observing Lamar, is moved and decides to approach them. As she walks closer to the men in distress, her stomach is full of butterflies and she begins to shake. She doesn't

He, Then Me, Comes You

say anything to Lamar but speaks to Derrick.

"Do you need anything, Derrick?" Jada asks.

Lamar looks up and to his surprise he sees Jada and his heart stops. He gets up and without hesitation hugs her and then stares at her face.

"Hey Mar."

"Jada what... what are you doing here?"

"This is my sister's funeral."

"Wow I'm so sorry, I didn't know. Derrick didn't mention to me his wife's sister by name."

"Oh, well, what did he call me?"

"He only referred to you as Jay."

Lamar looks to Derrick. Derrick excuses himself and goes into the bathroom. Without realizing it, Lamar takes Jada's hands as he continues to talk to her. Jada feels a shift in her spirit. It felt as if no one was around and the pain she felt for losing her sister had subsided and she was filled with joy and love. Jada didn't notice that she didn't hear Lamar speaking. As he was talking she was staring at him not acknowledging or comprehending anything that was said to her. Soon Jada snapped out of her gaze when Lamar notices she wasn't listening and stepped closer to her.

"Are you ok, Jada?"

"Huh? Um yeah... yeah... I'm sorry, what were you saying?

Lamar smiles an endearing smile, exposing his beautiful white teeth. He caresses Jada as she continues to stare. Moments later, as he is embracing her, God reminds him of the image he seen months ago, of his wife crying. Lamar then hears a small voice saying that Jada was his wife. Stunned by what God has revealed, Lamar smiles at Jada.

"Why are you looking at me like that?" Jada asks.

"I just didn't realize how much I missed you. When we saw each

Chapter Fifteen

other last time, I didn't get your number and I was hoping that we would see each other again, and here we are. I wish it could've been under better circumstances."

"Yes, I didn't know you and Derrick were close; why weren't you at the wedding?"

"We are good friends, but I was in Africa during that time, I did come by for a few minutes. That's where I met Mia."

"Oh, you're the man she was talking about."

"And you were the one she wanted me to meet."

"Wait - she tried to fix us up?"

"Well, Derrick wouldn't let her. It was as if he felt you weren't ready."

"Oh I can see that. What were you doing in Africa?"

"Missionary work. I helped build homes and clean water wells for villages and preached about Jesus."

"You are a preacher now? You didn't believe in God."

"No not a preacher, but a servant of God. And I didn't know what I believed. I was filled with anger and resentment."

"I think it's great! You look wonderful and so peaceful."

Jada and Lamar share a look. They both stand holding each other's hand, at peace. Lamar gingerly moves hair from Jada's face.

"I'm here. I'm not letting you out of my life again."

Jada smiles and Lamar pulls her close to him. He embraces her, holding her tight as if he never wanted to let her go. As they stand holding one another, Claudia watches her daughter being comforted by one of God's servants. She gets a sense of peace, knowing her daughter wouldn't be alone through her grieving period. As the funeral begins, Lamar and Jada are still holding one another, not caring what's going on around them. No one interrupts them but leaves them as they are. LD arrives and looks for Jada. As he locates her he notices her being held by someone. LD makes

He, Then Me, Comes You

himself scarce as the minister begins the sermon.

****

Jada awakens with a tremendous smile on her face. She looks to her window as the sun is shining bright and she can hear the birds chirping. She wipes away the crust from her bright eyes and jumps out of bed. She then grabs her phone and heads to relieve herself, wanting to call Mia and tell her about Lamar. She shakes her head, saddened that she won't be able to call her sister. She pushes the feelings of hurt from her mind. As she sits on the commode she smiles, admiring the text that Lamar sent.

-Good Morning my past, present and now my future, I can't wait to see you-

Jada begins to smile uncontrollably, while closing her eyes tightly and holding the phone with excitement. She can barely contain herself. She immediately jumps into the shower singing a praise song giving God the glory of this day ahead. As she is singing, she begins to dance, almost slipping and falling.

"Whoa, I almost fell." Jada says to herself as she begins to laugh aloud because of her silliness. She never expected to be this joyous and at peace after losing her sister. However, knowing that Mia is no longer in pain pacifies Jada's spirit and she is freed from guilt. Jada hops out of the shower, grabbing her plush towel. As she is drying herself off, still singing loudly, she notices people shouting from outside, telling her to be quiet. She laughs and raises her window up and sticks her head, full of curly hair, out of the window.

"No I will not be quiet! Praise the Lord for He is faithful!"

"Ok calm down lady," a stranger shouted.

"Hey man, get God in your life, it's wonderful." Jada says and then closes the window and begins to get dressed. Still singing, she notices a text from Lamar stating he will be there in five minutes to pick her up and she begins to get nervous. She grabs her sword

Chapter Fifteen

from her nightstand and drops to her knees.

"Lord I have been wrong on many occasions about this sort of thing. I know that I have made mistakes and feel confident that you have forgiven me for them. Please God, if Lamar is the man I'm supposed to be with, give me confirmation. I mean in a way that I cannot deny My Lord. I need a confirmation that will just give me an overwhelming feeling in my spirit. Thank you; in Jesus name I pray."

Jada rises and puts her bright white and yellow sundress on. She decides to not wear makeup because she wants Lamar to see all of her in her most vulnerable natural state. She trusts God will control the situation and outcome. Moments later Lamar is ringing the doorbell and she rushes down the stairs, again almost falling, ready to answer. As she stands at the door holding the doorknob, she takes a deep breath and whispers to herself.

"Trust in God, trust in God, trust in God."

She opens the door and there is Lamar, standing with a huge smile on his face, exposing those dimples. Jada's heart melts. He is wearing a white shirt with khaki pants; Jada admires his style. She looks him up and down, trying her best not to jump on him. They both stand smiling in amazement and disbelief. Lamar slowly moves towards Jada as they lock eyes and he grabs her and holds her tightly. Jada and Lamar both close their eyes as they feel each other's heartbeat. A tear slowly rolls down Jada's face as she allows Lamar to embrace her. Jada has never felt this sense of peace. She feels like Lamar is home. And there is nowhere else she wants to be.

"You look amazing. You are very beautiful," Lamar said.

Jada gives off a coy smile and replies thank you. Lamar hugs her again even tighter. He feels his spirit rejoicing as he has finally found his mate, the woman God has prepared him for. He vowed to himself that he would consult with God in his decision-making and allow him to be the lead in his relationship this go around. After Lamar embraces Jada, he grabs her hand leading her down the steps

He, Then Me, Comes You

to his vehicle. He opens the passenger door, helping her inside. Jada still smiling, is in awe of what is transpiring. She thought God had forgotten about her. She thought that he didn't hear her asking Him for companionship and love. Jada didn't understand then that God needed her to accept His love first and to seek Him and only Him. After Jada focused on what God wanted for her life, things started to fall in place in ways she never expected. She didn't think of writing a novel that would help women. She didn't think she had anything to offer anyone. Jada realized that she needed to know God. For her to know Him, she needed to experience Him in ways that He could position and design for her life that would require her to lean only on Him. This is what she needed all along.

"Where are we going?" Jada inquired.

"Don't worry about it. Let me do this."

"Do what?"

"The wooing..." Lamar said smiling exposing his white teeth and dimples. Jada felt a tug in her spirit as she gazed at Lamar. She looks suspiciously at his demeanor, wondering if he is in fact her mate. She's afraid of being wrong, afraid of making another mistake that might change the dynamics of her relationship with God. As she slyly watches him in her periphery, she feels another pull in her stomach pulling at her spirit, confirming that Lamar was the man God had chosen for her. Jada looks out her window, still apprehensive; she felt she needed more. She didn't want to be wrong again. So, she played it cool. Moments later they arrived at a park that was secluded where there was a private beach. On the beach was a picnic set up. Lamar pulls up and parks the vehicle. Jada perks up with excitement and amazement. She unbuckles her seat belt and leans in, observing the wonderful surprise that Lamar had planned. She had never experienced this type of love. Men didn't woo her. They only pursued her until they got what they wanted.

"Is this really for me?" Jada asked.

Lamar grabs Jada's hand and gingerly kisses it. "Of course, it is."

Chapter Fifteen

Lamar gets out of the driver's seat and moves to open the passenger door for Jada. He helps her out of the vehicle, leading her towards the beach, still holding her hand. As they get closer, tears form in Jada's brown eyes as she is shaking, now scared that this is a dream and that soon she would be awakened by the sudden urge to urinate. But as time went on, she knew it was no dream. This was really happening. Lamar helps her sit down on the big plush blanket that is nicely placed under a white gazebo. There, within the picnic basket is wine, vegan cheese, fruit, and crackers. Also within the spread are Jada's favorite stage planks cookies, from when they were kids. Jada used to love these cookies when she was a little girl. Lamar would buy them for her whenever he had extra change to do so, to help ease the pain of losing her father, and her mother abandoning them. He thought she would appreciate them after losing her sister.

"Are those stage plank cookies?! How did you...you remembered?"

"Yes, Jada, you were my..." Jada quickly hugs Lamar interrupting his sentence. The hug that Jada expressed set a fire between them. They were intertwined through the spirit of God. As Jada slowly let up and they were now face to face, Lamar takes his hands and embraces Jada's soft face. As they stare into each other's eyes a tear falls down Jada's face. Lamar wipes away the tear and leans in and kisses Jada tenderly on her pouty plump lips. They continue to engage kissing slowly taking in each moment never wanting to forget the first time they shared a kiss. Moments later they again embrace each other.

"I can't believe you remembered these."

"I thought you might need them to help you cope."

"You are truly amazing Mar. This is funny, after we saw each other at the restaurant and we didn't exchange numbers, I thought I would never see you again."

"I did too, but I'm glad we didn't exchange numbers. I wasn't the man you needed then."

He, Then Me, Comes You

"I too wasn't ready. God had brought me to a place of peace and comfort only He could do."

"Listen to you, talking about God; girl you better stop. That is a real turn on." Lamar says as they share a laugh. Jada embraces his face, still in shock that God has led her to this season, the season of courtship with her mate.

"I want to know things, tell me everything," Jada insists.

"What do you mean?"

"I mean what transpired with you since that day, what made you give your life to God?"

"He didn't give up on me. I had no direction, no sense of purpose and I asked and He answered."

"Yeah, that's our Father, ask and you shall receive."

"How are you really doing Bird, with your sister passing?"

Jada looks to the beautiful scenery set before her as she gathers her thoughts on what she was really feeling. She thought maybe she should be feeling sorrow or pain, but none of that is present. Sure she misses Mia, but God was graceful enough to help her prepare for her parting.

"I feel at peace really. I do miss her. But she is with Him now and I couldn't be happier for her. She was in so much pain here, suffering and without life. I feel compassion for Derrick being a widower within such a short period of time, but his strength enables us all to have strength. I can honestly say I'm better that she's better."

"I'm glad Jaybird. But you know you can lean on me to help you whenever you feel...you know."

"I know and I thank you Mar."

"You want to try some of this wine? It has been a long time since God has allowed me to taste alcohol. "

"I would love some."

Lamar pours Jada a glass of wine, handing her a piece of cheese to

Chapter Fifteen

cleanse her palate and taste the fullness of the wine.

"Um I'm a vegan, Mar."

"Oh, I know, this is vegan cheese."

"How did you know I was vegan?"

"Oh I had to do some research on you. No I'm kidding - Derrick told me."

"Ok that's cool." Jada says, as she tastes the wine. "This is amazing, I like this."

"Good, because it wasn't cheap."

"Oh please..."

"I'm kidding. I would give you my heart out of my chest if you needed it Jay."

"Awe I have enough cheese right here," Jada jokingly says as they share a laugh, throwing grapes at one another.

"Well being a man of God, I'm sure you are aware that I'm not dating Mar; I want a courtship that leads to marriage."

"I am a man of the Living God and I agree. We are courting, Jay. You will be my wife one day."

"How do you know?" Jada inquired.

"He told me."

"Really - when was this?"

"At the funeral."

"Makes sense. So then with this courtship you know there will be no sex until marriage."

"Yes. I'm so excited about you and our future. I can't wait until you meet Kyle."

"Kyle? You have a son?"

"No; well he has become more of a little brother. I took him in."

"Oh wow, that's awesome. Tell me more."

He, Then Me, Comes You

The two engage in more conversation talking for hours as the sunsets on them. Lamar wraps Jada with a blanket as the air chilled and they stare at what God has created with appreciation. Sure, they both have experienced a sunset or two but not in the presence of the Lord.

"Are you going to share your cookies?"

"Of course, Mar, you can have a bite."

"Wow just a bite? You're going to eat both cookies?"

"Mmm hmmm, sure is good." Jada jokingly places a piece of cookie in Lamar's mouth, then quickly takes it away as he tries to bite it. They become playful as Lamar begins to try and take the cookie from Jada. She gets up and runs from Lamar along the beach. Lamar chases her and catches up to her, picking her up and putting her over his shoulder. Jada kicks with excitement. He puts her down now facing him and they stare into each other's eyes.

"I can see Him, you know," Jada says.

"Who?" Lamar asked looking confused at her statement.

"God, I can see Him in you." Jada whispers. Lamar smiles and pulls Jada close to him. They continued to play on the beach and toss sand and water at each other, cheerfully playing as if they were kids.

The sun is rising and Lamar and Jada are asleep holding each other on the beach. As the sun kisses them, welcoming them with open arms they begin to awaken. Jada still amazed that this has happened, looks adoringly at Lamar as he sleeps. Moments later he awakens and looks to her and smiles.

"Hey you."

****

Jada and Lamar are at the art museum. They are holding hands, walking around, admiring the beautiful canvases that glorify the walls. As they silently admire the paintings, Lamar sensually and

Chapter Fifteen

vaguely caresses Jada's back and sneaks in a kiss or two. Jada smiles and tries to maintain her giddiness as he expresses his affection for her. It's early in the morning on a Tuesday and the museum is almost void of people. The two are hidden in a corner in the dark part of the museum and passionately kiss until they're interrupted by the security guard clearing his throat, allowing them to compose themselves and move along. They laugh playfully as they continue to walk around the museum. They stand at this one particular painting, drawing their attention as they stare. Jada puts her head on Lamar and grabs hold of his arm.

"This painting is wonderful. It's speaking to me..."

"I know it's so loud." Lamar says.

"It makes me want to cry and laugh at the same time."

They continue to stare, lost in the painting. Soon they move on and observe the other paintings.

****

Lamar is sitting at his desk, reading the Word and meditating. The doorbell soon interrupts him. Wondering who could be here, he gets up to answer. The man holding a package stands smiling, ready for a signature.

"Hi, are you Lamar Daniels?"

"Yes I am."

"Here yah go, just need a signature right here please."

Lamar signs the package and looks to see whom it's from. As he opens the package he perks up as he realizes it's from his father. He pulls out a letter and there is a picture of him. Lamar examines the picture closely. His father has his eyes. He is a dark-skinned man with a thick beard and mustache that is graced with specks of gray hairs. Lamar sits and reads the letter.

Dear son, I'm happy as I'm writing this letter. I finally received

He, Then Me, Comes You

confirmation from our Heavenly Father, stating it's time we met. After a long journey of getting my life right and building a relationship with God, I am stable enough and humble enough to offer answers to any questions you may have or any feelings of anger you may throw my way. Whatever it is son, I'm ready to receive. I pray this letter gets to you and you are ready to meet as well. I would like to meet you at a restaurant called Amélie at 7:30 pm this Friday. I look forward to seeing you there, son. Be blessed.

Love, your dad.

Lamar looks again at the picture in the wooden frame. Moments later Kyle walks into the house and notices Lamar in tears.

"What's going on? Everything ok?" Kyle asked with fear in his eyes.

"I got a letter from my father asking me to meet him."

"Whoa that's heavy."

"Yeah, God is answering all of my prayers. It didn't come right away but He did. It was a battle and I know there will be many more. But knowing he will be there through the battles makes it worth it. He's blessed me with Jada and now this."

"Are you going to take her with you?" Kyle asked.

"It's really a big deal; I should."

"Maybe you should go and invite her later, you know once you and your dad are better acquainted." Kyle suggested.

"Look at you with your helpful suggestions."

"I like Jada; she's funny and silly and is great at video games."

"I know she is something special."

"Hey is she the woman that we were praying for that day, when your heart was hurting?"

"Yeah it is."

Chapter Fifteen

"Wow, I want that. I want God to move in my life like he's moving in yours. Your walk in life is admirable and inspiring. I hope I can have what you have. A relationship with God where you depend on him."

"You can have that Kyle."

"I hope so."

"It won't be easy. But it will be worth it."

Kyle nods while smiling with approval. He has come a long way from when he broke into Lamar's house. He never thought he could ever be in a position where he would get help and the opportunity to be a great man. He always felt that God abandoned him and that he would end up in jail or dead. God is a mysterious person and Kyle looked forward to learning and leaning on Him wholeheartedly.

~ Chapter Sixteen ~

I will persevere, God is my strength…

Jada is in the room, pushing through with her cross. It is strapped to her back. She is stronger and focused. She no longer feels the struggle she once did when she first acknowledged her cross. She is walking and not crawling. She has her head held up high. She feels the Holy Spirit leading her and holding her up in strength. She is praying while she walks through the desert. She is thirsty but not for water. This thirst is for knowledge and the presence of God. Jada looks to the others as she watches them struggling; she smiles, remembering when she was at that stage in her walk with God. She prays for those struggling and moves forward.

Jada is having lunch with LD. As they continue to eat their meals, Jada is in her own world, smiling uncontrollably, looking outside the window. LD notices her "head in the clouds" attitude and smiles back at her. Moments later Jada notices LD.

"What?" Jada asks.

"What's going on with you? You're over there looking like a new woman. You are glowing."

"LD, I met the man God has prepared me for." LD leans back in his chair, astonished at Jada's news. He takes a sip of his coffee and admires Jada's giddiness.

Chapter Sixteen

"So... Miss Jada, how do you know that this man is your mate?"

"I prayed for confirmation LD, and I received it with an overflow of validation."

"I'm so happy for you. I hope I get to meet him soon."

"Of course. LD, you're like a second father to me. You've helped me so much, I wouldn't imagine not introducing you to him."

"That's wonderful. I actually have news of my own."

Jada takes a bite of her food in anticipation of what LD has to say.

"I contacted my son and we've agreed to meet."

"LD that's wonderful!"

"I'm so happy and scared."

"Why are you scared? You've been looking forward to this for over a year."

"I just didn't want to get my hopes up and then find out he didn't want to meet me."

"Well at any rate, it's great news! When are you going to meet him?"

"Are you still going to be there with me?"

"Of course, LD. I would love to meet him," Jada says.

"Yes, we can all meet for dinner."

"That sounds amazing. Is he married? Kids?"

"I believe he's married, no kids."

"Ok this is exciting." Jada and LD continue to finish their meals while smiling with excitement of the events to come. Jada is smitten over Lamar and is excited about meeting LD's son. She feels like things are going in the right direction and has a lot to look forward to.

He, Then Me, Comes You

****

Jada is looking in the mirror applying makeup. She is carefully putting on her mascara in anticipation of the surprise that Lamar has for her. She has butterflies in her stomach wondering if he will ask her to be his wife. They have been courting for several months now and are deeply in love. They have a deep connection that is bound by God and the foundation is solid. Jada is no longer a babe in Christ. She communicates with God on every aspect of her life. She has found that when she goes to God first, he will always lead her to the right path even if it's not the one expected. She never thought she would write a novel helping women to cope with loneliness and provide tools to help wait on God. Jada would show that she had strength she never thought she had before. She is not the same woman she was years ago. Jada stops to look at herself in the mirror. She looks to her hands and notices that she is trembling. As she rubs them to try and calm herself, she remembers a time when her sister Mia would rub her hands when she was nervous. She began to tear up as she thinks of memories of her wonderful sister. She finishes putting on her makeup and takes a deep breath. As she checks the time her heart begins to pound harder.

"You're not good enough for him; you're going to ruin his life."

Jada again looks to the woman looking back her and thinks that she is worthless, that she doesn't deserve to be this happy. She shakes her head and tells herself not to believe the words of the adversary. She battles with his manipulative ways increasingly since she started courting Lamar. She takes a deep breath and continues to get dressed.

Lamar walks up to Jada's door and stares for a moment. He takes out the box that holds a five-carat princess cut diamond ring that he purchased, and pauses. He takes a deep breath and puts it back in his pocket. He rings the bell and waits for Jada to answer. As he stands there he feels nervous and wonders why the feelings of fear disrupt his spirit. Moments later Jada answers with a big smile on her face. Lamar lights up. He moves in close to Jada and holds her tight. He embraces her for a sweet moment, smelling her coconut-

Chapter Sixteen

scented mane.

"Hello beautiful!"

"Hello my king." Jada says. She kisses him passionately and holds on to him. She smells his cologne and imagines herself living the rest of her life in his company.

"I don't want to let you go."

"I don't want to let you go either," Jada says.

Lamar pulls back and leads her out the door and to the vehicle. He decided to purpose to Jada before meeting his father. He felt the spirit leading him to do so. He planned a night that Jada will never forget. As he is driving to the surprise destination, he holds her hand caressing it and kissing it. Jada leans back enjoying her courtship with Lamar. He is everything she needs and ever wanted. He knows how to hold her. He knows what to do to calm her when she's upset about Mia or when she gets passionate about helping out the kids at the center. They have both learned that their ministry involves helping less fortunate kids and teenagers in foster care or in homes with single parents in need. They will glorify God through their joined ministry. Lamar suggested returning to Africa.

~ *Chapter Seventeen* ~

A Reunion well deserved...

LD and Jada are sitting in the restaurant; there are no words said. LD appears to be very nervous. God has been preparing him for this moment. He had faith in God but still had fear of the unknown. He didn't know if his son would be happy to see him or would stand him up and not come at all. Whatever the outcome, he is grateful for the opportunity to have a relationship with him. LD becomes fidgety and begins to tap his fork of the plate. Jada touches his hand and looks to him with comfort.

"It's going to be okay, LD. God has led you here. You trust in Him and what He wants for you, right?

"Yes."

"Ok then, take a deep breath and relax. You are an amazing person and he would be happy to have you in his life. Trust that our Father has also prepared him."

LD stops and looks to Jada. He can see the Holy Spirit in Jada and how she is allowing Him to speak through her. He is impressed with how far Jada has come in her faith. This is how God works. He can take something that appears to be so damaged and broken and show us that it is not in fact broken, but bruised. And just as muscles can be broken down, they can be rebuilt with strength.

"Jada, you are my sister in faith and I'm happy that you are here with me."

"I wouldn't be anywhere else."

Chapter Seventeen

They smile at each other and Jada leans over and kisses LD's cheek. She removes the lipstick mark she left. Moments later, as LD and Jada engage in conversation, Lamar walks into the restaurant. Jada's eyes widen as she perks up with excitement.

"Oh my…"

"What's wrong?" LD asks.

"The man I've been telling you about, he's over there."

LD looks over to Lamar and then Lamar locks eyes with him. He stands there in confusion. He notices Jada sitting beside his dad. Lamar walks towards the table.

"That's the man you are in love with?"

"Yes, but I'm not sure why he's here." Jada says.

"Jada, he's my son."

Jada begins to shake. Her eyes tear up. She begins to become frantic, knocking over her glass of water. Soon Lamar is at the table. LD rises, as he looks his son in the eyes. Lamar also begins to tear up as well as LD. LD looks Lamar up and down in amazement at how great his son looks. He grabs him and holds him tight. Jada is amazed and grabs hold her mouth trying her best not to scream. She can't believe that the man she learned to love, who helped save her life, was the father of the man she was in love with. She is now in full-blown tears. She is in awe of how amazing God is. She knows without a doubt that this was God. God put LD in her life to help him prepare for his son and to help her prepare for her husband. *How great He is, if we just rely on Him*, she thinks. *He knows already. We just need to trust in Him with all our heart and soul. Trust that He will deliver. Trust that He is God almighty and there is nothing too great for Him.*

"You are so beautiful son, you look so much like your mother."

"I'm so happy to meet you right now. I think my heart is about to explode." Lamar says as he hugs his father again. Some people in the restaurant are also in tears at this wonderful reunion. They couldn't help but cause a scene - they are hugging and crying in the middle of the restaurant. The people and staff are so moved that

He, Then Me, Comes You

they don't interrupt, only observe the greatness of God.

"Please have a seat, son."

Lamar sits, wiping his tears, and looks to Jada.

"I'm sure there is an explanation on why you are here, Jada. How do you know my dad?"

"'Mar, you are not going to believe this, or maybe you are, but LD is the man I told you about - he saved my life. He has been the father figure in my life. He has helped me with my faith. I can't believe all this time I have had a relationship with your father."

"God is good. When I was on my way here, I thought about calling you to be here, but God told me to trust Him and here you are."

"I am so happy you and your dad have reconnected."

"I need to hug you," Lamar says to Jada. She rises and leans in to hug Lamar. They hold each other tight, crying with joy. The waitress approaches the table a little warily, wondering if she should interrupt this wonderful emotional reunion. She stands for a moment.

"I'm so sorry but are you ready to order or can I bring you a drink?"

"Yes, please bring a bottle of your finest wine to the table, please." Lamar states. He is excited that not only is he reunited with his father, but the woman God revealed as his wife is also there for this powerful moment.

"I should have had some clue - I mean your initials are LD, your name is also Lamar Daniels."

"Yeah, my war buddies called me LD and it stuck."

"Jada told me how you two met but Dad, tell me from your perspective. Did God lead you to Jada?"

"I believe He did. I was praying to be reunited with you. I fasted for a breakthrough and He led me to Jada's street. He told me to walk and that's when I saw the young man leaving your house."

Chapter Seventeen

"Caleb? He saw you?"

"Yeah, I asked him if you were ok and he didn't seem concerned. I felt a tug in my spirit to wait or to at least see if you were ok; when I heard the gunshot I immediately ran in."

Jada recalls the night and begins to cry. Lamar consoles her and grabs her hand.

"I could have lost you forever if my dad was disobedient to God. I just want to thank you for reaching out and for being the man you are today. How you were before doesn't matter. I forgive you and I look forward to us being a family." Lamar explains.

"This is one of the greatest days ever. I just wish Mia were here. I want to tell her everything," Jada says, excited.

"I know."

"Ok let's order, it's on me! Anything you want."

"Oh yeah! I want a huge black bean burger with sweet potato fries."

"That sounds really good," LD says.

"I can't wait for you to meet Kyle, Dad."

"Who's Kyle?"

"It's this kid I'm helping, who broke into my house a while back. He is living with me and he is a really wonderful person. His faith has grown and I couldn't be prouder of him," Lamar explains.

"What made you help him? I mean I know you felt inclined to, but why him? Why allow him to stay with you?"

"The Holy Spirit led me. I couldn't call the police or let him leave, I felt he was going to harm himself or someone else and end up in prison."

"Well I'm proud of you son."

"This is really overwhelming. I thought I would be angry or have a lot of questions but I'm happy to finally see you and those questions I had are irrelevant."

He, Then Me, Comes You

"You sure? I'm prepared to answer any questions you may have," LD says with sincerity.

"I'm positive. God has given me the strength and courage to forgive you. I just want us to build a relationship now. There's no need to bring up the past. I want to know you as the man you are now. You have given me so much of you already in the journals you given me. Thank you."

"This is wonderful! I'm amazed at this day. I'm so happy to be a part of this. You two mean everything to me," Jada says.

"This is a day for a celebration. I have my dad back in my life and the love of my life is here. God is a faithful God. Glory be to Him!"

LD and Jada smile in agreement as they all lift their glasses and toast to God and what He has done for them.

"To new beginnings!"

~ *Chapter Eighteen* ~

Purposeful paths lead to great things…

Two Years Later…

Jada stands tall at the front of the room, waiting for the participants to enter. She looks to the empty blue chairs and women of all ages begin to enter one by one. They hold small personal conversations amongst themselves, smiling to Jada as they enter the facility. Jada smiles back politely at each one of them.

"Hello Ms. Jada," one of the ladies says, while waving in a coy manner.

Soon the room is full of bright-eyed women. They are waiting to hear Jada's testimony and gain knowledge from her experiences. Jada was led to write a book, and had written down how far God has brought her. She has been blessed with the mercy and grace from the Living God. Jada stands tall as the room becomes silent.

"Good afternoon, ladies, and welcome. I applaud you all for attending and giving me the honor of relaying God's Word and my testimony to you all. I have given this speech many times and it has never come out the same. The Holy Spirit has a way of using me for the benefit of others and I'm so happy to oblige our Lord and Savior. I see many of you with hope in your eyes - hope for answers, for confirmation or knowing that you are not the only one in pain or being tested; you are not the only one who has lacked

Chapter Eighteen

faith. I'm here to tell you that you are not alone. God has a way of bringing us together. He allows us to go through things so that we may help the next person who comes along who is going through the same things. You see, there is nothing new under the sun, and there's nothing like knowing that you are not the only one who's made those mistakes."

The crowd agrees and smiles as they intently listen to Jada. She has come a long way since the day she tried to end her own life over a man who was not for her. She begins to explain that to the audience.

"I was a complainer. I complained about a lot of things. 'Why don't I have a husband? Why don't I have any children? Why can't I have legs like hers or breasts perky like hers.' I was never satisfied. I didn't understand at first but then I decided to let God show me, and boy did He show me. I'm sure you heard the phrase 'be careful what you ask for because you just may get it.' Many of us believe that God doesn't hear us. We think that small, because we don't get the answers right away, or it doesn't come in a way we expect it. I remember when I asked God for my husband. He answered. But what we don't understand at times, is that we have to go through preparation. He prepares us for what we ask for. And when He begins to move and put things in line for us, a shift happens. He cleanses you. He removes people from your life who are way past their season. We think we can hold on to a man in our lives until we get the right one. We continue to have sex with them or take abuse from them until God saves us from the situation. He can deliver us, yes. But we have the choice and the power to take those opportunities that are presented before us. He will open a door or even a window. I'm sure if we all look back we can recognize a time when He gave us an out. But we, being stubborn, decide we can play God and change the man into what we want him to be."

As the women listen to the strong and powerful words, one of the women begins to move around in her chair; uneasy, trying to hold back. She starts to cry and puts her head down, ashamed. She screams out, interrupting Jada. The room watches as she continues to shout and cry, asking God for forgiveness.

He, Then Me, Comes You

"I'm so sorry God, I'm so sorry! Please forgive me!" The young woman shouts, looking up. No one stops her, for they all are moved by her repentance. Some share in her repentance and others pray for them. Jada stands as the Holy Spirit moves in the room. Jada silently thanks God and begins to tear up. She never thought that God would use her this way. Just a few years ago, she thought she was a broken person with nothing to offer anyone. But she was now being used to help others like her. She felt privileged and honored to be a servant of the Lord. Moments pass and the crowd are now at attention again before Jada.

"See how God works? You can be anywhere and have deliverance if you allow Him to work through you. I am here today to encourage you all. If you are serious about a life with God then be true to Him and allow Him to help you. Not for a husband, a car, a house or a job. Allow Him to work through you so that you can store up treasures that will never rust, that can never be taken away here on earth. Those things are nice but if you really are after God's heart, then He will reward you with things that are far greater than things that we deem important. Trust in Him with all your heart; do not lean on your own understanding. May peace be with you, my sisters and brothers. God bless."

The crowd stands with applause as Jada gracefully and humbly nods her head with gratitude. Lamar has helped her achieve many aspects in her walk with the Living God. She knows it is not her whom they are applauding, but the grace and mercy of God for allowing the Holy Spirit to work through Jada. They are not looking to Jada for answers and hope, but to the Almighty God. As everyone is meeting and greeting Jada, Lamar walks in with a smile on his face. He knows that Jada was a great vessel today due to the reactions of the people in the room. He walks over to her and greets her with a warm hug and kiss. Jada introduces him to some of the ladies. They are smiling with admiration. You can see the hope and glee in their eyes as they look to the love that Lamar and Jada exhibit. The Lord is present with them though their strength and glow. They complement one another, which is more evidence of Gods work.

Chapter Eighteen

****

Lamar and Jada are on their monstrous sized sofa, lying in each other's arms as they smile with comfort. They both have their eyes closed in awe of how amazing God is and how they came to be.

"Are you hungry, my love?" Lamar asks, keeping his eyes closed, holding Jada tightly against his chest.

"Yes I am. Are you cooking?"

"Of course."

"Is Kyle coming home today?"

"He is supposed to. Why?"

"Well I have some important news that I want to share and I need him here."

"Ok - must be very important. He texted and said he would be here for dinner."

Jada stares adoringly at Lamar as he walks into the kitchen. Jada follows and sits at the kitchen island.

"Are you helping or watching?"

"I'm watching. I love a man who can cook. It's so sexy."

"Oh yeah- even after two years this is still sexy to you?"

"It will never get old. I feel like I'm falling in love with you every day. It's like an overflowing extension of love, growing continuously all the time."

"That will never get old."

"What?" Jada asks.

"The way you use words to describe things. It's very intoxicating." Lamar says as he moves over and picks Jada up and sits her on the kitchen island. He passionately kisses her while caressing her crown.

They engage in each other; they have no insight of what's going on around them. Soon Kyle walks in and observes them. He clears

He, Then Me, Comes You

his throat but they do not hear him as they are intertwined into one another.

"Fire!" Kyle screams. Jada and Lamar stops kissing and look to him smiling.

"Hey Kyle," Jada says she grabs him and kisses his cheek.

"You two are really enjoying me being out of the house, huh?"

"Oh no we miss you, in fact I'm glad that you are here. I have great news that I want to share." Jada grabs a bag from the cabinet in the other room, reenters the kitchen and takes two gift bags from it, and hands one to each of them. They look to one another; each one is wondering if the other knows anything about what is about to transpire. They open the gifts and each one pulls out diapers. They look to each other and then to Jada. She is smiling intently to watch their reactions.

"Are you serious!" Lamar says as he smiles and grabs Jada, picking her up and holding her tightly.

"I'm going to be a big brother!?" Kyle says with excitement as he joins in on the hugs. As Lamar and Kyle are hugging Jada tightly, she thinks back on what God has done in her life. He is a faithful God, a loving God who wants us to be happy. She begins to cry with overwhelming joy. How happy she is to have waited on God.

"So does this mean you are having twins?" Kyle asks.

"Yes."

"Oh wow I didn't think about that? Oh I hope God blesses us with two boys! I will teach them to play basketball…"

"Uh no, I will teach them to play basketball, you have no game 'Mar."

"Excuse me but who schooled you the other day? It was me."

"Yeah out of a hundred games, you won one game." Kyle says with confidence.

"Hold on, what if they are girls?" Jada asks.

Chapter Eighteen

"So what, they will learn how to play too."

Jada shakes her head, happy that God has blessed her with two children. She is currently three months along and is healthy. The babies are healthy as well. Jada reflects back when she had a miscarriage and the pain of not knowing if she could ever carry a healthy child. She feared that she was not worthy because of having abortions before and all the men she gave her body to. She felt grateful that she turned her life around. She was happy that she endured and became close to her Creator.

~ *Chapter Nineteen* ~

Happy endings come those who wait…

"Breathe, Jada; you have to breathe, Baby."

"It hurts. I can't. I changed my mind. I want drugs, give me the drugs!"

"No Babe, we agreed to have a non-medicinal birth, you can do this."

"I don't care what we agreed to, I feel like my vagina is tearing into two vaginas!"

The nurse looks to Jada and Lamar. She smiles because she has heard it all before. A young mother with courage to have a natural birth then turns into someone else when that excruciating pain hits. Of course no one wants to use drugs that can be passed down to his or her child. They want to have courage and have the strength to get through a natural birth with no medicine. The nurse tries to help by encouraging Jada to be strong.

"Jada you can do this!" The nurse says, cheering her on.

"Oh shut up! You don't have to do it!" Jada says, screaming at the nurse, who walks away and then leaves the room.

"I would say I'm sorry but I'm not. She was getting on my nerves."

"I understand, Babe."

"You're getting on my nerves too; can you please get me some more ice chips."

Chapter Nineteen

Lamar kisses Jada on the forehead and leaves the room. She lies there, exhausted and in pain. She has been in labor for over ten hours and the pain is only getting worse. The doctor came in and examined her, informing that she is only dilated 4 centimeters. She closes her eyes and thinks of Mia. She can feel her in the room, telling her that she needs to be strong for her babies. Jada smiles at the thought of her. She imagines what she would say or do if she was in the room with her. As she lies there she speaks to God. She thanks Him for His many blessings that have transpired in her life. She asks for strength and courage to give birth to her babies. Another moment passes and Lamar reenters the room with the ice chips.

"Is it safe?"

"Of course my love. I'm sorry; I'm being a terrible wife. I love you but I also hate you so much right now." Jada says as she sincerely looks to Lamar. He smiles and hands her the cup of ice.

"I love you too, my queen. And it's okay to hate me right now."

"Oh, thank you. You are so sweet." Jada grabs the cup of ice and pours a few pieces in her mouth, sucking on it as if her life depended on it. Her face exudes pure exhaustion as her eyes droop, needing sleep. As she tries to get some rest, another contraction comes to interrupt. The nurse pops her head in asking if Jada is in need of anything. Jada gives her a scowling look and she immediately leaves.

****

Hours have passed and Jada is now ready to give birth to her twin babies. Her countenance is distressed as the doctor, nurse and Lamar surround her. Lamar is holding her hand with the encouragement that she can do this and that God is always with her. Lamar prays that she is graced with strength to get through this without any complications. Soon it's time to push and Lamar becomes anxious. You can see the concern on his face for his wife and children. He grips Jada's hand tightly informing her that she can do this and

He, Then Me, Comes You

he is here. She squeezes back with the acknowledgement that she understands. He smiles and begins to coach her to push. She bears down and pushes as instructed by the doctor. Jada continues on until her two beautiful babies are born into the world. Lamar and Jada are blessed with a healthy baby boy and girl. Lamar begins to cry with joy as he looks into the eyes of his son and daughter. He is taken away by the creation of his offspring. He then looks to his wife and is excited and grateful for her strength in giving birth to two amazing gifts. He kisses Jada passionately and then kisses his babies.

"Thank you, my queen, for giving me these gifts."

"They are amazing, aren't they?" Jada says as she holds on to her children. "Have you decided on the name for our daughter?"

"Yes, and you have a name for our son?" Jada asks.

"I do. I want to introduce you to our son, Lamar Jacob Daniels III."

Jada smiles. She remembers Lamar saying when they were children that he would never name his son after his dad, but here he is, giving him that name and happy to do so. She looks to their daughter and gives the baby her name.

"I didn't expect any other name. And this is our daughter, Mia Adrianna Daniels. In remembrance of my baby sister and your mom."

"I wouldn't have it any other way," Lamar says as he embraces his children. Moment later Claudia, Derrick, Kyle and LD enter the room with balloons and stuffed animals. Jada's eyes light up when she sees her family celebrating this moment with her. She tears up as she holds baby Lamar and Lamar is holding baby Mia. Claudia is in tears as she looks to her grandchildren.

"They are so beautiful. Can I hold one of my grandbabies?" Claudia asks, while she looks to Jada.

"And I want to hold my other grandbaby, please," LD requests.

Lamar hands baby Mia to his dad and Jada hands baby Lamar to

Chapter Nineteen

Claudia. Kyle watches and admires them, as he is secretly afraid to hold a baby. He fears he may hold them wrong.

"Wow congrats Bro, they are beautiful," Derrick says while he gives Lamar a hug and kisses Jada on the cheek.

"They are so tiny and precious. I love them so much!" Claudia says, while admiring her grandson.

"May I hold one?" Derrick asks. LD hands the baby to Derrick.

"What are their names?" Derrick asks.

Jada looks to Lamar. She nods for him to introduce their children.

"Well Mama Claudia, you are holding Lamar Jacob Daniels III, and Bro, you are holding Mia Adrianna Daniels."

Derrick looks to Jada. He begins to cry as he is holding on to his niece. He admires her small face and tiny hands. "You named her Mia? I know she would be so happy to have met her niece and nephew. I can't wait to tell them all about her and how wonderful and special she was."

"I know you will, brother, I wouldn't have named her any other name. She is a Mia and I hope she grows to be just as wonderful as her aunt was."

Derrick smiles as he is still crying with joy. He kisses baby Mia on the hand and looks to Lamar with admiration.

"Do you want to hold them Kyle?"

"Oh no not yet, they're so fragile and I'm too nervous." Kyle says as he shakes he head, adamant about his feelings.

"Derrick, Brother in law, we have something very important to ask you."

"Anything Jay; what's up?"

"We want you to be the godfather to our children." Jada says. Derrick looks to Lamar, his friend, and back to Jada, his sister and begins to cry harder as he feels blessed to be a part of their blessed union.

"Son, if it's ok with you I would like to take this time to thank

He, Then Me, Comes You

God for this occasion and say a prayer." LD asks as Lamar nods in agreement.

"Ok everyone, please lets hold each other's hand, bow our heads and give thanks to the one and only Living God." Everyone smiles and nods with agreement. They hold hands.

"Heavenly Father, we come before You on this occasion of happiness and blessing beyond what we could ever imagine. There are three generations that stand before You, thanking You for Your grace as You bless this family. We thank You, dear God for being an awesome Father and provider to us. We thank You, dear God, for giving us the courage to have faith so that You can lead us in our daily lives. We hope that You will continue to bless us as we humble ourselves and we praise You knowing that without You all these things would have not been possible, Thank You God, we love You, in Jesus' name we pray, Amen!"

"Amen!!!" Lamar, Jada, Claudia, Derrick and Kyle concur.

Made in the USA
Columbia, SC
08 October 2018